MARK FOUR

A Thriller

John Hindmarsh

Cover
Cover Design by Stuart Bache
www.bookscovered.co.uk

Editing
This book was copy edited by Sasha Paulsen.
Any errors were introduced by the writer.
Sometimes British terminology or spelling somehow finds
its way into the story; that's because I'm Australian.

Formatting
Formatting by Polgarus Studio.
http://www.PolgarusStudio.com

Beta Readers
A number of people took time out of their busy schedules
and read Mark Four in draft and pre-edit form, and they
made very helpful and constructive comments. You know
who you are – thank you very much.

Newsletter

Learn more about John Hindmarsh and his books. Sign up for John's newsletter.

You'll receive: updates on John's writing schedule, the occasional freebie (e.g., books, short stories, excerpts from John's current work in progress), advance details of discounts, and be part of John's street team for new releases.

Go here: John Hindmarsh

You can unsubscribe anytime! NO SPAM guaranteed! [John should be far too busy writing to send out spam].

Reviews

Oh yes, I almost forgot. Reviews are what keeps a writer going. Please review this book on Amazon or Kobo or other reseller [where ever you made the purchase].

DEDICATION

I want to thank my wife Cathy for her continuing patience,
for providing her utmost support, and finally
for re-reading many drafts.
This book is for Cathy.

Prologue

The eavesdropping swallow look-alike perched under the eaves, its visual and auditory sensors on the highest setting. It had earlier recorded and transmitted the arrival of a vehicle into the dusty courtyard. Now it reported that three travel-weary men, carrying their weapons, had disembarked and headed towards the front door of the building. Its position enabled it to capture an image of each face, which it transmitted to the Wyvern drone circling above, the short burst of data guaranteed to be undetectable. Now it was trying to eavesdrop on conversations inside the Islamic State-controlled safe house.

Three men, soldiers for Daesh, bearded, wearing camouflage jackets and pants, and in dire need of a meal, placed their rifles inside the small room. Their weapons were M16s, the A2 variant, looted from Iraqi military warehouses. They dropped heavy backpacks containing a number of STANAG magazines, all 30-shot, filled with 5.56 NATO cartridges. The packs, too, had been looted from the Iraqi Army. The house, a fortress with its high walls and armed guards, was on the eastern outskirts of Ar Raqqah, a town of a quarter of a million or so Syrians. The town was currently under the control of Islamic State forces. The men had traveled from Aleppo to report to one of the senior commanders. The journey of barely two hundred kilometers had taken them all night instead of a more typical four hours, due to their driver's extreme caution. Russian overflights posed a continuing danger.

The large room was stone-floored and bare of furnishings except for a heavy wooden table and a scattering of worn wooden chairs. A narrow window overlooked the front courtyard. There were containers of rice and meat stew and a plate of pita bread in the center of the table and the odors drifting from the hot food were a reminder that they had not eaten for more than twenty-four hours.

The youngest of the trio, tempted, moved towards the table, only to be stopped in his tracks by a comment in Arabic.

"Wait until you are invited."

He turned to the speaker, the senior member of their team, a questioning expression on his face.

"Westerners. You have no manners. Just because you can shoot—"

The softly spoken commencement of a disciplinary tirade was abruptly halted by the entrance of two men. One man was elderly, his long beard was all white, and he shuffled forward in his open leather sandals. He carried a copy of the Koran, its pages well-thumbed. He leaned on a heavy walking stick, a worn branch of a tree, as tall as he. Despite the heat of the morning, his heavy robe did not seem to be unwelcome. The other man was middle-aged, balding, clean-shaven, and had the air of a person accustomed to command. He was dressed in a finely tailored Western-style suit, with a pale lemon-colored shirt and a red striped tie. He wore a strongly scented aftershave lotion. There was a glimpse of a holstered handgun under his jacket.

The three soldiers stood silently, waiting—they were there to receive details of a new assignment. The mullah was one of the State's senior religious advisers and the other man, although a Russian, was a trusted and senior State commander renowned for his military skills. At last the commander indicated the food.

"Help yourselves," he said in Arabic. His accent had a slight Russian burr. "You must be hungry." He watched as the three newcomers scooped stew onto pita bread. As the youngest of the three, the one referred to as a Westerner, was about to take a bite of the wrapped bread, the commander spoke again, this time in English. Pointing, he said, "Except you."

Startled, the Westerner paused and held his food an inch or two from his mouth.

"What name are you using? Yes, it's currently Brent, isn't it. Not Eric, Eric Ferguson? Lieutenant Eric Ferguson?" The commander turned his attention to the older of the other two men. "Rashid—you understand you've been tricked? Brent— or Eric—is an American spy. He is a member of their Special Forces."

The oldest of the trio cursed and drew his knife; it had a long hunting blade and he had used it before on nonbelievers. His companion, closer to the door, dived for his M16.

The Westerner tried to protest. He dropped the stew-filled bread and held up his hands. "Whoah," he cried out. "It's not true—"

His protest was cut-off by a three-shot burst from the M16. He fell to the floor, now forever silent.

The Russian smiled. The mullah thumbed his Koran. The two men in camouflage stared at each other. Blood mixed with dust on the stone floor.

The operator of the Wyvern drone circling three thousand feet above the collection of buildings on the edge of the small Syrian town replayed an audio file, increasing the volume as he did so. He listened carefully. He signaled his duty officer. The man, a lieutenant, walked over to the operator's workstation and said, "Yes, Corporal?"

"Sir, I think we might've lost our resource. The sparrow-spy we put in place last night has transmitted an audio clip that includes a burst of weapon fire. There were some voices before the shots were fired and one sounded like our man. I think he said something like "It's not true." The other voices are too indistinct and I can't identify the speakers. They're all silent at the moment."

"Poor bastard. Drop your drone to a thousand feet. Copy the file to me and to Fire Command. We know the Russian is there with his religious adviser, one of the senior Daesh mullahs. FC may want to launch a Hellfire."

It was less than five minutes when the lieutenant returned to the drone operator. "Anything more?"

The corporal flicked his attention back and forth, between the screen showing the images relayed by the drone and the officer. "Yes, sir. Three vehicles just arrived. They're Range Rovers as far as I can determine. The drivers haven't exited. I suspect they're waiting for passengers. Yes, look, there's movement, people heading towards the vehicles. Two men wearing camouflage and a third person in a robe. It's a woman, wearing a hijab."

The lieutenant spoke to someone via his wireless mike. He listened. "Yes, sir. Will do." He returned his attention to the drone operator.

He said, "They're going to call back. Watch for any other departures."

It was ten minutes before the lieutenant returned to the drone operator's station.

He said, "Corporal, we've been authorized to drop two Hellfires, as long as we're sure the Russian is still in the house. What do you think?"

"Sir, only those three vehicles have departed. The Russian is still there, I'll bet on it. Both our targets—the Russian and his imam advisor—I'm sure they're still there."

"Good. FC is sending their authority reference to you. When you receive it, fire immediately."

"Yes, sir." In less than a minute, two missiles were on their short journey to the small collection of buildings. There were no survivors from the resulting explosions and inferno. At least, no bodies were found, although the searchers, locals, were not all that thorough. The resulting rubble from the buildings and protective wall was suitable only for road repairs.

###

Zarina was anxious. Her contact, when she phoned, did not seem eager to respond to her requests. Also, Rashid, her escort from Ar Raqqah, was proving difficult to disengage even though his duties were now at an end. It was not her fault his companion had been killed in an ambush along the highway to the Turkish border; it had been a negotiable situation, she was convinced. The man had been careless, exposing far too much bravado in his actions. For some reason, the older of her two-man security escort was blaming her for his companion's death.

At least she had entered Turkey without further difficulties. The bribes had been modest and her reporter credentials had been accepted without question. It had taken another two hours to drive to Diyarbakir where her contact had arranged accommodation. The hotel was a four-star Hilton, which was impressive given that most hotels in the town scored three stars or less. Her room, newly furnished, was on the tenth floor and had views across the old part of the city.

She had checked into the hotel using an American passport matching her cover as a journalist, the same documents she had used at the border to enter the country. The following morning she planned to fly to Istanbul; that is, as long as her contact delivered her tickets and replacement documents. She would revert to her Russian identity, her real identity, when she caught the flight and was waiting on her contact to deliver her genuine passport with the American green card visa and her other personal items.

Zarina folded her hijab and dusty clothes she had worn on the journey from Ar Raqqah into a small bundle. She planned to dispose of these; she had no intention of wearing them again. She had changed into jeans and a light blouse that she had carried on her trip, and which she had held in reserve. Later, she would change again, into far more formal dress, consisting of a skirt, blouse, and jacket, and heels instead of her favorite boots—another reason she needed her contact to follow through on his tasks. Not only did he hold her documents, he also had her suitcase containing her clothing and makeup.

Her ruminations were interrupted by a heavy knocking on the door. She checked via the spy hole. It was her escort. Cursing softly, she opened the door. The man pushed through and then sneered when he observed her jeans and blouse.

He spoke in English; she had not informed her escort that she was Russian and spoke fluent Arabic. "So you've reverted to harlot, yes?"

Zarina did not know the man's origin; she thought he was Iraqi. He had disclosed few personal details on the journey. She stood her ground as she lifted the dusty bundle of clothing. There was a knife hidden in the folds, its blade long, thin, and razor sharp. Her trainer had spent hours ensuring she was proficient in its use. She grasped the handle. She suspected the Daesh soldier was going to be more than a nuisance.

"Rashid, I don't like that attitude." Zarina was aware her words could provoke the man; however, she felt a passive approach would endanger her even more.

"Deny, if you can—you are the Russian's whore, no?" He grabbed at her arm.

Zarina stepped back, successfully avoiding the move.

She said, "Don't be ridiculous." She wasn't going to tell him the truth, that the man she had visited was her father.

"Ha," jeered the Iraqi. "It doesn't matter now. The Russians—or maybe the Americans—bombed the house, fifteen minutes after we left. Your lover—he's dead, for sure." He made another grab and caught her arm.

Shocked, speechless, not knowing whether to believe the man or not, Zarina dropped the bundle of clothes and spun towards her assailant. As she moved in closer, she used her momentum to push the knife as powerfully as she could, the sharp point penetrating up from under his jaws just above his larynx and finally penetrating his brain. He was dead before he had an opportunity to realize he was under attack.

Zarina stepped back as the Iraqi's body fell to the floor. She had to move quickly. If her contact wasn't coming to the hotel, she would have to go to him. She spared five minutes of her critical time to wipe off surfaces she might have touched. With luck, it would be morning before anyone discovered the body. There was a trace of blood on her hand and she washed it off. The knife she left where it was after wiping her fingerprints from the handle. She left the room, taking her folded bundle of clothes with her, making sure the door was closed and the Do Not Disturb sign was in place, hanging on the doorknob. She descended from the tenth floor using the emergency exit stairwell, controlling her panic to insure it would not override the necessary caution. Once she exited the hotel she would walk for a few minutes before hailing a taxi; she could not appear to be fleeing from the hotel. She would call her contact and force him to meet her, perhaps at a restaurant, somewhere public. She needed her papers. Her focus was on survival; it would be time to mourn later, if truly her father had been killed.

Chapter 1

Mark Midway examined the sagging metal gate; at least, he examined the bent metal remnants of the gate, which had once protected the entrance to his property.

A private militia member had used a slab of C4 to demolish the gate; it was an illegal act that had subsequently attracted both Mark's ire and the attention of the law. Once the small militia team gained access to the property, the members fired his home using hand grenades. The attack on the property, in return, garnered a number of .50 caliber bullets aimed and fired remotely at the attackers. Mark previously had mounted experimental, software-controlled "Cutter" weapon systems on top of each of the two now burnt-out farm sheds. When the men attacked what they thought was an occupied house, Mark, alerted by his security system, had aimed and fired the weapons from his London hotel room some three thousand miles away. The attackers were overwhelmed by his aggressive and accurate fusillade. He ceased his defense only when first responders, firemen and police alerted by smoke from the burning buildings, arrived.

Mark pushed the metal bars to one side to clear the entrance and returned to his vehicle. He drove towards the charred skeleton of the house; its carbonized chimneys and timber supports reached towards the sky like the blackened bones of a large prehistoric animal.

He was here to meet with an architect referred by friends in Boston. Mark intended they both would inspect the property, following which he wanted the architect to design and possibly supervise the construction of a new house. He had checked and the insurance company had agreed: there was nothing to be salvaged from the burnt-out remains.

Mark avoided the glass shards of shattered windscreens along the blacktop, the results of his marksmanship with the Cutter systems. Someone, he supposed the FBI, had retrieved the attackers' vehicles, which he had shot at and immobilized, presumably as evidence to support their prosecution of the militia members. He stopped short of the turning area in front of what used to be the entrance to the house and exited his SUV. He sniffed. Even though the fires had been months ago, he could still smell the smoke and ashes from the destroyed buildings. The odor of chemical residues from the weapons and grenades used in the arson attack added an acrid, pungent overlay. Mark stood for a long moment, trying to control his anger as he took in the results of the senseless, fire-driven destruction. This had been intended to be home; home for him and his partner, Anna, and for two Cerberus children who were in their care.

He frowned at his memories. He was not yet convinced that he should rebuild the destroyed structures; perhaps he should sell the property.

The sound of an approaching vehicle penetrated his introspective mood, and he turned to watch the newcomer carefully thread his sports car, a white Jaguar, along the access lane to park next to his Touareg. The rumble of the Jaguar's exhaust was counter-pointed by a roll of thunder from a looming thunderhead. Mark waited for the driver to exit his vehicle. The storm was receding, he hoped.

"Mark? Mark Midway?"

"Yes. You're Clancy—Joseph Clancy?" Mark unconsciously rubbed his fingers along the scar on the left

\ead. His hair had not yet fully grown back over
\ his scalp caused by the bullet that had nearly

The newcomer stopped and examined the burned remnants of buildings: the house, two barns, and a small cottage. After a minute or two he continued around the vehicles to Mark. They shook hands.

"Indeed. Call me Joe. Julian warned me to expect complete devastation, and I thought he was joking." Clancy was tall, thin, and exuded energy. He had a buzz cut and wore rimless glasses, jeans, and a Red Sox T-shirt.

Julian Kelly had provided Mark with an enthusiastic recommendation for the architect. "The man's a genius," Julian had said. "He will understand your needs and will deliver, I guarantee it. I like him. He works with ghetto children on most weekends; has a marvelous following."

Mark, the year before, had rescued Julian's daughter, Paula, from a possible kidnapping and they had more or less adopted him. Julian's opinion of the architect was a major plus.

He reached into his SUV and extracted a portfolio, which he handed to Clancy. He explained, "These are aerial photos before and after, images of the original buildings with interior shots of the house, approximate floor plans, and a map of the grounds. There's a memory stick with some aerial videos. It's the best of what I could get my hands on. It's to show you what we had, not necessarily what we want."

"Thank you. Let's walk around. I want to visualize the possibilities." The architect shook his head. "Such destruction. Sad. Why, do you know?" He walked to the left of the house remnants.

Mark paced beside him. "It's a long story. Perhaps Julian will tell you some day; he knows of my—ah—adventures, at least in part. The destruction was carried out by a gang of thugs, apparently a private militia, at the direction of a pastor. All from the South."

Clancy shook his head. "I oversaw the rebuild and decoration of his apartment after it was wrecked last year. He mentioned a debt he owes. I understand you helped protect him and his daughter after someone tried to kidnap her?" He looked at Mark. "These people hated you enough to do this?"

"The events aren't related." Mark waved his hand at the blackened timbers. "This was done from more of a mercenary motive, I suspect. Someone paid them. I heard they were forthcoming with details after their arrests. Their trial is scheduled for late next month. They all pleaded guilty. Given they were in mid-assault when the police arrived, I doubt they could do otherwise." He smiled. It was a grim expression. He wondered how Maeve Donnelly, with her current responsibilities for management of Cerberus US, was going to minimize publicity— the news media had been quick to report details of the attack, describing him as some kind of mystery man.

"Hmm. Julian mentioned they used hand grenades to fire the buildings. Is it safe to walk here?"

"The local police and the FBI have searched the area for evidence. I understand they removed anything of a dangerous nature. I'm certain they found everything." He didn't mention that twenty or so soldiers from the 145th MP Battalion had also conducted a thorough search. He made a mental note to arrange for a contractor to remove the burnt residue of the buildings.

"The risk is low; that's acceptable. The woods here, behind the house, will remain?"

"Oh, yes." Mark said.

He could feel the presence of a watcher. However, there was no threat that he could discern. At the moment.

Mark continued. "I'd like some protective features in the design. If you have ideas that you can include—?"

"I'll do that. I've consulted on two or three properties where the owners needed to be safe. I can provide strong elements of security without constructing a fortress." Clancy continued to the trail that led away from the rear of the house into the woods. "An escape path?"

"Yes, it's intended as such. We have a shed about a mile away, well-hidden and large enough to store two vehicles, if we needed to. From there we have easy access to the main roads. It's not obvious that the building belongs to this property." Mark indicated the remnants of his former home. "At least, unless someone reconnoiters the place. There's also a small shed in a clearing about three hundred yards into the woods." He made another mental note, to remember to check the smaller shed once the architect had departed.

They walked on. Mark followed the lead of the architect as they wandered the rough circumference of the destroyed buildings examining the ruins. Clancy used his camera to take additional photographs. As they walked, Mark described the interior of the house and summarized his personal preferences for a new building. He hoped Anna would agree; he would check with her when he returned to Boston.

Clancy waved his hand at the buildings and said, "The sheds are straightforward. I suggest you replace them with simple New England-style farm buildings, basically identical to what you had. Perhaps with additional fire protection. The housekeeper's cottage—we can copy it. Modernized, it will remain a simple residence. For the main building: I'll have one of my team come out in a day or so and take detailed measurements. We'll produce a set of concept drawings for you. That will take perhaps a week or so. When I've reviewed those and made sure they're presentable, we'll be in contact, yes?"

"In two weeks?"

"Indeed. Two weeks. At my offices. I'll arrange a time. My team will present their ideas. We'll do some costings, all preliminary. Okay?"

"Definitely." They were back at the architect's vehicle. Mark watched as the man drove off. Now, he would explore deeper into the woods. He wanted to find whoever had been watching them as they walked around the burnt-out buildings. He also needed to check on Gabrielle's hidden treasure, as she described it.

Before he moved away from his vehicle, Mark reached inside, took out his Glock and attached the holster to his belt, under his jacket. As he straightened, his cell phone rang. He looked at the caller ID. Maeve Donnelly.

"Yes, Maeve?"

"Where are you?"

"New Hampshire. At the property."

"Alone?"

"Yes."

"Damn."

"Why?"

"There's been a lot of social chatter in the last hour or so. Linda Schöner's analysts think it's something to do with you."

"Already? We've been back only a week."

"Someone is on the move. Linda's team is trying to discover who and why."

"Okay." He paused. "There's an intruder here, although I don't sense any threat. I still have a couple of chores to do."

"I'll contact Winter Security; they'll provide an escort for you back to Boston. The team will take a while to get there, though. I'll talk to the local police and arrange for them to send someone to you. You can wait where you are or accompany the police back to their station in Redmont. My recommendation? Go to the police station."

"You think it's that serious?"

"Yes."

Chapter 2

"Jamie, what's the position regarding Schmidt? Are you up to date?" The man posing the question, Ross Cromarty, was seated in a soft leather chair. Cromarty was a major stockholder in a number of large international corporations, most of which were based offshore for tax purposes. He had a glass of Scotch at his left elbow and held a cheroot in his right hand. The man he was questioning, General Jamie Grovers (retired), sat two yards away, in a similar chair, also with a glass of Scotch. A third man, Ken O'Hare, an assistant director with the National Security Agency (NSA), responsible for FORNSAT Resources, a section of the Foreign Affairs Directorate, listened intently. He was taller than the general and in far better physical condition. He was drinking bourbon. They were meeting in the library in one of four houses that Cromarty owned across the country. This one was located in Texas; it was situated overlooking the Colorado River, north-west of Austin. The locals called it Cromarty's Castle.

Grovers took a sip of his drink while he considered his reply. He placed his glass down and joined his hands, reaching his arms out.

Cromarty interpreted the gesture as a subconscious cry for help. Grovers, he had decided, did not have the strength that he required in a senior executive. He could still make use of him, though.

"A good question. He suffered severe injuries in that helicopter crash. A pity the Russians didn't do a better job, if you ask me." He had never matched the other general's ability to always pull victory out of adversity. Envy was an acid that burned without leaving a visible mark.

"We know that much," said O'Hare. "What about now? It's been over three months."

The retired general stared at his second questioner.

"Well?" O'Hare stared back. He was standing; he had been looking out at the water view as the sun set. He was a non-smoker and waved away a cloud of smoke.

Grovers wilted. "He's recovered, physically. I've seen portions of his fitness report. It states the man is extremely fit. With reservations, apparently."

The first man spoke. "Is your emphasis on his physical condition indicative of other issues?"

"Yes. There are rumors of some residual issues."

Cromarty looked up, suddenly interested.

Grovers continued. "Well, I don't think he's any crazier than usual—I heard dizziness, so it's more likely his heart than his brain." He shrugged. "Donnelly is guarding him like a mother lion with her cub; it's difficult to get anything insightful."

"O'Hare, what do you know?"

"Sorry, Ross. My people can't get close, either. I could push, but I don't need that exposure."

Cromarty stubbed out his cheroot with a savage motion. He stood with his back to the lake view. "Listen to me, both of you. Schmidt, and Donnelly, now that she's running that Cerberus organization, are potential—major—stumbling blocks to my business plans. I'm in the midst of developing my strategy for two financially significant takeovers. I'm also setting up a super PAC for a good friend and business associate. I need to make sure no one—I mean no one—can impede my plans. Grovers, it's your task, as head of my

15

security, to work out an action plan. O'Hare, you will consult and advise. Between the two of you I want to know that any potential threat can be neutralized. More than a token 'can be'."

"Do we have a budget?" O'Hare asked.

"Half a mill for planning and five for execution."

"You know the execution part has been tried before, without success? Some from other agencies—Mercante, for example—have tried and failed," said O'Hare.

Grovers was still considering the implications of the conversation. Cromarty thought the general was unsure he wanted to be involved with the implied activities.

"Mercante was a fool. A pathological idiot. You know that." Cromarty lit another cheroot. He didn't offer one to his visitors.

O'Hare shrugged. "I'm just sayin'."

"The budget might be enough for planning," Grovers said, brave for a change. "Not sure about the rest. It will depend on what we plan, the risks and, of course, the resource costs."

Cromarty looked at O'Hare.

"I agree," O'Hare said.

"All right. Let's say one mill for planning. I'll add a bonus of another mill, which you can share if I approve the result. After that we'll determine the execution budget. Bring me a bloody foolproof plan, though."

Grovers and O'Hare exchanged glances, silently agreeing to work together.

"What about your bid for the Cerberus intellectual property?" O'Hare asked, apparently unaware of the nerve he struck.

"Totally bloody rejected. Kelly and RDEz are in the driving seat. He's establishing a pharmaceutical company to develop and market whatever products can be created from the DNA research and laboratory work done by the late Dr. White and her team. He's acquired the Lifelong material— the Midway-related research. I heard he's got access to some material from the UK, value unknown, via Midway."

"So Kelly's cornered the genetic engineering market, huh?" commented Grovers, unintentionally provocative.

"Yes, and I can't stop him—his stock position is a total block. Why don't you work out a solution to that problem?" The snarl was not disguised.

"Outside my scope," Grovers said. "I'll take on security and related issues, but leave marketing to those experts."

Cromarty was unsure whether Grovers had purposefully misread his comment. He said, "Fair enough." He checked his watch. "We've guests coming and my wife will be upset if I'm not ready. O'Hare, spend some time with Grovers, and both of you get a plan together. Find out whatever you can about Schmidt's current physical and mental condition. Send me your updates. We'll meet and review in ten days. Feasible?"

"Sure."

"Works for me," Grovers agreed. He turned to O'Hare. "I'm heading to the airport—do you need a ride?"

"No, thanks. My chopper's due in minutes. I'll give you a call on Monday—I'll be in Washington all week."

"Okay." Grovers gave a half salute.

"I'll show you out," Cromarty said. He and Grovers left the room. O'Hare turned back to the view of the lake and waited for Cromarty to return. The beat of a helicopter signaled its approach.

Cromarty was back in less than three minutes. "Anything else?"

"Are you seriously considering major acquisitions?"

"If I can remove stumbling blocks that might embarrass me, yes. I have some friends who want to join with me—it'll cost big money, and I mean big, and the returns are huge. I could self-fund it all, of course. The problem is the FBI either holds or has access to material I'd prefer not to see the light of day. Donnelly will be aware of it. Schmidt is worse; he knows everything, or his people do. If it's released, it will kill my offers."

"We'll have to see what we can do." The helicopter was closer, landing.

"Indeed. By the way, there's a larger bonus if you can neutralize another potential problem."

"He shouldn't be too difficult," O'Hare pointed outside. "That's my ride—I'll talk with you through the week."

Cromarty watched the NSA officer walk out the door. Minutes later he heard O'Hare's helicopter depart. His dreams could become nightmares if he wasn't careful. He poured himself another glass of Scotch.

Chapter 3

After Mark finished his discussion with Maeve, he called Anna. She was in Boston with Niland and Gabrielle, their two unofficial Cerberus wards. All four were genetically engineered. Mark did not know his origin; records of his early childhood were non-existent. Anna and the two children had been processed in embryo by Cerberus scientists. Maeve headed up Cerberus US, and Mark, during his recent visit to London, had been appointed CEO of the UK organization.

"I met with Joe Clancy. He seems to understand what we need. He said he'll have some ideas, concepts, for the house, to show us in two weeks."

"That's good. Does the place feel sad?"

"Heartbreaking. The house is like a blackened skeleton. The barns and cottage are burnt rubble."

There was a pause as each absorbed the emotion.

"I should've come with you."

"No, it was best I came alone."

"Did anything survive the attack?"

"I don't know whether the shed is still standing. I haven't had a chance, yet, to go look. I've sensed an intruder. I'm waiting for the local police to arrive."

"They'll love that. They probably think our place is a vortex of violent crime. Is there anything else?"

"Maeve called. She said there's been a lot of social chatter and Linda Schöner thinks I'm the focal point. Her analysts are trying to discover who's behind it."

"Be careful."

"Maeve wants me to wait at the Redmont police station until one of Winter's security teams can escort me back to Boston."

"She's that worried?"

"She's being extremely cautious. I'll stay with the police, though, until my escort arrives. I can't ignore her advice."

"I should hope not. I'll be anxious until you return."

"I'm armed. I'll wait here until the police arrive. I'll see if they'll go with me while I check the shed. Expect a text from me when I leave the police station."

He ended the call. He knew Anna would worry until he returned. He wanted to explore, to look for the intruder, and to check for Gabrielle's art books containing her drawings. She had left them in the small shed at the back of the house. She'd planned, a week or so before they had departed for London, to use it as her studio, and had begun to take possession by moving in an easel, paints, a chair, and some of her artwork.

He was tempted to wander and on reflection, reconsidered, deciding it was more prudent to wait by his vehicle as he had indicated to Anna. There would be time enough to look around once some of Redmont's law enforcement arrived.

The sound of the approaching siren roused him from his reverie. He checked his watch. Ten minutes. Either they had been nearby or they were driving well in excess of the speed limit. He watched as the police vehicle threaded its way through the entrance and around the patches of broken glass. The driver brought the vehicle nearly up to Mark's toes.

Two officers exited the police car. One, a senior officer according to his rank chevrons, approached him. His hand was on his weapon.

"Midway? Mark Midway?"

"Yes, that's me."

"I'm Lieutenant Harkness, Redmont police. Can I see some identification?"

"Yes. I'm armed. Can I remove my Glock, first?"

Harkness drew his weapon. "Leary, get over here. Search this person. He said he's armed." He turned back to Mark. "You should know the routine. Turn around, hands on the vehicle. Make anything like a wrong move and you'll wake up in hospital. Maybe."

Mark turned around and placed his hands on his SUV. He spread his feet. "I thought you said you understood Major Dempsey's message—what was it? Ah, yes: Don't mess with the people who live here."

Leary laughed.

Harkness said, replacing his weapon. "Shit—you must be Midway. No one else would know that. You guys haunt my dreams. I'm still trying to explain to the chief what happened here when Dempsey's men blew up his MRAP. We haven't seen the promised replacement, yet."

Leary reached under Mark's jacket and removed the Glock and its holster. He dropped them onto the front seat of the police vehicle. "Anything else?"

"No. My wallet's in my jacket pocket—mind if I get it out?"

"Go ahead."

Mark withdrew his wallet and opened it to show his driver's license. He handed the wallet to Leary who passed it to Harkness.

"Okay," confirmed Harkness, returning the wallet. "You can stand easy. You appear to be the person we're supposed to meet. You think there's an intruder here? Also, your contact—Maeve Donnelly—said your safety's been threatened, and she'd like us to take you to our station. She's arranging a security escort for your return to Boston?"

"Yes, she's a cautious person. She was the director of the FBI—you might recall she was kidnapped a year or so back.

Her driver was shot and killed by the Russians who kidnapped her, and she resigned shortly afterwards."

"I remember that," said Leary. "And Cox—what was his name—ah, Nikita Yanovich—he was Russian, too."

"Don't mention that guy to me, please. So it's a problem with Russians?" Harkness asked. "Or is it something to do with the terrorists who shot up your house? Although I must admit, you did a damned good job of fighting them off. Where were you, London?"

"Donnelly's team has identified a threat aimed at me, but not who. Yes, we were in London."

"That was some weapon you used. Software controlled?"

"I can't discuss it; I'd have the US Army on my case. I occasionally work with them, as you may recall."

"I understand," Leary said.

"Now what's this story about an intruder?" Harkness asked.

"I was walking around with an architect, discussing what we needed to rebuild. You know how you get a twitch, sometimes, when someone's watching you? It was that. Plus some sounds." He added the latter point to make sure his concerns were more credible. "I thought I'd explore after the architect left. Before I could do that, Donnelly phoned and told me there was a possible threat. So I thought I'd wait until you arrived."

"Sensible," Harkness said.

"Do you mind coming with me? There's a utility shed a few hundred yards into the woods that I want to check."

"Sure. We'll come with you and see what's there."

The three men, with Mark leading the way, walked to the rear of where the house used to be. When they reached the narrow path into the woods, he turned and followed it. There were no signs of use, no footprints, and the grass, undisturbed, was tall and hanging down, hiding the trail. Trees, mainly maples and birch, provided shade. They stopped at a small, solidly constructed shed, which was set away from the path and partially hidden from casual passers-by. It was in its own clearing. Three ravens watched from a high dead limb, hopping from branch to branch, as though they were intending to move closer. A wind generator spun its vigorous round and a row of solar panels added to the power supply. The shed door was partially open, the lock broken. Mark pulled on a corner of the door and pulled it open.

The shed was unoccupied. A sleeping bag had been folded and placed on a small bench. Cans of food and some cooking utensils were stored near a small camp stove. There were electric cables and controls on a side wall. An easel stood against the other wall, and there was an artwork folder nearby, on an old table. He stepped into the shed and checked. The folder was empty—there was no sign of Gabrielle's drawings.

He could hear the ravens cawing in the tree above the shed.

'Looks like someone broke in and is camping here," Leary said, following Mark. Harkness stood at the door. Leary continued, "Whoever it is, they're undoubtedly hiding somewhere in the woods. Probably the same person who was watching you."

"I remember this shed," Harkness said. "It was set up with hydroponic irrigation. We raided it two—three years ago. There were a couple of young guys who were giving us some trouble. They knew the son of the owners, although we couldn't prove anyone else was involved. They were using it to grow pot. It was a sophisticated operation. They had their own power for light and heating, and an underground well for irrigation. They grew fifty or more plants, which were about four foot high when we took them out."

"This damage and break-in definitely happened after we left for London," Mark said.

Harkness groaned. "That's all I need—another crime on this property. Is anything missing?"

"Some artwork of our ward's. Otherwise nothing of commercial value as far as I can tell." He sent a brief text message to Anna.

"Okay, we'll make a note. We could search around and see if we can find the perp. He's probably well out of sight now he's heard the siren."

"Agreed. I'll return with some help in a day or so to search the woods. We might be lucky."

"Do you want us to treat this as a crime scene? There's likely to be prints all over the place," Harkness asked. "We might get lucky."

"Would you mind? There's damage to the door, illegal entry, and trespass. I wouldn't be bothered normally, but we've had too much damage done to this property."

"I understand—the house and main sheds are a write-off. Okay, I'll arrange for a crime scene team to visit. With luck, they'll be here this afternoon. I'll radio base when we get back to the car. Leary, I'll find out if the team is available, and if so, you can return here and keep an eye on the shed until Lieutenant Pierce arrives. I'll escort Mark to the station, so he can meet up with his security team."

"Sure thing."

As they returned to the vehicles, Mark was certain he could sense the attention of the hidden watcher. Apprehension was mixed in with the caution he had sensed earlier.

The three ravens flitted from tree to tree, escorting them out of the wooded area.

Chapter 4

Mark followed the police vehicle to the Redmont police station where Harkness signaled for him to park in the official section. They both exited their vehicles and Harkness beckoned.

"You won't get a ticket," the police lieutenant said. "Well if you do, give it to me. You can wait in Leary's office, if you like. It's next to mine. Fortunately the chief's in Boston; otherwise, he'd want to know who you are. Not sure the Midway name would excite him in the right way."

"Whoa. I'm not one of your—ah—clients. I've been raided, my property shot up and burnt out, and now have an intruder apparently damaging a shed and trespassing. Also, some personal property is missing."

"Yeah, but he loved that MRAP. I know, I know. We don't encounter that many mine-based ambushes around here and it was totally unsuitable for a small town. Anyway, if we can help with your intruder, we'll do so. Oh, I'll carry your Glock. I'll return it when you leave. We've a metal detector for visitors, and it'd be best if you go through without causing any alarms."

Mark settled into the small office, using one of the visitor's chairs. He sent another text message to Anna, letting her know where he was. He tried to get comfortable on the chair, which seemed to have springs in the wrong places. After an hour, Mark was bored with re-reading a year old copy of Hunter & Shooter and had no interest in the police magazines on Leary's desk. As he stood up to stretch, Harkness entered the office.

"There are people here for you. I assume they're your security, but we'd better check."

Mark stifled a yawn. "I agree. Is there somewhere we can meet with them?"

"I've commandeered an interview room. They're waiting for us. Two of them. They look as though they might be ex-military."

Two men were waiting in the interview room; one was seated at a table and the other was pacing. Mark did not recognize either one. Harkness kept back as Mark stepped forward.

"I'm Midway." He used his cell phone to take a photograph of each man. "Let me send these images." He addressed a message to Maeve and attached the two jpeg files. His note was simple, seeking confirmation of the identity of each of the two men. He expected a reply within minutes. He looked at both men. "Do you have IDs?"

"Yes, sir," replied the man seated at the table. He stood. "I'm Andrew Reeves and this is Tomas Strong. Please call me Drew. We're both members of Winter Security. Brian said to convey his greetings. I understand you advised Paul Kelly when Brian installed his security system." Each man handed over identification documents to Mark.

Mark looked at each driver's license photo and at the men who would escort him back to Boston. The faces and photos matched. "Tell me more."

"Yes, sir. We're both ex-military. Iraq. Served with Dempsey, whom you knew, I believe. We've been with Brian for three years. We have another three men waiting with two vehicles. I'll drive back with you in your SUV, and the other vehicles will provide escort. Our task is to get you back to Boston in one piece—alive."

Mark checked his messages. Maeve had replied to his message with a simple 'Yes.' He handed back the identification documents. "Very well. I've received confirmation. I'm ready to go. Lieutenant Harkness, I appreciate your courtesy."

"Our crime team should have some details within a day. I'll call you."

Harkness escorted them out of the building and once outside he returned Mark's Glock. The police officer checked Mark's vehicle while Reeves retrieved some gear from one of the escort vehicles.

"It's clear, no tickets," Harkness said. "Safe journey."

"Thank you." Mark said.

Harkness returned to the police station.

Mark opened the driver-side door of his vehicle, ready to drive to Boston. Reeves intercepted him.

"I'll drive, sir," Reeves said. He was in the process of installing forward and rearward facing video cameras with wireless links back to their base. "I know how our team works, if we need to take counter-measures."

Mark handed over his keys. "I don't mind, at all."

When they headed out of Redmont, Mark made a phone call. "Anna? Yes. We're on our way back. I'm with Winter's escort. Tell the children there was no trace of Gabrielle's artwork."

Anna said, "I'm relieved you have security. Gabrielle will recover, I'm sure."

After they completed their conversation, Mark messaged Maeve that he was on the way back to Boston. He sat back and tried to ignore the questions surrounding the intruder he had sensed.

Mark was jarred out of his relaxed state by the sudden swerve of the vehicle and his driver's curse. There was a major confusion of vehicles about a hundred yards in front, which they quickly overtook. He looked back; an SUV had slid sideways towards the edge of the road, some yards before the emergency lane. He was unable to discern details. They were on the Northern Expressway, heading south towards Boston, into a splatter of raindrops from the storm he had seen earlier.

"What's up?"

Drew said, "Our front escort was taken out. I think someone dropped a concrete cinder block on the vehicle, from the Chandler Road Bridge—the one we just went under."

"Check your other vehicle."

The driver reached for his radio handset; he'd installed the radio in Mark's vehicle before departing the police station. "Tomas, did you see that?"

"Sure thing, boss. It was nasty. Mike slid off, missed everyone, fortunately. I couldn't see him when I passed. He's not answering the radio. I've called 911 and reported an accident."

"We need to be careful from here; the traffic volume's getting lighter."

"They'll probably try something after the 495 intersection. There's swamp and forest on either side; it restricts the public view."

"Okay. Let's go to high speed. We'll call the state troopers and let them know we're under attack. Keep an eye open for anyone matching our speed." The SUV was accelerating before Drew had finished speaking.

"Make sure you're strapped in," he directed Mark. "Call 911 for me. Tell them it's Winter Security, and we have an emergency. Ask for Desk 301 and say it's Code 25."

Mark used his phone to make the call. It was connected to the SUV's cell phone system and was on speaker. The 911 operator patched his call through to another responder without hesitation or question.

"Desk 301. Sergeant Trevors."

"Code 25. Winter Security, providing security for a client.

I'm the client. We're heading south on the Northern Expressway, approaching the 495 junction. One of our escorts has been taken out, we suspect by a cinder block dropped from the Chandler Road Bridge." Mark completed the details, uninterrupted. He concluded, "Traffic is light. Our two vehicles are traveling at speeds of 90 to 100 mph. We're in a dark blue Touareg—Volkswagen—and our second vehicle is a red Expedition. Can we have police assistance?"

"One moment, sir."

The officer came back online after a short interval. "Yes, sir. We can arrange vehicles to meet you."

Mark could hear Tomas's voice but did not absorb his message. Drew said, "Tell them there are two, possibly three, chase vehicles."

"My driver advises there are two or three chase vehicles." He relayed the details provided by Drew.

"We have troopers approximately eight miles in front of you. Three marked vehicles. They will wait for your arrival. Two will intercept the chase vehicles, and the third trooper will escort you. Please do not disconnect this call."

"Drew, can we hold out for eight miles?"

"Sure. I think. Contact Tomas, see what he says."

"Officer, I need to contact the other driver."

"Yessir."

Mark used the radio. "Tomas, we'll have troopers to assist in about five minutes. Can you cope with the vehicles chasing you?"

"One tried to side swipe me. He's an *imbécil*—his little car can't stand up to mine." There were noises; they sounded like shots. "*¡Qué chinga!* They're shooting at my tires. This is hot." There were some louder, closer, shots. Tomas came back, "We've discouraged them for the moment."

Mark spoke to the police sergeant. "They tried to crash our escort vehicle. They fired shots at it and at the occupants. Please communicate to your troopers that this is a dangerous situation."

"Yes sir. Please turn on your hazard lights."

"Drew, hazard lights."

"Okay."

"Tomas, please turn on your hazard lights. We're getting close."

"Sure thing. This *cabrón* is going to try again, that's for sure."

"Hang on." Mark hoped that was possible.

"You should be within a mile or two, now," advised Trevors.

"Drew, a vehicle got past while I was defending. It's close to you—" Shots interrupted whatever Tomas wanted to add and the radio fell silent.

Drew cursed.

Mark caught a glimpse of a black sedan, a BMW, approaching the driver's side of their vehicle. He glanced to his right and saw a second black BMW approaching. A passenger in the second vehicle had opened the rear window and was leveling a weapon in the Touareg's general direction. He thought the gunman was aiming at their tires.

Drew cursed again.

"I've lost control. They've taken over the electronics—no steering, nothing." He hit the steering wheel with both hands. He was struggling to regain control.

The gunman on the right fired a burst from his weapon. A ricochet scorched a streak of pain across the back of Mark's hand. His anger grew; he had been shot at too many times. He dropped the cell phone. He aimed and fired his Glock: two shots at the passenger trying to shoot out their tires and two at the driver. The BMW slid sideways; it was as though it had hit an unseen barrier. He saw it roll off the roadway as it receded in the distance.

He turned his attention to Drew, who was fighting the Touareg's refusal to respond. The people following them were maintaining at least partial control of the Volkswagen.

Drew said, "They keep switching their penetration. It

seems random—loss of brakes, next was power steering, followed by accelerator. I've managed to select neutral and now all I can do is try to come to a stop, hopefully, without hitting anything."

"There are blue lights ahead. See if you can get to the troopers."

"Our pursuers also can see them; that might give them second thoughts." Mark reached for his phone. "You still there?" he asked.

"Sure. It sounds as though you're experiencing a rocky ride."

"Let the troopers know we're being attacked electronically. We've eliminated another vehicle, as far as I can determine."

Chapter 5

She was young, about twelve years old, and wore jeans, a long-sleeved shirt, and a light jacket, all of which needed drastic laundry intervention. Her sneakers were once bright red and now the color was uncertain and the shoes were worn and scuffed. Her hair, blond, was long and tied into a mix of plaits and pigtails in a juvenile attempt to disguise her need of a sympathetic hairdresser and a serious shampoo. Her baseball cap did not adequately cover the mixed style. Her face was rubbed streaky clean and two or three freckles spotted each cheek. As the driver eased his old truck to a halt she smiled her thanks and pushed on the door handle. It and the hinges squeaked in unison as the door creaked open.

"Are you going to be all right?" The driver of the truck, an old farmer, frowned his concern.

"Yes, sir. My mom will meet me here. Thank you for the lift."

"Well, if you're certain?" There was something odd about a young girl walking along a road by herself. These days—for some reason he did not continue that thread of thought. He watched the girl clamber down to the road, dragging her empty backpack. "Now, you know my name and have my phone number, so if you and your mom ever need some assistance, give me a call."

"Yes, sir." She used all her weight to push the truck door closed. The window glass rattled and slipped down half an inch.

The driver nodded and shifted into first gear. The truck shuddered as he released the clutch and slowly moved back into the traffic. It lurched as he changed up through the gears to match the speed of the other vehicles. A small suggestion, one of those added when he had reached out to help the girl board his truck, threw off its dormancy. Within seconds he had forgotten completely about his recent passenger.

The girl watched as the farmer and his old truck drove off. He had believed her story, as unrealistic as it was. That did not surprise her; she had added small suggestions when he touched her hand to help her climb up into the cabin of the old farm truck. The first was to ensure her safety. The second was to suspend his disbelief. The third was to ensure the man forgot all about her once she left his vehicle. Her expertise was increasing, contributing to her survival. She swung the empty backpack onto her shoulders and headed towards the small store.

"Hello, Missy," The store owned called as she pushed through the swing door. The greeting was genuine. She had been here before, a while back. She did not like repeating her visits too frequently, in case people began to ask questions she was not willing to answer, at least, not truthfully.

"Hi, Mr. Mason."

"Shopping for your mom, again?"

"Yes, sir. She's not feeling well. I know what to get."

"Good. I'll look after you when you're ready."

She put her backpack into a shopping cart walked along the modest aisles, looking for supplies. She avoided candies, foodstuffs with high sugar content, and crackers. With one exception; she selected a small packet of crackers; her feathered friends always expected a treat. She ignored frozen food unless it was something she could eat within a day or two. Packets of pasta, some sauces, cans—she had a can opener, although sometimes it was a struggle to use, fresh vegetables and a box of protein bars. Soon her backpack was full; at least, as full as she could manage. She pushed her cart around the other aisles, observing, listening to whispers, low conversations, and snippets of thought. At last she pushed the cart to the checkout where the storekeeper was waiting.

She watched and waited while Mr. Mason keyed her purchases into his register and repacked her backpack.

"Did you hear anything I need to know?" the shopkeeper asked.

"There're two men in the far row—I think they're planning to rob you. One of them has a handgun. Nothing else." She kept her voice low; fortunately there were no customers within hearing. On her last visit she had discovered one of the store employees was skimming money from a cash register amounting to fifty to a hundred dollars each day. She thought that revelation balanced her own skimming and Mason did not express any disagreement.

The storekeeper did not change his expression. He had a shotgun under his station, and two of his storemen were ex-police, retired and working part time. They would come to his assistance as soon as he signaled. He picked up the phone that connected to the store's PA system.

"Thirty-one to Delivery. Thirty-one to Delivery." He replaced the handset. The coded message would alert his team. Mason looked at the register slip.

"I'll keep this for your mom, all right?"

"Yes, sir. She should be better in a few days."

Mason nodded. There was something he needed to say, but the thought was too elusive. He helped the little girl shoulder her now loaded backpack. As their hands touched, a gentle reinforcement flowed from the girl to the storekeeper. In three or four days he would tear up the unpaid register slip and would welcome her when she next visited.

She struggled under the load and headed out of the store to the bus stop, a distance of only a hundred or so yards. A small bus, part of a regional service, was scheduled to depart in twenty minutes and she planned to be on board. She did not want to spend time in the small town where people could ask unnecessary questions. She had enough money for the fare, at least, for a short journey, and the bus driver never questioned how far she traveled once she boarded his bus.

The girl halted her quiet progress along the overgrown track, suddenly extra cautious. Her backpack was heavy, and its weight was an obvious struggle for her. She was worried she had too much to carry. She had only walked a short distance from the road near the locked shed and still had a long way to go along the narrow path through the trees. Perhaps she should make more than one trip. She decided to hide half her purchases and return for them later.

She explored the trees off the path and found one that she thought would provide shelter from the rain if the storm came. It was far enough into the woods to be safe from casual inspection. She unpacked a good half of her backpack, stacking the items against the tree trunk and covering them with leaves. No one, she was confident, would find her cache. She returned to the path, her pack now much easier to carry.

A raven landed in front of her, out of arm's reach. It hopped towards her, its head on one side. She smiled. She patted her pockets, found what she was seeking, and brought out a small handful of crackers. She dropped three in front of the raven, which was now peering at her, its expression unfathomable. It hopped forward and pecked at one of the treats. A second raven landed beside the first one, and dropped something bright and shiny from its beak. It retrieved the object, hopped forward, and dropped it again. A third raven watched from a branch above her head.

She eased the backpack off her shoulders and set it on the ground, relieved at the excuse to stop awhile. She stepped a pace forward, towards the two birds on the ground. They stilled, watching her with heads to one side, their eyes bright, intent. The second raven hopped sideways, towards one of the crackers, leaving the shining object on the grass. It was a key, a brass key. She wondered where the bird had found it. She put it in her pocket.

The third raven flew down to claim his cracker. Its comical hops and quizzical expression made her laugh, the sound quickly hushed—there could be anyone in these woods. She gave the ravens another cracker each, silently enjoying their antics as they fed.

The backpack, even half-empty, seemed to be heavier, she was certain. She struggled with the shoulder straps and untwisted one that was trying to dig its way into her skin. She set off again along the path. The ravens, their snack completed, flew above her head and landed in the low branches of a tree less than ten yards ahead. It seemed to her that they were having a conversation. The three birds flew down to land on the path in front of her, cawing, tentatively blocking her progress. She stopped, wondering what they were trying to communicate. One flew back behind her in the direction she had come. She turned to watch the bird as it hopped back along the path. The other two ravens flew back and joined the first one. They all hopped in the same direction. Well, she thought, that's a clear message.

The girl walked back along the path to where she had hidden half her load of groceries. She bent down to avoid low branches and headed to the tree she had found earlier. She removed her backpack and placed it on the side of the tree away from the path. She covered it, too, with leaves, camouflaging its appearance. She checked her handiwork, and satisfied, made her way back to the path.

She sat beside the path and thought for a minute or two,

watching as the ravens watched her. They had no opinion to offer, she decided, so she would make up her own mind. She gave the birds another cracker each and when they finished their snack, she headed up the path in the direction of the shed she was using as her home. As she approached what she thought of as her shed, she slowed, moving quietly from tree to tree, avoiding the path. Leaves crackled underfoot and she slowed even more. She came up to her shed from the rear and slowly walked around to the front where it faced the path.

To her alarm, someone had broken the lock on the door. A person stood further away, closer to the house ruins. She thought he looked like a policeman; at least, he wore a uniform. He was facing away. She didn't want to be found by the police; it was far too risky. She had used her abilities to steal things, mainly food to survive. They would send her to prison. She crept slowly back to the rear of the shed. The ravens seemed to be ignoring her activities. They did not appear to be alarmed so she lifted a loose board and dropped down a makeshift panel that someone, perhaps the owner of the shed, had put in place as an emergency exit. She lifted herself up and slid into the narrow opening.

Rays of light filtered through the panel opening and through other gaps and narrow slits in the walls. She waited. When her eyes adjusted to the dimmer light, she checked her small collection of clothing, her sleeping bag, and utensils. To her relief, nothing was missing. She gathered everything up into a makeshift bundle and returned to the panel opening. She pushed her bundle through and quickly followed, dropping onto the grass at the rear of her shed. She closed the panel and pulled down the loose board.

Again, she wondered what her next steps should be. The ravens were silent, watching from the high branches of a nearby tree. The key presented to her by the ravens might unlock the shed near the road. She would check; it would not take her long. If it worked, and the shed looked suitable, she would move her possessions there. Alternatively, she would camp out, hiding in the woods for a few days until she was sure no one was tracking her. She had to stay away from the path; otherwise the policeman would find her. She headed into the trees with her bundle of possessions.

Chapter 6

For some reason, the road was free of vehicles apart from the one following them. Mark looked back to check, twice. Drew caught his concern.

"Someone, police or thugs, have blocked the road, stopping anyone from getting in the way. Another mile, then we should be safe," Drew said.

The blue lights ahead were blocking the roadway. The black BMW still trailed them and Mark wondered at the driver's intention. The presence of the police should have deterred his pursuit. Perhaps he planned to bluff his way past the blockade. Their SUV began to slow.

"Are you in control?"

"Not yet—the BMW guys are still hacking us."

The SUV braked sharply and slewed across the road, heading towards the nearest police vehicle. Drew held on to the steering wheel, struggling to steer out of the slide. His efforts may have been successful because the Volkswagen came to a stop mere inches away from the rear of the nearest vehicle in the police barricade.

"Hell," breathed Drew, hitting the steering wheel with both hands.

Mark didn't comment. He was watching the BMW through the rear window. It halted close to the rear of their vehicle. The driver and his companion appeared to have no concerns about the police presence. He and Drew were blocked in, with one of the barricade vehicles in front and the black BMW behind.

"We've got trouble," Mark said to the listening sergeant. "We have five patrol cars blocking the road; they're all Highway Patrol. Troopers are standing next to their vehicles, with weapons pointing at us. The guys following us are confident, perhaps too confident. Maybe there's some collusion. We'll get out and see what this is all about."

Four police officers were standing in front of the Volkswagen, weapons drawn and aimed at Drew and Mark. At the same time the two occupants of the BMW had exited and were approaching on either side of the Touareg. Mark was not surprised to see other troopers had weapons at the ready—something strange was happening. Two police vehicles left the barricade, heading down the highway.

The man closest to Drew motioned with his handgun. "Exit your vehicle. If you have a gun, leave it behind. As you exit, raise your hands."

"Come on, let's see what this is about," Mark said.

"I have a bad feeling."

"You're not alone."

They opened their doors simultaneously and stepped out. Mark dropped his cell phone and his Glock on the car seat and noted Drew did the same with his gun. Mark stood straight and raised his hands high. He felt the presence of one of the men from the BMW behind him. He couldn't see the other man and assumed he was standing behind Drew.

"Our weapons are in the vehicle," he said. "Why are you stopping us?"

"Shaddup," commanded the closest police officer.

Another one said, "We've all seen the FBI BOLO alert."

"I'm with Winter Security," Drew said. "We were under attack, as I reported to your base. Look—"

The police officer who had instructed them to get out of

the SUV struck Drew across the face with his weapon.

"I told ya—shaddup."

Drew staggered and lurched forward, towards the police officer who had attacked him. Mark heard a shot and realized it had come from the man standing behind Drew. He saw Drew fall to the ground. Mark felt the pressure of a gun barrel in his side.

"Don't move, don't utter a word, unless you want to join your friend." The voice was soft, close to a whisper.

"I think you can write that up as shot while assaulting an officer in an attempt to escape." The speaker was the driver of the BMW. He leaned down to check the body. "No pulse." He sounded satisfied. He addressed the senior officer. "Thanks for your assistance. We've been after these people for some time. We'll take the other one—you can have the body. Our boss will be in contact with your boss to express his thanks. We owe you, all of you."

"You're welcome. Glad to help the FBI. Did you lose anyone?"

"As far as I know all of my people are alive. Perhaps some broken bones. One or two vehicles were wrecked along the way. I'll make sure you get a full report. Our chopper is due to arrive shortly—it's going to land here. Can your men drive these two vehicles to your base? We'll have someone pick them up later. We want to get this one behind bars as quickly as we can."

Mark listened with disbelief. He didn't believe these men were FBI agents. Before he could object, he was reminded with a sudden jab that the weapon barrel was still pressed into his side. The threat was obvious. Mark held back his response—he would pick a better time.

The senior police officer said, "Understandable. I'll arrange for the vehicles to go to our garage."

The whomp, whomp of an approaching helicopter caught everyone's attention. They all watched as the aircraft settled down on the highway, a hundred yards back. The man with the handgun poked Mark's side with the weapon.

"Hands behind your back. My associate's going to cuff you."

The man who had shot and killed Drew approached, readying handcuffs. Resigned, Mark allowed the man to cuff him without protest. He felt a jab in the side of his neck.

"Wha—?" He tried to jerk his head away from the sharp pain.

"It's only a little something to make sure you don't give us any trouble. It'll take effect in a few minutes. Now come on, we have a chopper to catch." The speaker turned back to the police officers. "Thanks again, everyone. We owe you." He grabbed Mark's arm and pulled him towards the waiting aircraft. He spoke in a softer voice to Mark. "You've given me enough trouble this morning—two of my men are dead. Give me any more and I will shoot you. No, I won't kill you. I'll make sure you hurt, though."

Mark's head began to spin. He knew they were approaching the side passenger door of the helicopter. He did not have the strength to step up into the cabin and someone pushed him from behind. He fell, sliding across the cabin floor. He hit his head on something unyielding. He was lifted and pushed into a seat. There was a jumble of voices and activity. He heard a voice, as though from a long way away.

"You've got him—good. Expect the bonus—"

The rest was lost in the noisy acceleration as the helicopter lifted off. Everything went dark, silent, and he floated, floated, floated.

Chapter 7

The two-person Redmont Police crime team arrived at what they called the Midway Property some minutes after 4:00 p.m. The driver of the van, Lieutenant Kelsi Pierce, cursed to herself when she saw broken glass on the blacktop on the way towards the ruins of the house. She slowed the vehicle and wound around the clumps of glass fragments.

"Someone made a heck of a mess of this," she commented to her assistant. Kelsi had the rank of lieutenant, in part because of her Boston experience and in part because of her medical qualification.

"A gang of some kind attacked the property a month or so before you were recruited, Doc," her assistant replied. He was a trainee laboratory assistant, young, eager for experience.

"Can I ask you a question?" the lieutenant said as she stopped the van in front of the burnt wreckage of a house.

Her assistant was cautious. "Sure, Doc. I suppose."

"Why does everyone call you Ladder? I mean, the alliteration works—Ladder Lasher—but what's the reason?"

Kelsi watched as her assistant grew red in the face—the way the color spread she realized his entire body was blushing.

"Aw—do you have to?"

"No, of course not. However, it would make a positive

contribution to our working relationship." She hid her smile. She opened the rear door of the van and pulled out her evidence kit and camera. "Here, carry this. I'll take the camera. You can tell me as we explore. Harkness said Leary would be here. Can you see anyone?"

"No."

"Come on, it can't be that bad."

Ladder mumbled as he took hold of the evidence kit.

Kelsi thought he said something like "You don't know the half of it."

She smiled. "Harkness said there was a track away from the house, at the rear. We need to find the small shed a couple of hundred yards along that track, right?"

"Yes, Doc."

"Good. Come on. Let's find this mysterious shed. Now, your story."

"Aw, Doc, don't do this to me. Look, there's the path."

"Where the heck is Leary, I wonder?"

They headed down the path and stopped outside the door of the shed. He set the evidence kit on the ground.

"Gloves," instructed Kelsi. "While this is probably a wild goose chase, we need to follow the rules." They both donned latex gloves. Kelsi took photos of the front of the shed and moved in closer to photograph the broken lock. He watched, hopeful that the lieutenant would forget her question. Kelsi pried open the door and stepped inside.

"Flashlight," she requested. Ladder reached into the evidence kit, found the flashlight, and handed it to his boss. He stood beside her, to watch her process.

Kelsi steadied the beam, moving it carefully from corner to corner, progressively checking the interior of the small shed. She stopped and shifted the beam back to what appeared to be a collection of old clothes. Men's clothes. She froze for a moment and then her training kicked in.

"Stop. Don't move any further into the shed. That's a body. It may be our missing Officer Leary. Whoever it is, I need to check for life signs. Wait outside the door for me."

Ladder quickly exited the shed and Kelsi followed shortly after. "It's Leary. He's dead. Shot. We have to go back to the van and call it in. Take care where you walk."

She led the way back to the crime team vehicle and called in her emergency. The duty officer was as shocked as she was.

"Yes, it's Leary," Kelsi said. "No, he's not breathing. Yes, I'm a doctor. I know if someone is dead or not. Get some help here as quickly as you can. I feel exposed. There's only me and my assistant." She listened for a while. "Good, we'll be here." She ended the call.

Kelsi turned to Ladder and said, "They're sending Harkness and an investigative team, an ambulance, and the ME. Probably twenty minutes. We should remain in the vehicle until someone gets here. Plenty of time for you to tell me how you got your name."

Ladder was pale; this was the closest he'd been to a dead body, and he realized the killer could still be around.

"Yes, Doc. Do you—do you think the—?"

"The killer is still here? No, long gone. Well, if he had any sense."

Kelsi took her seat and Ladder sat in the passenger seat. He reached over and turned on the ignition and pressed the button to wind down the side window. The glass slowly recessed into the door. He turned to look out and jumped back with a shrill scream.

A head, with blood streaks adding to disheveled hair, had rested on the glass and now fell towards him, stopped only by a half-conscious restraint of the body that thumped lightly against the door panel. As he watched, the girl's face slid slowly out of sight.

"Help me." The request was faint as she disappeared, falling to the ground.

Kelsi leapt out and ran to the other side of the van where the slight form lay crumpled on the tarmac. Ladder watched anxiously, still recovering from his fright. His boss knelt down beside the body and checked vital signs.

She said, "The girl's alive, unconscious. Her heartbeat is strong. Her matted hair is full of partly-congealed and crusted blood—she has a head wound. I can't check it any further without cutting her hair back. I'd prefer the hospital to do that. Ladder, come on out. I need to settle her on the seat. Come on, she won't bite." She lifted the child carefully from the blacktop parking strip.

"Um—sure, okay Doc." He struggled out of the vehicle and held the passenger door open while Kelsi deposited her burden gently on the seat.

"There's a blanket in the back. Get it for me, please. Also a large bottle of water, some wipes, a towel, and a plastic cup. Quickly."

Ladder moved with purpose, quickly returning with the requested items. Kelsi first wrapped the girl in the blanket and used the wipes to clean her own hands. She washed some of the blood away from the girl's face. She pushed her hair back from where the blood was still oozing. It looked as though she had been struck by a bullet. She checked further, as gently as she could. The girl moaned.

Kelsi straightened up and breathed deeply. She said, "That's possibly a bullet wound. Not deep, the bullet didn't penetrate. She'll live. As long as we get her some hospital treatment."

The girl stirred and her eyes opened. "Thank you." Her eyes closed again.

"She's a tough one," surmised Ladder.

"She's drifting in and out of consciousness. I don't know whether to take her to hospital or wait for the ambulance. Let me contact base again. Stand here, make sure she doesn't move or fall."

Kelsi returned to the driver's side of the vehicle, reached in, and picked up the microphone. She pressed the transmit button and made contact.

"Who is it—Harriet? This is Kelsi. I've an update for you.

There's a shooting victim here, a girl. Probably twelve or so. Head wound. Alive. Needs emergency treatment. Where's the ambulance? Should we take her to emergency ourselves or wait?"

She listened to the reply. "Five minutes? I agree, the ambulance is better equipped. The van would be a rough ride. Okay, we'll wait. Yes, if she regains consciousness, I'll try to find out what happened."

Ladder waited for Kelsi to end her call. "I think I can hear the siren, so they're close," he said.

"Good. Yes, you're right. I can hear it, too. Relax, Ladder. Your secret's safe. For the moment."

Kelsi and Lieutenant Harkness stood by as the ambulance crew lifted the stretcher into their vehicle. The little girl opened her eyes and, in panic, sought Kelsi.

"You'll come and visit me?"

"Why, yes, I will. You're in good hands." She reached out to hold a tiny hand.

"There's a car shed at the end of the trail," the soft voice whispered. "That's where they shot me. They're both dead." Her eyes closed again. Kelsi stood back and let the ambulance crew complete their task.

"She'll be okay," the driver said, detecting Kelsi's concern. "We'll get her to emergency as quickly as possible. Do you have any details? Name, parents, address?"

"No, not a thing. She was only conscious for seconds, and I didn't want to interrogate her. I'd like to follow up, see how she is, perhaps some time tomorrow?"

"I'll let the hospital know you'll be visiting. Okay, we've gotta go."

"Don't forget you have to come back."

"No problem—we won't be long."

Kelsi and Ladder watched as the ambulance accelerated

along the drive towards the road, its lights flashing. She turned to her assistant. "We'll both visit her, if you like?"

"Yes, Doc. I'd like to."

Harkness intruded. "We'll interview her once she's cleared by her doctor. Now I'd better see where this other shed is and check whether there really are another two bodies. You coming?" He headed off without waiting for a reply.

Ladder followed Kelsi and Harkness, his dragging footsteps providing an accurate measure of his enthusiasm at the thought of attending multiple crime scenes with a total of three bodies.

Chapter 8

Maeve Donnelly tried to relax as her driver threaded his way through Washington's evening traffic. The driver was Cerberus-engineered, as was her guard seated beside him. She had her briefcase, with papers that she should read later in the evening. Leading and managing the Cerberus organization was not, she thought, a walk in the park. A walk in the dark, more like. She had worries that would overwhelm those she'd experienced when she was director of the FBI.

Schmidt—now he was one of her more significant worries—would be waiting for her when she arrived at her apartment. She had invited him to join her for dinner and she hoped to detect some progress from the therapy he'd been undergoing. When the Russians shot down the helicopter, which was taking him to a scheduled Defense meeting, it surprised his rescuers that he had survived. Unfortunately Major Dempsey, CO of the 145th, had not.

Schmidt had recovered—well, nearly. He had not yet resumed his military duties, and his medical issues were severe enough to reduce the value of his advice to her. She reflected on the drastic step he had taken before the accident, of undergoing a series of Cerberus nanite-based DNA medications. She wondered, had they helped his recovery or delayed it?

Doctors—specialists who oversaw his immediate treatment—were surprised that Schmidt had survived the missile explosion and the crash-landing. They were also surprised at the rapidity of his physical recovery. They could not, however, account for his central nervous system disorder. Their diagnosis was that nerve cell activity in his brain was experiencing random disruptions, resulting in short term bouts of loss of consciousness. Their conclusion: time and therapy would tell.

The car was approaching her apartment building—the driver had worked wonders to find his way through the peak hour streets without too much delay. She sighed. The papers in her briefcase weighed heavily on her mind. What could she plan for the future of Cerberus? That's where she needed Schmidt's insight and advice. Especially now, that he, too, was Cerberus engineered. The driver stopped the vehicle at the allocated parking space in the underground car park, two floors below ground level, beneath the block of apartments. She waited for her guard and driver to move.

Her security processes were, she thought, extreme. However, no matter how much she protested, her Cerberus people would not reduce their level of care and caution. The two men watched their security monitor, waiting for the clearance from the team on duty in the apartment building before they would exit the vehicle.

Initially, when Maeve first moved into her apartment, other apartment tenants had protested the heavy security presence, so Cerberus purchased the building. Now they had the freedom to manage the building security as they wanted, and any tenant who objected was politely requested to terminate their lease and leave. Not many did so—most appreciated the increased level of security, for Washington was not always a safe town.

It was thirty seconds before the monitor screen displayed the all clear and the guard rushed to open her door. They both—the driver and the guard—escorted her to the elevators where another security guard waited. No one else was in the elevator and it delivered her to the tenth floor without interruption. At last, she reached her apartment where she could relax.

Archimedes Schmidt handed her a cocktail. "To your precise requirements," he said. He appeared fit and healthy. He was dressed casually, for once forsaking his more military style.

"Oh, I need this."

"You need a vacation, more likely." They touched glasses. Schmidt was drinking sparkling water, Maeve knew.

"Yes, I do. Not likely, though. How about you?"

"I'm healthy, as you can see. I think I've regained some of my youth—seriously. I suspect it's a side effect of the Cerberus treatment. Now to convince everyone my head is screwed on properly." He smiled ruefully. "I won't get medical clearance to resume my duties until I do."

"Perhaps you're subconsciously avoiding that responsibility?"

"Now don't you start. It's bad enough all the witch doctors trying that approach." His smile took the sting out of his words.

"I'll stop, I promise. It's—" Maeve sipped her drink.

"You're worried, concerned for me, I know. I do think the worst is over—the Cerberus nanites have completed their tasks."

"Indeed. Now Bennie is going to prepare us a nice meal. Your contribution is to read some of my papers. I need your insights."

Her cell phone buzzed before Schmidt could reply. She checked the caller ID. "That's Brian Winter. Let me take his call."

"Yes, Brian?"

"Maeve, we've lost Mark."

"What? Hold on, Schmidt's here—I'll put you on speaker."

"Hi, Schmidt. I have bad news. We've lost Mark. One of my primary teams was escorting him. They were intercepted somewhere along the highway back to Boston from Redmont. My team was eliminated: two are dead, two badly injured, and, fortunately, two will recover without hospital time."

Maeve said, "Please accept our condolences for your losses. That is so sad. Any details you can add?"

"It's all confused. There's a report my senior man was shot resisting arrest. I haven't found out why he was being arrested. There's a report of FBI involvement and some rumor of Mark being taken off in a helicopter. There's a lot of obfuscation—the local law is putting up major roadblocks in response to our questions. We're trying to make sense of it. Maeve, can you check with the FBI to see if they had an ongoing operation on the Northern Expressway?"

"I'll get on it right away, as soon as we're finished here."

Schmidt spoke up. "Can we provide you with more people?"

"Thanks for the offer—I've pulled some of my people off less important duties. I'll let you know if I need more."

Maeve added, "Good. Don't hesitate to ask. Let's review the situation tomorrow morning. Get what you can. I'll work with the FBI to see what they can add."

"Yes, Maeve. I'm sorry. We should have been better than this."

"Now don't condemn yourself. Mark has managed to attract some powerful enemies. We'll combine forces to find him. Now, is there anything we can do for your people? For families?"

"I'm taking care of them. As you can imagine, it's painful when you lose someone on duty, more so for the surviving families, of course. We can discuss details later after we've rescued Mark, if you like."

"Yes, indeed. We'll call for an update tomorrow at 10:30 a.m? Will that work for you?"

"Done. I hope we have good news."

Maeve ended the call and turned to Schmidt. "Dinner may be full of interruptions. I need to call Linda; she's leading, well not only leading, she's managing your team of analysts. Doing a good job, too."

"She's more than capable, as is the team." He frowned. "I need to get involved, tomorrow. That will shock them all."

"She can get everyone focused—they'll work all night if they need to. They're mostly Cerberus, and Mark is their hero."

"Not at all unexpected. He's helped more than a few Cerberus people."

Maeve decided to try a number of approaches. There were hundreds of Cerberus people in the FBI organization, from agents to office workers, from programmers to scientists, who would respond to informal questions from Linda's team. Indeed, the team could reach out to all the Cerberus resources, to see if anyone had news of activities against Mark. That would encompass the military, CIA, and numerous other governmental and law enforcement agencies. Sometimes Maeve shuddered when she considered the extent of Cerberus penetration into core government organizations. She would ensure this wider network responded to Linda if they discovered anti-Cerberus activities, especially if it involved harm to Mark. She would also make more formal inquiries, using her senior government contacts.

She said to Schmidt, "I'll contact Robbie Fisher. He's been a good friend since taking on the responsibilities of director, after my retirement. Linda can launch a Cerberus-wide search. I'll inform Jenkins, because this has national security ramifications and he'll filter details up to the president. I'll tap other contacts, as we go. Read while I make phone calls."

Maeve handed Schmidt a set of files. He began to read the contents as Maeve spoke to Linda and made her other calls.

Dinner was not the relaxing meal she had intended. She was worried about Mark. She had many reasons to like and respect the young man. Whoever had planned and conducted this assault—including murder and kidnapping—was going to feel heat, lots of it, before she was finished. She said as much to Schmidt and his reply was straightforward.

"I'll hold the bastard's feet to the fire for you."

Chapter 9

"You idiots did what?" exploded Ross Cromarty, spilling his Scotch. His face reddened, as he appeared to struggle to restrain his anger.

"Relax, Ross," said O'Hare. "We're covered."

"I'm not so sure," countered Grovers. "I disagreed with this venture. I told you not to proceed, that it had the potential to expose all of us."

"So this is what the media is full of: a major police chase on Interstate 93, cars wrecked, three or four people killed, others in hospital?" Cromarty asked.

"Yes, and none of it can link back to us."

"For this little piece of mayhem, what do you have to show?"

"I have Midway."

"Midway?" Cromarty's voice rose in pitch. "Midway? It's Schmidt I want to deal with, not bloody Midway."

"Midway will give us Schmidt."

"This is not in the plan you both provided me." He looked at Grovers. "Were you involved in this madness?"

"No, Ross. I had no knowledge of this."

Cromarty turned his attention back to O'Hare. "I thought you were the sensible one. I'm totally—totally—amazed that you carried out this little adventure without my knowledge or approval."

"Ross, if you don't want Schmidt, I know others who do—the Russians will take him and pay us any price—well, within reason. He's exposed some of their network in this country, killed some of their senior people, plus he's had substantial access to the genetic material you've been after. They'd love to get their hands on that knowledge. There are indications he's been genetically modified, too."

Cromarty paced the floor of his study. This time they were meeting in his upstate New York mansion and his study was larger than most average-sized houses. There was a bar and wall long wine rack at one end, a home theater system at the other, and a huge desk half way between the two. He stubbed out his cheroot, anger still evident in his flushed face. He was trying to show he was controlling his fury at the NSA agent.

"Note for the future." He glared at O'Hare. "I don't care if you're NSA or something else. I call the shots if you want to work for me. I. Call. The. Shots." He punctuated his words with a stubby forefinger. "Do you understand?"

O'Hare shrugged. "I used my discretion. If you don't want me to do so in future,"—he shrugged again—"that's okay with me. We'll lose opportunities."

"More to the point, we won't see rogue activities that will come back to bite us."

O'Hare replenished his bourbon. "As you say."

"Where is Midway?" Grovers asked.

"I don't think that's in your need-to-know box," O'Hare replied. "Take my word, he's safe and secure."

Cromarty regarded the speaker. "I think we have a need to know," he stated.

O'Hare pondered for a long moment. "He's in Gitmo. We have a facility—a camp—that's secure. Code-named Botany Bay. It's one of our new detention camps. He's our first resident."

"Guantánamo? How the hell can we access him there? Assuming we wanted to, that is."

"General, I have staff who will find out anything and

everything he knows. Tell me what you need."

"I'm not interested—this is a flawed approach," he said, dismissing the suggestion. "NSA will have access to whatever you extract from Midway. I'm more interested in how you're planning to use him to catch Schmidt."

"Likewise." Cromarty poured himself another dram of Scotch.

O'Hare stared at Cromarty. He did not look at the general. "I believe we can use Midway as bait. Schmidt will have to rescue him, or at least make the attempt. We can catch him in the act. We'll have both Midway and Schmidt, snap."

"So that's your plan? This is how the NSA operates?"

"No, General Grovers, it's not how we operate. I'm not going to disclose aspects of our operations to either of you. Take my word. We have more than one black site at Gitmo. This new one is under my control. As I said, Midway's our first guest. I've an expert there, who is looking forward to taking care of him. Schmidt will be our second guest. We caught Midway and now his location is untraceable. We'll catch Schmidt, be assured."

Cromarty raised his hand. "Very well. It's done. I didn't approve your actions and won't. For the record, O'Hare, I don't agree with what you are doing."

"In that case, I need to get back to New York. My pilot's expecting to lift in ten minutes."

"If you don't wish to stay for dinner? No? Let me see you out. Stay here, Jamie. I won't be long."

Cromarty led the way out of the room and O'Hare followed. The NSA AD did not acknowledge Grover's half-hearted farewell.

The two men were silent as they walked across the atrium towards an outside door. O'Hare looked back to make sure he couldn't be overheard. He said, "You're a good actor, Ross."

"You think so? I simply pretended I was angry with one of my poorly performing CEOs."

"It worked."

"Now, you're certain there are links that can be disclosed, if need be, showing our general was the key person in yesterday's activities?"

"Oh yes, he's well involved. There's enough evidence to make a *prima facie* case against him. We have him, now."

"Do you intend to process—question—Midway while you have him at Gitmo?"

"Of course. It's an opportunity I don't want to lose. He caused some good agents to go down. Their friends want revenge."

"Let me have copies of any DNA-related information you obtain. When will you lure Schmidt?"

"Of course. I want my people to spend at least a week or so with Midway, to get what we can from him. When we're ready, we'll let Schmidt know where Midway's being held. It'll be entertaining to see how he reacts."

"Don't underestimate the man. That's happened before, and people, smart people, have gone down."

"We're safe, Ross. We'll be insulated from any heat. Schmidt will get an anonymous tip-off."

"Good. Okay, safe trip back. We should plan on meeting next week. I'd like you to keep me informed regarding Midway and anything you discover."

"Will do."

Cromarty watched as O'Hare boarded the helicopter. He returned to his other guest.

Chapter 10

Schmidt stepped out of the elevator and pushed through the security door into the foyer of his Cerberus office. The building was located on Pennsylvania Avenue, near the International Monetary Fund (IMF) headquarters. His pass worked, the security guards knew him, and he was eager to get to work. He headed to the smaller of the two conference rooms, the one he favored because of its more personal setting. Office staff had not yet arrived; he would have to wait for coffee.

First he contacted Major Helen Chouan; she commanded the 145th and had direct management of its MP resources, particularly Bravo Company. Of course, they were all Cerberus.

"Helen, it's me, Schmidt."

"You're on duty early. Is everything okay?"

"Yes and no. I'm back, that's the good part. The bad part—someone has kidnapped Mark. They also killed members of his security escort and may have killed a police officer on Mark's property. This happened yesterday in New Hampshire. I want fifteen of your best heavies and a team of five investigators to be ready to move when I say. Actually, seven or eight of the heavies and the investigators should leave in the next half hour, for Redmont. They'll also spend time in Boston. Use one of your choppers. I want them there as soon as you can get it done. You need to be there. Maeve, Linda, or I, will forward briefing papers. Keep men in reserve, ready to move out on the instant. Understood?"

"Yes, sir. Good to have you back, Archimedes."

Schmidt disconnected and decided he needed coffee. He encountered three early starters and they took pity on his caffeine-deprived condition. Ten minutes later, a steaming pot of coffee was delivered to the conference room. In the meantime he had managed to follow the user instructions to connect up the video system so he could meet with members of his analysis team.

"Linda, I need your support."

"Schmidt—you're back!"

"Yes, it's me, in full formal dress. As Maeve told you, we want a briefing session at 10:00 a.m. She'll call Winter at 10:30. I want to know what happened in New Hampshire and Boston—feed me details as soon as you have them. An additional item: a Redmont police officer was shot and killed late yesterday afternoon. He was on Mark's property waiting for their crime team. Another two, civilians, were found dead on the property. That's still vague, but one seems to have killed the other, after which he committed suicide. No identification. A girl, twelve or so, was also shot. Fortunately she survived. I'm heading to Redmont after our conference to speak with her or her parents. I've arranged for a copy of the police logs and their report, as much as they have, to be here for the briefing. There's something else—oh yes, I've arranged for Helen to send an investigative team and some heavyweight support to Redmont. When you talk with Maeve, ask her to give me a call as soon as she can, please."

"Yes, sir. Welcome back."

He disconnected the video and poured another coffee. Schmidt frowned; he hoped people stopped saying that before the morning progressed too far. He was back; somehow, something, overnight had lifted whatever had been inflicting him and now he felt fitter and sharper than ever. He emailed a long list of people to let them know he had resumed duty. The formal clearance by Army pill pushers would have to wait; he had things to do.

There were three people he dreaded contacting. Maeve had spent twenty minutes on the phone with Anna and the two children last night, and he was planning to do the same this morning. He reached for the phone as the conference room door was opened, interrupting his call attempt.

"Sir, General Schmidt?"

"Yes, Rosalie?"

"There's people to see you. It's Anna, Gabriel, and Niland. They said they're here to help find Mark."

All of Cerberus, he realized, would know by now that Mark had been kidnapped. Their support would be total, he was certain. "Show them in. I'll see if they need anything, make sure they've had breakfast, and let you know."

"Yes, sir. And wel—"

"Don't say it."

"No, sir. Yes, sir." The Cerberus PA backed out of the room and, shortly afterwards, Anna and the two children entered.

"I was planning to call you—I was about to pick up my cell phone."

"We know. Niland said you would."

Schmidt hugged Anna and the two children.

"How did you know I'd be here?"

"That was me," said Gabrielle. "I knew this would break through the barriers."

"We agreed."

"It was my idea."

"Whoa." Anna halted the flow.

"You're all welcome here, of course. But why did you come?"

"You need to be north of here, perhaps Boston. We'll take you back with us," Niland replied. "There's something—" He stopped, unable to define their reasoning.

Schmidt smiled. "It's early. You've all had breakfast?"

"Yes, thank you. It was a nice hotel buffet—all you could eat," said Niland.

Anna explained, "We caught a late flight last night and stayed at a hotel. The children wanted to surprise you this morning."

"You certainly did that. I haven't had my breakfast. I'll order something from our kitchen. You'll have to watch me eat."

"In that case—" The children spoke in unison.

"I'll order four breakfasts. The chef should be in by now." He headed out the door to find Rosalie and gave his breakfast order. At his direction, she added extras for his visitors.

"I have an update. No, we don't know yet where Mark was taken. Late yesterday, when the Redmont Police Crime Team arrived, they discovered a body in the shed behind the house." He relayed all the details he'd received in an early morning call. "We don't know who the girl is."

Gabrielle looked pensive. "She's Cerberus. No evidence. Only my intuition. She was shot by the man who killed the policeman. She made the shooter kill his companion, and she forced him to shoot himself."

Schmidt stilled for a moment, considering. He looked at Gabrielle. "You know, there's a certain logic in what you said that I find attractive. I'm not sure we'll be able to explain it to the local police, though. We'll check and confirm, and if she's Cerberus, we'll protect her, of course. I'm going to Redmont once I finish up here. I have MPs from the 145th on the way. I'll manage investigations from there. You all want to come with me?"

There were no dissensions. Gabrielle rushed out to get Rosalie and another PA, and Schmidt provided instructions for travel.

"Anna, you'd better go and pack, if you three are coming with me."

Niland laughed. "We packed and checked out. We brought our backpacks. We're ready to go."

The general sat back in his chair. "I think I've been out-Schmidted," he mused.

Maeve and Linda joined the video meeting at 10:00 a.m., and Schmidt, Anna, and the two children sat around the small conference table to hear the details.

Maeve said, "Linda's team is doing their usual outstanding work. They cracked the Highway Patrol's call recording system and have copies of the communications between their people and Mark. Linda, can you play a portion of the tape from where they were stopped on the highway."

"Sure. Give me a moment. We think Mark had suspicions about this chase. He dropped his—or Drew's—cell phone on the seat of the vehicle. He spoke loud and clear. He also left the side window open. He knew we'd be able to get to this. Winter also has video, so we'll be able to verify it all."

The tape began with Mark speaking. "*We've got trouble. We have five patrol cars blocking the road, they're all Highway Patrol. Troopers are standing next to their vehicles, with weapons pointing at us. The guys following us are very confident. Maybe there's some collusion—let's get out and see what this is all about.*"

Linda continued, "We're enhancing the tape from here on to get clarity. People were speaking outside the vehicle and some of the voices are muffled and difficult to hear. The call was disconnected after three minutes or so. The following points are critical. It may have been a governmental action; the people following Mark used software to disable and remotely control his vehicle, a Volkswagen SUV. That software is not generally available. At least, we haven't seen any criminal use of it. Accents—where we have clarity—are American. The police mention an FBI BOLO alert and that they were helping the FBI. However, the driver with Mark was shot and killed without cause. There are eyewitness statements stating Mark was transported out by helicopter."

Maeve added her perspective, "The FBI comment is important. We suspect the Highway Patrol was misled. We're looking for the drivers and crews of the five Patrol vehicles; we'll determine who was involved and why. I've already arranged DoJ warrants, full search and seizure, and I've arranged for an FBI team to be in New Hampshire by early afternoon, under one of their top special agents—someone I know. Half the FBI team will be Cerberus, and no, Fisher doesn't know about them."

"Excellent. I've already arranged for a team from the 145th to get there. I'll lead the meeting with the Highway Patrol," Schmidt said. "They are going to think their building has collapsed on them."

"We're currently checking aircraft flight plans—the pilot must have lodged some indication of its flight," Linda added.

"A good start. Keep me posted while we're in New Hampshire. I want transcripts, results of your search for a flight plan, anything else discovered by our teams. We're leaving shortly. I've arranged a helicopter to pick us up in"— he checked his watch—"fifteen minutes. I won't wait for your call with Brian. You can update me, if necessary, while we're in transit. Oh, Maeve, tell Brian he's welcome to join us in New Hampshire."

"Schmidt—I have one thing to add—welcome—"

"Don't say it, don't say it!"

Chapter 11

"Tell me your earliest memories." The voice was insistent, imperative.

The young boy watched from afar as village children boarded their school bus, their joyous shouts pealing across the countryside. It was early morning and spring had not yet arrived. The tree under which he sheltered was winter-dormant and three brown leaves clung hopelessly to an upper branch; they would soon be replaced by spring buds. His hand tightened on a low branch. He subconsciously understood he would never be allowed to join in the fun enjoyed by children in groups, small or large. As he watched, the bus roared into life, its lights swinging across the village green as it headed towards the road out of the village.

His reverie was interrupted by an angry shout. The housekeeper had noticed his absence. He pulled the worn, oversized coat around his shoulders and turned towards the decrepit farm building where smoke now drifted from the kitchen chimney. The boy shouted back and walked across the frozen mud to the kitchen door.

"Lazy child," said the old woman who was setting a frying pan onto the stove. "Your task is to light the fire and make sure it's burning. Next time you leave it you'll get a thrashing." She spoke English with an execrable accent.

He ignored the threat. He had been thrashed before. It hurt only for a while. He moved nearer to the stove to warm himself and then sat at the table after the old woman dished out half-cooked porridge. He knew it was the best she could prepare. He ate heartily. He always had an appetite and would not reject food even if it was represented by badly prepared meals.

"When you finish, go and wake that lazy tutor of yours. Tutor, huh." She sniffed.

He knew the man who was supposed to be his tutor was not so much lazy as wine-soaked. His tutoring ability was suspect even to him, young as he was. He learned more from reading the books the man had brought with him than from his teaching. As usual he struggled to waken the sleeping man. Each day it was becoming more and more difficult to penetrate his alcohol-fueled fugue. Eventually he succeeded and left the tutor to his morning affairs.

"No, that isn't what I want." The voice sounded disappointed.

He wondered why.

He twisted and turned. His neck burned. His head ached. The back of his hand was on fire. His hands were strapped to a metal frame. He tried to move his legs and discovered they, too, were strapped down. He tried to sit up. A strap across his upper body held him down. He was able to lift his head, barely an inch or so. He built up the energy required to open his eyes. His eyelids were glued together. He struggled and at last managed to open both eyes. They were full of grit, aggravated, painful.

There was nothing to see—the room was pitch black; there was no light, anywhere. He could hear faint, distant noises, so presumably it was daytime. He tried to recollect what had happened. The car chase, Drew shot and killed. The injection in his neck. Presumably he'd fallen unconscious after the injection had taken hold. He'd probably recovered faster than expected, because of his genetic enhancements—possibly his captors would not be aware of those. It might be early—very early—morning.

His nose itched. He couldn't scratch it. His knee itched. He couldn't reach that, either. His neck, where his captor had applied the injection, burned. The back of his hand stung; it felt like a wasp was drilling into his veins. He could move his head. That didn't help. He blinked. His eyes felt less gritty. He realized he was wired, he could feel pads on his body—perhaps he was being monitored.

The flow of electricity into his body and the sharp agony that accompanied the shocking voltage negated that thought. The pain seared. There were electric connections all around his limbs and torso, some in places he didn't want to think about. This, he realized, was going to be a challenge. The torture technique likely consisted of sensory deprivation followed by electric shocks at unpredictable times. A second rush of electricity spasmed his body. How much respite would he get, he wondered, until the next shock? The voltage, he assumed, would be increased, perhaps to a level that would render him unconscious.

There must be something—his body spasmed again. Someone, he thought, after the electric flow stopped, was enjoying this. He hoped they realized he would provide their last opportunity to enjoy anything. If he could escape, it would be a welcome duty—and if he didn't escape or wasn't rescued, Schmidt and hundreds—no, thousands—of Cerberus members would take up the task. He was confident, one way or another, his captors faced certain death. He gritted his teeth against the next flow—it spiked at a far higher voltage than the prior shocks. He spat blood; he had bitten the side of his tongue.

He focused his thoughts. Perhaps he could use the nanites in his body. He must be able to direct them to mute the agony and help heal damage that he was suffering. However, there was more. Each conductive pad required a direct contact with his body. If he could somehow persuade the nanites to gather at each point of contact and build an insulating layer, enough to act as a barrier—that would protect him. His nose itched again. He hadn't heard of any Cerberus person attempting what he was planning. He could experiment on one of the pads. He knew which one; it was stuck to his scrotum. He would wait a while before commencing his experiment. First he wanted to see what other torture techniques his captors planned.

As he explored his predicament he again felt the wasp sting in the back of his wrist. That wasn't, he now recognized, an insect, accidentally released into the blacked-out room. It was a needle, probably attached to some chemical delivery system. They were drugging him. Hell, he thought, they think in clichés—pain followed by what—hallucinations? He was confident he could handle that. His failure to react might be cause for someone to come and check him. He focused on the pain point. He could block the needle—that was something the nanites could readily achieve. He might have to suffer first, before the nanites were in full deployment. He shuddered.

Why, he wondered, was the previously blackened room now a swirl of lights? Faint and distant sounds were now ear-shatteringly near and excessively loud. It was as though he had been dropped into the midst of a furious clamor of metallic presses, each trying to outdo the other with the volume and discordance of their sounds. He spun, the center of a spiral, sharp colors piercing his eyes. He tried to close them. His muscles—his eyelids—would not respond. The vortex altered its shape and he realized it was a spinning propeller, moving closer and closer. He sunk down to the hub, the razor sharp blades slicing his head, his mind, his brain, even his body, into millions of tiny pieces. He fought to focus, trying to override the strange visions. Perspiration ran down the side of his face, out of reach.

His captors were, he was certain, exploring his genetic enhancements, measuring his reaction and recovery times.

His heartbeat, respiration, possibly level of muscle spasms, and other measures were being charted to show how long he was out of action. Damn, he thought, that's another challenge. He needed to control his reactive functions to thoroughly confuse whoever was conducting experiments on his body. It was going to be an interesting day and it was still, he thought, early morning.

"I want later memories—tell me about the laboratory." The voice was adamant, commanding.

He fought back and failed.

He reached the house without misadventure and climbed the front stairs to the entry porch. He tugged off a glove and tucked it into his belt. The front door was ajar and he stepped inside, Glock in hand. He pushed the door back into its almost closed position, ensuring it did not latch. Even though he was now living in a small apartment in the laboratory complex, this was his home, and he was familiar with the layout of the rooms. The building was two-storied, with bedrooms upstairs, and kitchen, dining and living rooms downstairs. In addition, there was a study downstairs towards the rear of the house.

No lights showed and after a moment of consideration, Mark decided first to explore upstairs. The main bedroom was on the right. While he was aware he was intruding into personal areas, he was convinced something evil was in the house, which was justification enough for his actions. He stepped soundlessly up carpeted stairs. He had no desire to be detected by the deathly presence which was clamoring silently for his attention. He moved with extreme care.

As he eased into the main bedroom he tugged a small LED torch from a side pocket of his backpack and switched it on. Mark was careful to select the red light to preserve his night vision. He quickly scanned the room and froze for four or five seconds. Fear mounted and he could feel his heartbeat racing. There was a body in the middle of the large double bed. It was Dr. Anna, and she had been shot. Just once, in the center of her forehead. There were no signs of a struggle. It seemed she had been asleep when her killer acted. He must have fired his single shot from the position where Mark was standing.

He moved around the foot of the bed, exploring further. He was at the edge of hyperventilating. His unvoiced fears were realized as he saw Dr. Otto's body, crumpled on the floor beside the bed. He too had been shot, once in the center of his forehead. Mark did not need to check either body for life signs. He switched off his torch and returned it to his backpack. Shaking with grief, restraining nausea, he stood at the top of the stairs, considering his next move. His anger built. The two doctors were the closest he would ever come to having real parents. He brushed away tears. He could not afford to mourn until he had revenged the deaths of his friends, his family.

"No, not that—tell me about the laboratory."

For a moment he wondered what the voice really wanted.

"Tell me."

The order had to be obeyed.

He cursed as he made his way through the building. Offices had been trashed. Alarmed, he rushed to the incubator room. The door was open and he stopped, momentarily reluctant to see inside the room. He edged forward. Fetal containers had been smashed, destroyed with deliberation, their contents released to the open air. Four lifeless bodies glared at him with unseeing eyes, blaming him for his failure to protect them. He dropped to his knees, careless of the fetal fluids which had spilled from the broken containers.

"I'll find whoever ordered this," he promised, wiping his eyes. "When I do, I will destroy them. I promise."

"No, stop. This is all nonsense." The voice was querulous.

He twisted and turned. His neck burned. His head ached. The back of his hand was on fire. His hands were strapped to a metal frame. He tried to move his legs and discovered they, too, were strapped down. He tried to sit up. A strap across his upper body held him down. He could lift his head, only an inch or so. He worked up the energy to try to open his eyes. His eyelids were glued together; he struggled and at last he managed to open both eyes. They were full of grit, aggravated, painful.

There was nothing to see—the room was pitch black; there was no light, anywhere. He could hear faint, distant noises, so presumably it was daytime. He struggled to recall—something. Presumably he'd fallen unconscious after the injection had taken hold. He'd probably recovered faster than expected, because of his genetic enhancements—possibly his captors would not be aware of those. It might be early—very early—morning.

His nose itched. He couldn't scratch it. His knee itched. He couldn't reach that, either. His neck, where his captor had applied the injection, burned. He could move his head. That didn't help. He blinked. His eyes felt less gritty. He realized he was wired, he could feel pads on his body—perhaps he was being monitored.

At last he remembered—this had happened before. He'd had these exact same experiences the previous morning. At least, he assumed a day had passed. Perhaps it had not been an entire day, perhaps it had been only an hour or two. He had no way of knowing.

Something warned him, a subtle cue, unidentifiable, and he tensed and recalled that he needed to relax—he didn't want to bite his tongue again. His body spasmed as the current flowed. He panted; he could feel his heart racing, the muscles in his legs cramping. The current flowed again. He repressed a scream.

The current eased. He remembered an idea, a thought, that he should be able to control the savage voltage-induced muscle spasms. It needed something else, he couldn't quite recall—

The back of his hand stung—that was it, the hypodermic was attached to some form of chemical release system. He was being dosed with narcotics, hallucinogens, pain accelerators—nothing that was good for him.

His lips were dry, his throat parched. He couldn't recall drinking any water, nor could he remember eating. He knew he stank. He estimated he had not been released from his restraints for at least two days and his bodily wastes were not being removed. He had no way to clean himself. This was, he assumed, part of the torture program, establishing a lack of dignity, showing that he was not worthy of being treated humanely. He smiled in the dark. They did not know—the electric shock charged through his body. He'd missed the cue.

His body now understood it needed to react. His mind pushed and pulled at various possibilities. He decided first to block the flow of injections; it would take a small sacrifice of nanites. He focused on the pain in the back of his hand, delving deeply into his mind. He relaxed. He hoped the needle was blocked. Next, he recalled his idea and commenced to build a nanite-based insulation layer under each conductive contact point—starting with the most painful contact. He concentrated, visualizing the effect he sought. If nothing else, and if it worked, his actions would cause someone to explore, to determine why their processes had halted. If only he could release some of his restraints. He panted, his heart racing—the cue—but no electric shock. It had worked.

If he could free a hand, his arm. He tried to move, twisting his hand, his wrist, his arm, testing the restraint. Was it—? Yes, he felt movement. There was a slight give in the restraint. He repeated his moves, stressing his body. He could feel the straps cutting into his flesh; he could feel blood on his arm. Suddenly—he could feel his arm move. He relaxed and tried to flex his hand. It felt freer, not yet free, closer, but still restrained.

Chapter 12

Dr. Kelsi Pierce found her way to the single-patient ward where, she'd been informed, the girl was recovering. It was the first opportunity she'd had, since starting her shift early that morning, to take a break. She checked with the duty nurse who directed her further down the hallway.

"She's a popular patient," the nurse commented with a smile.

"She is? I didn't think anyone knew her?"

"Your trainee lab tech—Ladder—is with her."

"So that's where he disappeared to."

"There's a police officer on duty outside her door. I understand the FBI's also sending someone," added the nurse.

"That's a lot of law enforcement interest—I wonder what her story is?"

The nurse shrugged. Kelsi walked to the indicated room and smiled a greeting to the police officer seated outside the door; she recognized him, although she couldn't recall his name.

He nodded back and said, "Hi, Doc. Welcome to the party."

She cautiously opened the door and peered in. The girl was sitting up, a wide-awake expression on her face. Someone had made a half-hearted attempt to tidy her hair and her face was clean. There was a bandage across the top half of her head.

Ladder was sitting beside her on the edge of the bed. The girl was holding his hand. Neither had noticed her entrance. The room contained two beds, one of which was empty. There were two small sets of drawers beside each bed and four visitor's chairs, pseudo-modern, in yellow plastic and chrome—probably even more uncomfortable than they appeared, thought Kelsi.

"Oh, no," said the girl to Ladder. "What color were they?"

"Black, of course."

She giggled and after a moment so did Ladder.

"But I do like your real name—Oxley—it sounds so manly."

"Oh, pul-eze."

They both realized Kelsi was in the room. Ladder blushed and the girl giggled again. Ladder slid off the side of the bed and straightened the bedclothes where he had been sitting.

"Doc. Good morning."

"Can I call you Doc, too?"

The girl's eyes were surprisingly vivid, Kelsi thought, a blue that seemed to have strange depths. "Good morning, both of you. Yes, you can call me Doc. What's your name?"

"Alex—it's short for Alexandra. Thank you for rescuing me."

"We did our best, didn't we, Ladder?"

"Yes, Doc."

"How's your head?"

"The pain's eased. I think I was lucky."

"I agree." Kelsi quickly checked the dressing and when she was satisfied, she sat on a visitor's chair. "What do you remember—can you tell me who your parents are?"

"I already asked, Doc. She can't."

"Everyone's been asking me questions," Alex said. "I really, really can't answer them."

Kelsi had been told earlier by the admissions clerk that details on the young patient were scant. "I understand. Perhaps when you've recovered some more."

A doubtful expression flitted across Alex's face. "Yes, I suppose."

There was a knock on the door and it opened slowly. A woman entered. She had, Kelsi thought, thoroughly researched power dressing. The newcomer was wearing a masculine jacket and pants with a white blouse and her blond hair was pulled back in a severe ponytail. Her black shoes had low heels and seemed practical. It made Kelsi's usual ripped-knee jeans, working shoes, and man's shirt approach to style very *passé*. At least today she was wearing the regular Redmont police uniform.

The newcomer looked around the room obviously assessing its contents, including the patient and her two visitors. "Good morning, everyone. My name is Gail Prentice."

Kelsi thought there was a thread of recognition in the eye contact between Alex and the newcomer.

"You—you're—?"

"Yes, I'm an FBI agent." She held out her badge. Kelsi thought the question Alex had intended was not the one the agent answered. The girl seemed apprehensive. Ladder looked from one to the other.

"Is that a real FBI badge?" he asked, standing up. He took a step towards the newcomer and reached out his hand.

Kelsi was surprised at the degree of confidence in his demeanor.

"Oh, yes, it's real," the FBI agent replied. She held out her ID and badge for Ladder's closer examination.

"I agree, Ladder," Alex said. "She's FBI, I'm sure."

Ladder raised his eyebrows. "You are? She is?"

"Oh, yes. I—I know she's telling the truth."

He looked more closely at the photograph and accompanying details. He made eye contact with the agent. "Thank you, Agent Prentice."

Kelsi was impressed—this was a side of Ladder she had not previously observed.

The FBI agent returned her wallet to her shoulder bag.

"Good—Ladder, isn't it? And you're Alex, according to our records?" She turned to Kelsi. "Dr. Pierce?"

"All right, what's going on?" Kelsi asked. The tension in the room had somehow escalated.

Agent Prentice replied, "There's no problem. Rest assured, Alex is important to us. I'm here to provide protection until some other people arrive."

"Who's coming?" Alex was anxious.

"Let me see." She consulted her cell phone, reading off a text message. "General Schmidt, and some other people—Anna, Gabrielle, and Niland."

A huge smile creased Alex's face and she jumped on the bed with excitement. "Oh, good, that's so good. When will they get here?"

"Some time this afternoon. I believe they're traveling by helicopter."

"Okay, now I'm really confused," said Kelsi. "Can you clarify what's happening? Who are these people? Are they Alex's family?" She looked at the FBI agent and back to Alex.

"Yes, they're family. Well, not General Schmidt, of course," said Alex. Suddenly worried, she looked up at Agent Prentice. "What about Mark—you didn't mention his name?"

"We—that's a problem—Mark is missing. There may be a connection with yesterday's events. We don't know for sure. That's why Schmidt and some other FBI agents, more senior than me, are all heading here to Redmont. I don't know enough to help you with questions, though; my task is to make sure you're protected. We'll have two more agents outside your door and a Redmont police officer to keep an eye on you. You're an important person—Mark would agree."

"But Mark—"

"General Schmidt will find him."

Agent Prentice seemed, Kelsi thought, to have every confidence in this General Schmidt. She was surprised at the number of law enforcement personnel. Three FBI agents and a police officer seemed overly protective for a girl who looked to be no more than twelve years of age.

"Ladder, we need to get back to work. There's still more for us to do at the crime scene."

"Uh—Dr. Pierce?" The speaker was the FBI agent.

"Yes?"

"I'm supposed to tell you—the FBI have jurisdiction; our team's out at the Midway property, now. They've taken control."

"I suppose I shouldn't be surprised. It did seem more than an average shooting. Alex, here's my card. Contact me if I can help with anything. Or Ladder. Let us know." She signaled her lab assistant. "It's time to go; we need to wrap up our report."

"I'll visit you again, Alex." Ladder waved.

"Thank you, Doc and Oxley." She giggled. "I mean Ladder."

Anna arrived with Gabrielle and Niland some thirty minutes after the departure of Dr. Pierce and her assistant. An FBI agent was seated with the local police officer, a second agent was at the reception desk, and Agent Prentice was inside the small hospital room, reading material on an iPad. Alex had dropped off to sleep. The external guards waved them through, into the room.

Anna spoke quietly to Agent Prentice, "We've been cleared for a private conversation with Alex. Do you mind waiting outside?"

"Sure. I received an email. Let me know when you're finished."

Anna nodded and, after the agent left the room, said to Gabrielle, "You can wake Alex now, if you like."

Gabrielle gently shook Alex's shoulder. Niland stood at her other shoulder. They spoke in complete unison. "Stop dreaming. It's us; wake up."

Alex opened her eyes and looked from Gabrielle to Niland and back to Gabrielle. She burst into tears. Gabrielle offered her handkerchief. Niland looked at his and returned it to his pocket. Alex, after wiping her face, reached out a hand for each of the two children, and between sobs, said, "I thought I'd never see you again." She looked up to Anna, "Oh, Anna, thank you for coming."

Anna smiled, and with her clean handkerchief, wiped Alex's face again, drying the tears. "There, now you're nearly presentable. Next, a trim of that hair, don't you think? We can arrange that for tomorrow, if you like."

"Tell us," urged Niland, "What happened?"

"Who shot you?"

"How did you get there?"

Anna realized the questions would continue at a rapid fire pace and interceded. "Stop, both of you. Alex has had a traumatic experience, is recovering, and doesn't need to be hassled by you two."

As Anna was speaking, the door opened and a voice offered, "Although I believe we'd all like to hear the details." The speaker was Schmidt. "Always assuming Alex is strong enough, of course?"

Niland whispered to Alex, "That's General Schmidt—he's a good friend."

"I thought you had meetings to attend?" Anna said. She ignored the wide-eyed expression on Alex's face.

"Later. For now, I'd like to hear Alex's story. Do you think you can cope?" He directed his question at Alex.

"Yes, sir," Alex whispered. "From the beginning?"

"That's usually the best place to start any story, I'd say. Can I sit here?" He indicated a chair next to the bed. "Anna, you should sit, too. I suspect this is going to take a few minutes. These two live wires can stand. They look as though they're not letting Alex go—or maybe it's the other way around?"

The three children smiled. Niland said, "We thought we'd

lost Alex at the—at the place where all those killings took place—Camp Brewer." He turned to Alex and asked, "How did you escape?"

"I hid in my room when the shooting started, when I realized what was happening—those men were going from room to room killing everyone. I worked out how to do what you do, you know, making people not see or hear you. It's as though you turn invisible. I did that. The people—the killers—opened my room door and I hid. I turned invisible and they didn't see me. I could hear them shooting as they went. I was so f-frightened." Her grip tightened. Neither Gabrielle nor Niland protested. "After an hour or more, I heard some more shooting. Later, after a long time, I heard an aircraft arrive. I decided I had better find out what had happened. I kept myself hidden, in case, when I went outside. I saw all the dead soldiers and some dead children, I knew them all—they were from the same birth group—my sisters and brothers. And I saw you all with Mark and someone else."

"Scott Gilmore—he's Cerberus and an ex-FBI agent," Anna clarified.

"I-I suppose. I didn't know what to do. Mark went away and returned with a motor vehicle. You loaded it up—I couldn't speak, I couldn't release whatever was making me invisible."

"Go on," urged Schmidt when she paused, his voice gentle.

"I climbed into the back of the vehicle—it was large, there was lots of room. I curled up and slept. When you—with Mark—arrived at his house—I still kept hidden. I was so frightened. I waited for you to unload and when you finished, I hid at the back of the house. Later, I found the shed and decided to stay there, where I felt safe. I used to raid the kitchen for food. I thought you would be mad with me because I'd kept myself hidden and no one could see me. My other brothers and sisters—they all died. I lived. I don't know why. I cried every night. When you left, when you went away, when you left me all alone, I didn't know what to do."

Gabrielle reached her free arm across Alex and hugged her tight. "We're here. You're safe with us. We'll look after you, I promise."

Anna nodded her agreement. Niland squeezed her hand.

Schmidt said, "We'll make sure of that. Tell me, how did you survive after Mark and everyone left?"

"There was some food in the pantry, so I had that until it ran out. Some people arrived and set Mark's house on fire. I was so frightened with all the shooting and explosions. The police came and arrested those criminals and I stayed hidden. Everything seemed to be—overwhelming. I kept hidden. I cried."

"How did you survive afterwards—the pantry was empty—when there was no more food?" Anna asked.

"I—I won't get into trouble if I tell you, will I?"

"No, my dear, we'll all protect you. That's what we're here for." Anna looked at Schmidt.

He nodded his head, a reassuring expression on his face. He said. "Alex, don't worry, no one is going to punish you for anything. I agree with Anna, we'll protect you."

"I worked out how to go shopping. I hitched a ride into Belmont, I think the town is. I went to the closest shops. The first time I—I was attacked by a man, the driver who picked me up. When he grabbed my hands, I was able to stop him. After I stopped him, I made him take me to the shops, made him forget he'd seen me. I—I stole food—I couldn't pay, I was starving."

"So you made visits, did your—er—shopping, and afterwards returned to your hideout?" Anna asked.

"There's a bus service—most of the time I rode without paying. When a shopkeeper gave me some cash—it was a reward, cos I told him one of his employees was robbing him—I was able to buy a ticket." She looked shamefaced. "Sometimes."

"The winter must have been freezing cold for you?" Schmidt questioned.

"I found things in the house and in the sheds—before those men destroyed everything. A sleeping bag. Some blankets. The shed had electricity and a heater. It was solar-powered and had a storage battery, I think. The water was cold, though. I—I didn't wash every day."

After a pause, Schmidt said, "Are you able to tell us what happened yesterday?"

Alex bit her lower lip. "Y—yes, I think so."

"You were aware of the police presence?"

Alex nodded her head. "I'd gone to do some shopping. There's another way to get onto Mark's property—there's a track down to a road, and another shed—it's for cars, I think. I always go that way, it's closer to the main road. When I came back, after I did my shopping—some birds—ravens—three of them—they're my friends—stopped me. Well, they hopped in front of me so that I had to stop. I feed them crackers, and they like me."

"The ravens stopped you?" asked Gabrielle.

"They knew something was wrong, that I was in danger. They gave me a key."

Niland and Gabrielle spoke in unison. "They gave you a key?"

"Yes, one of them dropped it on the path for me."

"Was the key for the garage?" Schmidt asked.

"I—I checked. It opened the garage. It was empty, no one had been there."

Anna said, "What did you do after that?"

"I got my things from the shed—there's a hidden way in through the back. I took my sleeping bag and some other things back to where I had left my backpack with my shopping. It was too full. I couldn't carry it all, and I'd hidden it off the trail."

"And?" Schmidt prompted.

"I heard a shot. It came from near the shed. I went back as quietly as I could, to see what had happened. Someone had shot the policeman."

"What did you do?"

"I was afraid, so afraid. I ran back down the trail. I must have forgotten to hide myself, because two men followed me. I reached the garage and was trying to unlock the door, to shelter inside, when one of them shot me. It hurt." She touched the dressing on her head. "It's not bad, now."

"What did you do?" Anna reached out and held Alex's hand, sharing it with Niland.

"I—I'm not sure. I hadn't touched their hands. I was afraid because they had shot the policeman. I—I suppose I was angry that they'd also shot me. The man without the gun was telling the other man to shoot me again; he said I could identify them. The man with the gun started to aim at me. I reached out and told him to shoot the other man. After—after he did that I made him shoot himself." Alex looked at the general, her face fearful, her eyes damp with tears. "I didn't know what else to do. They were going to kill me."

"We'll look after you," said Niland.

"No one is going to do anything to you," confirmed Schmidt. "You defended yourself. I agree with Niland, we'll look after you. Thank you, Alex, for telling me what happened. I'm sorry I made you relive the horror."

By now Alex was crying into Anna's shoulder and Niland and Gabrielle still were holding onto her. Anna hugged Alex. "Shhh. We're here. We'll take care of you."

Chapter 13

"Major Dunlap, I'm General Schmidt. I'm leading a presidential task force responsible for investigating certain recent events in Massachusetts. With me are FBI Special Agent in Charge Charles Thoroughgood, Special Agents Dennis and Thompson, and Major Helen Chouan. I believe you've received an email from the State Governor's office instructing you to extend every possible assistance to us?" He did not introduce the three MPs from B Company.

"Er—Yes, General. Please, everyone take a seat." Dunlap indicated seats around the meeting room table. A whiteboard covered an end wall. Various police banners and photographs haphazardly decorated a longer wall. The opposite wall was blank. Steel cabinets were lined up along the wall with the entry doorway. Major Dunlap was uniformed, as were Schmidt and Helen Chouan, although Dunlap's was the formal dress of the Massachusetts State Police. "I think we have enough room—we use this room for training and briefings. I really don't know if I can—tell me, what is this about?"

"We have reason to believe that some members of your troop were engaged yesterday in a road blockade on the Northern Expressway. We would like to interview them as soon as can be arranged. The vehicles involved are on this list." He handed a printed sheet to the State Police major. He didn't mention the details were from a camera in Mark's Volkswagen, which had uploaded clear video images to Winter Security. "In particular, we wish to interview Lieutenant Joyce and Sergeant Trevors."

"Well—I don't know. These men are on duty. I doubt you have jurisdiction—"

"Charles, please present the warrants to the major." Schmidt waited for the FBI agent to hand copies of the warrants to the police officer before he continued. "Dunlap, if I hear another negative or uncooperative word from you, I will arrest you for obstruction. Those warrants give me and my team the authority we need."

The major paled. "You can't come in here and ride roughshod over me and my men—"

"Your men were involved in criminal conspiracy, murder, and kidnapping. Possibly terrorism. I don't know how far these criminal activities reached—perhaps you were involved? Certainly both internal staff and your state troopers are of interest to us. There were at least three deaths yesterday and your men were involved. There was a major traffic incident: your people blockaded the Expressway, and a number of civilian vehicles were damaged—you're certainly aware of all this?"

The major nodded his head. He licked his lips but did not speak.

Schmidt continued, "We're looking for two vehicles." He handed Dunlap a printed sheet with details of the black BMW and the Volkswagen Touareg. "These appear to have been taken under control by your men."

"I'll have to contact my—my senior officer. There is a chain of command for this type of inquiry, you know."

"You have already received a communication from the governor—he's top of the chain of command pyramid for you. I'll read out the message he sent to you, in case you've forgotten what it says."

"Now, listen, this is most irregular. I'll protest—"

"Major, I have a letter of authority signed by the governor, which will allow me to remove you from your post, if I want to. You've seen the warrants we have for your arrest for obstruction of justice, one federal and one state. Do I use these or will you co-operate?"

"Damn you. Joyce is one of my best troopers." He looked towards the door. It was blocked by a large MP. "Okay. I'll arrange for him to be called in. Yes, and the other troopers."

"Don't create any alarms. Get them here for a review meeting at 5:00 p.m. Tell them the governor wants to know why the Expressway was closed and you want personal—face-to-face—reports. I assume you have a larger room where we can all meet? Good. Special Agent Dennis and two members of my team will be your new best buddies for the remainder of the day. They'll help you make calls, re-arrange your schedule for the afternoon, safeguard your cell phone, and so forth."

The two other men were from the 145th. All—including the FBI agents—were Cerberus. Schmidt did not mention that the major would be accompanied by his new best buddies until all the troopers had reported in. Indeed, their escort would continue for some time after that, until he, Schmidt, was convinced the major was not involved in any way in Mark's kidnapping. Without that conviction, the trooper would be placed under arrest. "We need some space here to set up an operations center."

"Sure, sure. This room, the one next door. Take control of whatever you need."

"Dennis, return with the major once he's organized calls to bring in the troopers involved. He needs to include the desk guy, too."

"Yes, General. We'll look after our best buddy for you."

The small group headed out of the room, Dunlap in the lead. Schmidt addressed his team after the door to the meeting room closed. "Of course, we're going to encounter obstructions. However, we've got the state governor's support, plus the state attorney-general's, and from a federal perspective, everyone from the president down has been briefed, and are in full support. We'll use the next thirty minutes for catch-up, make sure our people are up to date."

He called Linda Schöner and when she answered, he said, "Linda, you're on speaker. Charles and his team are listening, also Helen. Did you get more details from Brian Winter?"

"Yes, he's been extremely helpful. Not unexpected; he lost some good people. His team, when they picked up Mark, apparently installed cameras in Mark's vehicle; the cameras transmitted videos back to Winter's monitoring team. We now have videos of the chase, of the shooting of the driver, of the shooter, and of most of the police involved. The image quality is excellent. Audio also, in support. We've confirmed the license plates of the five patrol vehicles."

"You have enough to identify the shooter?" Schmidt had not heard that item of information.

"Yes, my analysts are using facial recognition software against a large number of government databases to see if we can discover who he is. Also, the helicopter's landing and take-off were caught on the rear-facing camera installed by Winter's senior man. While the helicopter was emblazoned with large letters indicating it was FBI—which we consider to be false—we hope its registration numbers are genuine. We've only partials, so it's a bit of a struggle. My team are researching, both for ownership and flight plans."

"Good, good." Schmidt rubbed his hands together. "We've met—that is, Anna and the children and I—met with Alex. It's an interesting story. Yes, she's Cerberus, survived the Camp Brewer massacre, and hid herself for months. She was shot and remained conscious long enough to have the shooter take out his associate. She forced the shooter to kill himself. Alex is one dangerous young lady. I'm going to recruit her when she's older." He looked at the FBI special agent in charge. "Charles, anything yet on that dead shooter and his companion?"

"They had no papers; we haven't found a vehicle anywhere nearby, and assume they were dropped off for whatever reason. Tattoos indicate they may be Russian. Their prints are being checked by Homeland Security and by our people. We should have feedback by end of the day."

"Russians? Their involvement must be a coincidence, surely?" Schmidt mused.

"That's our conclusion, too. We can't work out what they were doing. Perhaps they heard Mark was visiting his property and wanted to—er—kidnap or kill him—revenge motive, most likely."

"Sounds about right. At least the shooter did us a favor; he shot himself after killing his associate. Helen, you've set up an outside command post?"

"Yes, I have some able people involved, as you know. They're monitoring cell phones—at least those we've traced—of the troopers involved. Sergeant Trevors is top of our list. He's a desk jockey working inside the state offices and is more likely to hear of our presence. If he does, he could try to escape or at least warn his fellow-conspirators. We're using voice delay on his cell phone calls, which will cause his call to drop out if it looks as though he is warning anyone. If that happens, we'll immediately arrange for his arrest."

"Good. Let's hope he doesn't pick up on anything. Anyone—anything else?"

Linda said, "General, we've received a trace on the helicopter. Well, we have a candidate based on the partial registration numbers in the video. Surprise, it's not FBI. Corporate owned—Delaware. We'll try to track down the shareholders, which likely to be a lost cause—I expect their names and addresses will be cutouts. As soon as we discover a flight plan, I'll let you know."

"That's good news. Charles, tell your people it wasn't an FBI chopper—they'll be relieved, I'm sure."

"I'll do that, now."

"Thanks everyone." Schmidt disconnected the call. He checked the time. It was 3:00 p.m. He had hours to wait. He set off to find coffee.

Chapter 14

Jamie Grovers was perplexed. He knew of Archimedes Schmidt, who was probably ten years younger, although he had never worked with the man. He'd certainly been on the path for rapid promotion. Grovers didn't fully comprehend why O'Hare and Cromarty were so determined to get their hands on him. Midway, he thought, was a more useful resource, given his genetic engineering knowledge. He was both intrigued and alarmed at the apparent actions undertaken by O'Hare to protect Cromarty's business plans. But capturing Schmidt? That project was doomed to failure—Schmidt was not someone you tried to capture.

Grovers had retired at sixty-three, only two years after his promotion to brigadier general. He'd realized his promotion had been rushed. The Army had wanted someone to hold a post that was responsible for a sensitive nuclear establishment while it dealt with the previous incumbent. Grovers held that post for two years, after which he had been quietly asked to retire. It was either agree or face the public humiliation of a trial for conduct unbecoming—he and a major's wife had been caught *in flagrante delicto*. He had retired without any fuss. The MPs from 145th had done an efficient job of gathering and presenting evidence.

His perplexity now wasn't anything to do with his promotion or retirement.

The last meeting with O'Hare and Cromarty had raised the hairs on the back of his neck. The NSA AD had gone way out on a limb, in Grovers' assessment. Cromarty had been angry; at least he had appeared so, although subsequently he had taken no punitive action against O'Hare. Indeed, a week later he had authorized payment of a substantial amount to a numbered account with a bank in Curaçao. Grovers had traced details of that account and without surprise, had discovered it belonged to O'Hare. This contradiction in Cromarty's behavior had triggered an alert reflex and Grover was now trying to assess his own position within the corporate organization.

Grover suspected he was likely at risk, a sacrificial component, a pawn, in Cromarty's plans. The man was Machiavellian. His planning was for far more than the next quarterly financial release by one of his companies. Grovers was convinced the man planned not only for the short term, but five or ten years out. He knew moves for his game when no one else realized the game even existed. That meant, Grovers decided, there were moves in place, which already placed him at risk. He needed to discover them. If he couldn't do that, he needed to leave a trail to bring both men, O'Hare and Cromarty, into jeopardy—perhaps even open up a door for Schmidt to explore.

The risks were substantial, if he had accurately assessed Cromarty's personality. He'd been a part of the tycoon's inner circle for two years, planning and plotting devious but always legal activities designed to further the man's ambitions. Some months previously he had accidentally accessed computer files apparently maintained by his predecessor. At first, he'd thought Cromarty had engaged in activities that shaded criminal laws, perhaps sometimes—inadvertently—crossing over to the darker side. The details in the hidden computer files had persuaded him otherwise; Cromarty operated on the dark side. Grover had uncovered more than simply threads of proof; he had uncovered certainties.

There was one trail—it led to the Middle East—which had fatal potential, fatal to him, that is, if Cromarty ever discovered he'd been digging into the files. There were links between Cromarty and Iran. He was aware Cromarty's family had been refugees in 1975, a few years prior to the revolution that had unseated the Shah. However, he had never considered the man himself would have current links to Iran. Grover's research indicated one of those links was possibly to VAJA, the Iranian Ministry of Intelligence. Shaken, he had stopped exploring and still shuddered whenever he thought how fatal his data surfing could be. He was conflicted, partly not believing the small threads of evidence and partly in fear for his life if his suspicions were correct.

Absently Grover wondered whether O'Hare was aware of the full scope of Cromarty's current Iranian links.

He thought back, re-examining what had attracted him to accept the position with Cromarty. Obviously he had been tempted by the money. Cromarty paid him more than double what he had achieved in the Army. The additional income had helped—somewhat—to pay for the medical treatment and hospital expenses required by his wife. Perhaps Cromarty had known and traded on his need; he had no way of discovering if that was so. His wife had succumbed six months ago; her chemo treatments had failed to counter the fatal structure of the cancers that had attacked her body. He had no children, no close relatives, no one to share his cares and excitements. In some ways, he was a lonely man and to counter his loneliness he immersed himself in his work, exploring, always exploring.

While he now avoided the folders with fatal potential, he still explored. Occasionally he would discover—or uncover—another vein of gold. His ability to override security credentials allowed him to read files on near and remote servers. Cromarty's IT gurus had decided to move a large number of corporate files to the cloud—third party storage providers—and they had inadvertently included files from Cromarty's offshore offices. These were files Cromarty would have regarded as top secret, containing extremely sensitive contents. The IT types, however, had failed to ensure network and cloud security matched internal strictures, and Grovers had probed and uncovered the weakness. He would, at a convenient point, let the network people—and Cromarty's CIO—know of this failure. In the meantime he was enjoying hours of system surfing, which is how he had discovered the payment authorization to the Curaçao numbered account. Another file had provided the link between the account and O'Hare.

More troubling at this point in his file surfing activities were the unexplained emails in his own business email account. They had appeared only recently, and although a sophisticated attempt had been made to bury them in innocuous folders, Grover had entered an unrelated search, which had accidentally revealed their existence. The contents appeared to be laying a foundation that was both false and likely to do him harm at some point in the future. He suspected they represented a component of Cromarty's longer term game plan, and he, Grovers, was the sacrificial pawn.

Additionally, he had discovered a small number of encrypted files in cloud folders, locations that he thought he had secured. He had thought he was the only person with access and authority to create new files. He had no encryption software, no decryption skills, and no idea of what the contents of these strange files might be. He had tried to delete them, without success. The resulting computer message was along the lines of: *unable to delete file while it is open in another application*. It wasn't a problem he could expose to others in Cromarty's offices.

His self-defense antennae were quivering.

It was time for him to build—not a counter, because his IT skills did not reach that far—but rather a revenge. Okay, Grovers thought, it might be that he's getting more paranoid than either Cromarty or O'Hare. If his fears were never realized, nothing would happen. If, however, they were realized—exposure material would flow to people whom Cromarty regarded as his enemies. Grover began to construct his trapdoor process; he knew what files to copy and how to transfer them to his own personal cloud. Schmidt would sure as hell get the surprise of his life when it was triggered. As would Maeve Donnelly. And others.

Chapter 15

The troopers filed into the large conference room—it was really a media room with seating for twenty-five to thirty people—making comments that reflected their annoyance at the need to report in person.

"I hope this is overtime," one commented.

"I've reached my sixteen hours; I'll need to swap time."

"I'm missing my hot date."

"You're always missing hot dates, we've heard."

"Hi, Allen," one of the troopers said as he entered.

Sergeant Allen Trevors was talking to Major Dunlap. The sergeant nodded to the man who had greeted him. Schmidt identified the newcomer as Lieutenant Joyce. Special Agent Dennis was standing close to the major, ensuring Dunlap had no opportunity to warn or contact any of the men streaming into the room.

The troopers sat carelessly in the rows of seats near the podium. Schmidt took a head count, checking the presence of all concerned. He walked to the podium from the back of the room, watched with interest by some of the men. The remainder ignored his presence.

"Well, Major, what are we here for?" The question came from Joyce.

"Ask the man," Dunlap indicated Schmidt.

"What the shit's the Army to do with us?" The questioner was anonymous—Schmidt couldn't identify the speaker.

Schmidt turned on the microphone and waited a moment. Ten members of the 145th filed into the room and stood at the back. They were armed. Their entry had not been noticed by any of the troopers except the major.

"Gentlemen, this meeting is being recorded. I am General Schmidt. I'm assisting the FBI—we have five special agents in attendance and the agent in charge is Charles Thoroughgood. In the back of the room we have ten members of my MP Battalion; they're here to observe. Unless, of course, there is a reason for them to act."

He paused while the troopers first looked at the rear of the room and then to their commanding officer.

"What the hell is this, Dunlap?" asked Lieutenant Joyce. Angry murmurs underscored the general reaction.

Schmidt said, "The major is not in charge here. I am. You can address questions to me; I may or may not answer you. Yesterday you each participated in a blockade on the Northern Expressway. We will interview each of you, separately, to discover why. I'd point out that a man was murdered and another was kidnapped as a result of your actions. And no, there will be no union representation here."

"Hell, there won't," shouted Trevors.

"Ah, Sergeant Trevors. You played a key role in yesterday's criminal activities. Play the Trevors tape."

Linda and her analysts had dialed in to the media control room adjacent to the conference room. They were ready, when they received an instruction from Schmidt, to play a number of audio and video files prepared from camera and audio recordings the team had gathered from Winter and police sources—the latter without permission, of course. Schmidt's microphone was connected to a radio link back to Washington. One of her team members played the file they had labeled the Trevors tape.

"Desk 301. Sergeant Trevors."

"Code 25. Winter Security, providing security for a client. I'm the client. We're heading south on the Northern Expressway, approaching the 495 junction. One of our escorts has been taken out, we suspect by a concrete block dropped from the Chandler Road Bridge. Traffic is light. Our two vehicles are traveling at speeds of 90 to 100 mph. We're in a dark blue Touareg—Volkswagen—and our second vehicle is a red Expedition. Can we have police assistance?"

"Just one moment, sir."

There was a short pause.

"Yes, sir. We can arrange vehicles to meet you."

"My driver advises there are two or three chase vehicles."

The caller provided vehicle details.

The speaker who had identified himself as Sergeant Trevors replied. *"We have troopers approximately eight miles in front of you. Three marked vehicles. They will wait for your arrival. Two will intercept the chase vehicles and the third trooper will escort you. Please do not disconnect this call."*

Schmidt looked at Trevors and said, "I'm sure you recognize your own voice. The FBI will arrange technical validation to confirm our identification. The other voice was a passenger in a Volkswagen SUV. Now let's have video tape 2."

The large wall monitor beside Schmidt clicked on, under remote control. Linda's operator selected the video taken from within the Touareg as it stopped inches away from the front of a patrol car. Her team had added audio from the cell phone recording that she had earlier played to Schmidt. The operator played the composite audio and video file.

"Are you in control?" The speaker's voice identified him as Sergeant Trevors.

"Not yet—the BMW guys are still hacking us." The reply was from the caller.

The video showed the nose of a dark blue SUV as it braked sharply and slewed across the road, heading towards the nearest police vehicle. It came to a stop only inches away from the police barricade.

"Hell."

"We've got trouble. We have five patrol cars blocking the road, they're all Highway Patrol. Troopers are standing next to their vehicles, with weapons pointing at us. The guys following us are very confident. Maybe there's some collusion—let's get out and see what this is all about."

Police officers had their weapons drawn and aimed at the occupants of the SUV.

Two police vehicles left the barricade, heading down the highway.

The trooper closest to the camera motioned with his handgun. He was clearly identifiable as Lieutenant Joyce.

The trooper said, "Exit your vehicle. If you have a gun, leave it behind. As you exit, raise your hands."

"Come on, let's see what this is about."

"I have a bad feeling."

"You're not alone."

"That was an FBI operation," shouted one of the troopers.

"Shut up," instructed Joyce.

"I have another tape for you," said Schmidt. "Video 3, please."

Video 3 contained scenes from more than one camera and included audio from the cell phone that Mark had dropped on the seat of the SUV. Linda's team had done an excellent job of enhancement and recovery of the sound. The video commenced, continuing from the prior file.

Both the vehicle driver and passenger exited the SUV.

"Our weapons are in the vehicle," the vehicle passenger said. "Why are you stopping us?"

"Shaddup," commanded the closest police officer.

Another one said, "We've all seen the FBI BOLO alert."

"I'm with Winter Security," the vehicle driver said. "We were under attack, as we reported to your base. Look—"

The police officer who had instructed them to get out of the SUV struck the driver across the face with his weapon.

He said, "I told ya—shaddup."

The driver staggered and moved as though to defend himself. A shot was fired and the man fell to the ground. The video showed the shooter at the moment of firing his weapon.

The shooter said, "I think you can write that up as shot while assaulting an officer in an attempt to escape."

He leaned down to check the body. After a moment he said, "No pulse."

He stood and continued, "Thanks for your assistance. We've been after these people for some time. We'll take the other one—you can have the body. Our boss will be in contact with your boss to express his thanks. We owe you, all of you."

The trooper replied, "You're welcome. Glad to help the FBI. Did you lose anyone?"

Schmidt looked around the conference room after the video stopped playing.

"I think we all can recognize Lieutenant Joyce from those images," said Schmidt.

None of the troopers spoke; there was a hush as his audience attempted to assimilate details from the files they had watched.

After a pause of thirty seconds or so, Schmidt said. "Well, there you have it. Criminal conspiracy, assault, murder, and kidnapping. You all were involved. At no stage did you check the so-called FBI agent. At no stage did you protest a clear homicide. You stood there, like fucking dummies, and allowed one man to be shot to death and another to be kidnapped. Personally, I think you're all guilty and deserve whatever's going to happen to you. Other charges are being prepared. The list is long, believe me."

Three or four of the troopers stirred, as though about to object.

"Yes," said Schmidt, acknowledging the possible protest. "Two vehicles drove off before these last events took place. I'll leave criminal conspiracy on the table and remove murder and kidnap; but only for those troopers who departed. For the remainder—I'll do everything I can to see justice done."

"Why is the Army involved in this?" shouted one of the troopers.

"National security," replied Schmidt. "The man who was kidnapped is a valuable person from the perspective of this country's security. His kidnapping represents a potentially severe loss to the military, to the country."

"If it wasn't FBI, who was it?" questioned another trooper.

"That's what we're investigating. That's what you should've asked yesterday."

"I want to talk to my union rep," shouted the trooper sitting next to Joyce.

"As of this morning, yesterday's events were classified as acts of domestic terrorism by the DoJ. Now, all of you— including Major Dunlap—are suspended from duty. You're all on administrative leave without pay as a precursor to dismissal and possible legal action. Any rights you think you might have, in terms of union representation, are suspended. You each will be interviewed this afternoon—I should say evening—separately, by FBI agents. They will determine charges based on the evidence, your cooperation, and your answers. Help yourselves—help us. Oh, you won't be going home this evening, hot dates or otherwise. You'll be held as either suspects or hostile witnesses. If you object and refuse to cooperate, I have a military helicopter ready to take you to our base and from there it will be a quick journey to Gitmo. Your choice." He shrugged.

One of the troopers jumped up from his chair. "Come on, this is all bullshit. They can't do anything. We were helping the FBI—Joyce said so. Let's get out of here." He headed to the door.

Schmidt signaled. Two of the MPs at the back of the room moved to intercept the protester and hustled him outside, crashing the trooper through the door. Dead silence followed, both inside and outside the conference room. Three minutes later the two MPs returned and resumed their positions against the back wall. Neither man was ruffled. Schmidt waited for another minute. No one spoke.

Schmidt said, "Well, that's one way to volunteer to be interviewed. Other interviews will commence now. Junior ranks first. Wait your turn. We'll call you by name. Please refrain from any discussions. I can arrange for you to be held separately, if need be."

It was, thought Schmidt, going to be a long night. He didn't think Joyce or Trevors had many friends, at least none friendly enough to stop disclosure of details that would seal the fates of those two officers. He knew—as undoubtedly did some of the troopers—he was walking on thin ice with his approach. He hoped the FBI would be able to cope with objections, if they arose. He was prepared, however, to carry out his threat, and move troopers to Camp Brewer and isolate them as suspected terrorists. He was confident he had communicated that certainty to his audience.

They had better believe it.

Chapter 16

Was it the sixth time—perhaps it was the tenth time? He had lost count. Numbers now had no meaning. He twisted and turned as he sought to identify where he was. The room was, he knew, pitch black. He kept his eyes closed—there was nothing to see. He realized—this time someone had entered his prison. He knew if he opened his eyes the light would flood in and cause more pain. He kept them closed, as tight as he could. He did not want to open them, not yet. A voice, female, soft, low, pierced his eardrums.

"Mr. Midway, we're going to clean you up. Afterwards, we can have a little talk, yes?"

He was beyond anger. His captors had strapped him to a bed of some kind—he suspected, from the fragile impression he had gained, it was a zinc autopsy table with drain holes—and they hadn't released him for toilet purposes. Now someone was hosing him down with cold water. It was fortunate, he supposed, that he had not been given anything to eat or drink while he was strapped down. Perhaps the IV had helped.

His jailer—or nurse—it made no difference—turned off the cold water. He'd kept his eyes closed; he knew the glare would be blinding. He waited for her to approach.

He did not know how long he'd been strapped down. The

total, isolating darkness of the cell had prevented him from estimating the passage of time—days may have been hours or hours may have been days. He was hungry. Thirsty. Tired. His entire body felt bruised.

Next, someone threw a towel over him. It covered most of his body. Still there was no conversation. How he was supposed to dry himself he had no idea. His arms—well, except for the one he had managed to free and so far his captor had not noticed—and his body and legs were firmly strapped down. He couldn't raise his head more than an inch, if that. He waited and listened. It sounded as though someone was rolling up a hose. He tried not to shiver.

There was silence for a couple of minutes. At last there was a voice, the same one, female, who had spoken before the hosing began.

"There, that's an improvement. For me, anyway."

She was talking to herself, Mark thought, *rather than to me. Perhaps she does have a conscience and is trying to hold it in check, by ignoring me.* He did not move. He did not speak.

"I suppose you can hear me? It would be difficult to continue if you're deaf. No one mentioned that possibility. I suppose I can dry you. Well, at least your face. This is not a full body wash service center."

The speaker rubbed his face with the now semi-damp towel. The fabric was harsh and his nerve ends sensitive. Still he did not move. She partly dried his chest and left the towel covering the lower half of his body. As he sensed her moving closer, he opened his eyes. He ignored the pain. She was close, very close. She was probably in her late twenties and was wearing a white uniform. He reached out with his free hand and grasped her arm.

"I didn't see that coming." She tried to shake her arm free from his grip.

She was wearing gloves that reached up to her elbows. The thin latex had stopped him making direct contact with her arm. The sleeves of her medical uniform reached down to the top of her gloves. He pulled her down, towards him, and shifted his grip. He tugged the edge of the glove and pulled it down. When his hand touched her bare skin, she froze and did not protest as he continued to remove the glove. Her eyes were moving back and forth, their movements fed by anxiety. There was no worry, yet. He examined her as best he could while he took control.

"Don't speak unless I tell you to. Now give me your hand," Mark instructed. She did so and Mark held it firmly for a minute. He strengthened his links.

"Remove the needle from the back of my wrist." He did not flinch when she somewhat carelessly removed the needle. The puncture wound bled drops of dark red blood.

"Release my right arm." He watched as she undid the fastening.

"Now my head and the rest of my body." Two minutes later, he was no longer restrained.

"Help me sit up."

He was correct. His bed was an autopsy table. He used the towel to dry the lower parts of his body. He knew his next action was going to hurt.

"Help me stand."

He held back a scream when his feet first touched the floor. He stood carefully, fighting back waves of agony. His entire body was an aching mess. The needle, he thought, had managed to inject some pain-enhancing drug before he had succeeded in blocking it, or there was some residual drug that now was taking effect. He felt as though the lines traced by his nervous system were on fire. He fought the surges of pain that threatened to overwhelm him.

"Is there any clothing here that I can use?"

She shook her head.

"You can speak. If you try anything to prevent me doing what I want, I'll share the agony I'm experiencing." He opened up a narrow pathway and fed a sample of what he was experiencing from his seared nerves. She screamed. He blocked it off.

"See what I mean?"

"I didn't—I didn't know you would suffer like that."

"You've been dosing me, and probably others, with all kinds of chemical junk," Mark challenged. "What do you expect it to feel like? Do you think this is some kind of joke?" He gripped her arm until she flinched. "Yes, my pain is real."

His agony slowly reduced and became more manageable. "What's your name?" He knew the answer. He wanted to reinforce his control.

"Emma."

"What do you do—what's your responsibility?"

"I'm a psychologist. I prepare prisoners for questioning."

"Where are we?"

"Gitmo."

"What? Who brought me here—who do you work for?"

Her face paled. "The—the NSA."

"Damn. And you're simply following orders."

"All the people we arrest and bring here are terrorists."

"No evidence, no trial, no judge, no jury—only you and your bosses. So the NSA is kidnapping American citizens and bringing them here for torture?"

"Kidnapping? No—no, that's illegal."

"So what you're doing is not? How long have I been here?

"Five days. We try to confuse the prisoners by applying different drugs. Semi-starvation is part of the destabilizing process. The objective is—"

"Yeah, I know—to torture them."

"Oh no, what I've been doing to you isn't torture. That comes later."

"Who's your boss? When will he be here to follow up on your work?"

"I report to a senior person. His name is Ken O'Hare, and he's one of their top agents."

"Good for you and him. Now, can I have some water?

Some food? Can you get me some clothes?"

"I—I'm not authorized to allow that."

His exasperation escaped. "Emma—I don't give a damn what you're authorized to do. I need to recover, to start feeling human again. Food and water is the best way to begin." Mark gripped her hand in both of his. "Listen to me. You're going to do everything possible to help me recover and escape. You'll bring me a meal and water. While I'm eating, you'll find clothes and shoes and bring them to me. Do you know if my own clothes are here?" She shook her head. "All right, any reasonable clothing—men's, something that won't look out of place. Weapons—do you have a weapon? A handgun? Do you have access to one?"

"Yes, but we're not supposed to—"

"Will anyone notice or stop you getting one?

"No."

"In that case, this is what you will do, without raising an alarm. You'll bring me a meal and water. While I'm eating, you'll get me a weapon—a handgun and suitable ammunition. You'll find some clothes for me. Understand?"

"Yes."

"Go. Be as quick as you can."

The water was easy. Emma handed him a plastic bottle with a straw. He drank.

"I'll get you some human food—it's what I eat. It'll take about ten minutes, maybe more."

She returned after a long fifteen minutes and handed Mark a foil wrapped tray. The tray contained some kind of meat stew, bland, with over-boiled vegetables. His mouth watered. The cutlery was plastic.

Emma stared at him as he started to eat. She said, "I'll go see if I can find a weapon for you."

He enjoyed the meal even though it was definitely low cuisine. He ate slowly, allowing his body to gradually resume its functions. After he'd eaten, he waited patiently. It was half an hour before the young psychologist returned, carrying a wrapped bundle which she handed to him. She waited for his response.

Mark unwrapped a handgun and two magazines of ammunition. Enough to cause trouble, probably not enough to support an escape.

"Good. Next—clothing. Oh, and do you have a cell phone? With a service to call the US?"

"I—I can try and get clothing. I have a cell phone that works here. I can bring it."

"Bring the cell phone first, okay?"

"Sure."

After waiting for what he estimated was close to fifteen minutes, Mark started to worry. The door to the small cell was unlocked, and while he had only a damp towel to wrap himself in, he decided to take the risk of venturing out into whatever room was adjacent; he suspected it was the monitoring area where Emma worked. He wrapped the towel firmly around his waist.

It was not as though the temperature was low—this was Cuba, after all. He held the handgun—a Glock, lightweight, .38 caliber automatic, a model that he was not familiar with—ready in his right hand and carried an extra clip in his left. That gave him twelve shots; after that it would be all over. He pulled the door open cautiously and peered around the edge of the opening. As far as he could determine, no one was in the room.

It was full of medical monitoring equipment, which, up to an hour or so prior, had been used to monitor him. He checked for paper printouts. Nothing. There was a small computer and a video monitor so presumably all his records were filed somewhere on a computer drive. He was in what seemed to be a metal building, flat-roofed—or at least, the ceiling was metal and flat. He recalled from some memory—probably not his; it felt as though it belonged to the psychologist, Emma— that he was in a converted container—a CHU—what the military called a containerized housing unit. Normally these units were used for setting up temporary military housing in places like Iraq and were large enough to accommodate a number of soldiers. This one contained torture facilities.

He was tempted to try to access the details on the laptop and decided that would be a diversion he could not afford. The room measured about ten feet by twenty feet, with small cabinets along one side. A door gave access to a longer corridor, which, he surmised, led to an exit. A cabinet door was half-open and he caught a glimpse of bottles and pre-loaded hypodermic needles. Probably the same as whatever had been used on him before he was loaded onto the helicopter. He shrugged; he could only guess. There was a telephone on the desk next to the computer.

He was tempted.

He sat down and placed the spare ammunition clip on the desk. He picked up the handset as slowly and quietly as he could, aware that his hand was shaking. He could not control it. He hoped the phone did not create a signal somewhere in the building or complex. He raised it to his ear. A female voice, familiar, was apparently reporting to someone on the other end of the call.

"Yes, he's awake. Yes, I hosed him down, cleaned him. No, I don't think so; he doesn't seem unduly affected. He said he was hungry and thirsty. I fed him, variation twenty. That will put him out for another six hours. What do you want me to try next? Uh-huh. Yes, I know the one. I'll report to you again, once he's unconscious. When will you be back? Tomorrow? Good, I'll look forward to seeing you. It's lonely here, by myself. Yes, Ken, me too. I'll see you tomorrow."

Mark heard the disconnect click and looked at the handset in disbelief. He replaced it quietly and turned towards the door into the office. Emma entered, carrying a bundle of clothes. She gave a jump when she saw Mark and nearly dropped the items she was carrying. Her burden included men's clothes, Mark noted, as he closed the door behind Emma.

"I have my cell phone, too. I thought it would be quicker if I brought everything instead of making separate trips."

"Where did you find these?" Mark asked as he sorted out a shirt, pants, shoes and socks. There was even a pair of underpants. He steadied himself with one hand on the edge of a desk and leaned over to pull on the underwear.

"What? Oh, I raided Ken's room. I thought I'd better phone him, to give him an update. He said to say hi, by the way."

Chapter 17

"How does he do it?" Linda was serious.

"Who—Schmidt?" Maeve asked. They were in Maeve's office.

"Yes. He knows things before we do, and we've got a darned good network. How did he know there had been a shooting at Mark's property? We hadn't been advised of that. Schmidt arrived at his office yesterday morning, early, ready to roll—he knew as much as we did about Mark's capture and more than we did about the little girl and what happened there."

"That's why he's Schmidt. Always one step ahead. Well, until Russians fire missiles at him."

"He's really recovered, hasn't he?"

"Yes. He needs his formal medical clearance, though."

"I can't imagine anyone will block that."

"Let's focus. What's your latest?" Maeve pushed her pen aside, a token clearing of her desk space.

Linda opened her folder. "We're waiting on a briefing from Schmidt after he completes interviewing those troopers. In the meantime—and I haven't briefed him yet—we've identified the man who shot Andrew Reeves, you know, the Winter Security operative." She passed a sheet across the desk to Maeve. "Here's a summary. The shooter's name is

Boyle, Nathan Boyle. Probability we're correct is 99%. He's ex-CIA. Had difficulties with a black op, resigned to avoid prosecution, and has had run-ins with the law. Violent stuff—assault, assault with intent, assault with a deadly weapon. Not guilty on most—Boyle has good friends, we've heard, and perhaps there's been some witness tampering or payoffs. No one marked him as a killer, though."

"Well done. You have a file? Good. The FBI will be interested. Send a copy to Chuck—Charles Thoroughgood. He'll arrange a warrant."

"Yes, ma'am. Now, the helicopter. As we'd reported earlier, it's privately owned via a shell company. Shareholders are untraceable. No—no, it's not a dead-end. We've been able to collect two years' worth of flight plans—a number of them originate from or end up at Langley. It's really surprising how careless—"

"Or how arrogant?"

"Yes, or how arrogant some people can get. We have over a hundred flight plans. Thirty-five involve Langley. What's of additional interest is the network of flight destinations and starting points, other than Langley. Look, here's a map of ninety-three flight plans, covering one hundred and eighty-six start and end points." Linda unfolded a printout. "We've marked them as heat maps—the more they've been visited, the larger the red indicator. See the patterns?"

"Now that's what I call interesting. Have you dug deeper?"

"Yes. This, the blue-circled point, is a property owned by a wealthy businessman—you may have heard of him—Ross Cromarty. This one—the green circle—is, we suspect, someone's mistress. We had one of our external analysts visit that address. It's a property in a sheltered country location, upstate New York. There's a handyman, foreign, who maintains the grounds. Our man managed to speak with a woman at the house. Her name is Zarina—he didn't get her surname. She sounded Russian. Our investigator tried to sell her fire extinguishers. No sale, unfortunately. The extinguishers were bugged, of course."

"The work your people do continues to astound me. What about this, with the black circle?"

"Our conclusion—tentative, but high probability—is whoever lives there is the primary user of the helicopter. Interestingly, the aircraft and the property are owned by the same Delaware company. We discovered the company arranged mortgages for these purchases. However—this again is where people slip-up—both the mortgages are guaranteed. We accessed some bank records, unofficially, of course."

"You delight in drawing your exposés out to the last, don't you?"

"Yes, ma'am. Specially when it's as good as this one. The guarantor is Ken O'Hare, assistant director, NSA."

"Damn."

"Definitely."

"Schmidt will be pleased."

Linda frowned. "You don't think he already knows, do you?"

Maeve laughed. "I doubt he's that good. He'll be impressed, don't worry. Now, what about possible destinations for the helicopter after they kidnapped Mark?"

"We've made some progress. There was a plan filed yesterday for a flight to and from a small private airfield, south of Boston. It was probably used for re-fueling. The departure point and return destination were both O'Hare's residence, the location we circled in black. We suspect they offloaded him at the same time they re-fueled, that Mark was transferred to another aircraft. We don't think he was transferred to a vehicle. Unfortunately, we haven't found a flight plan for any other aircraft matching the approximate arrival and departure times. We need that flight plan. We've reached a temporary dead-end. It requires a more hands-on investigation—live bodies on the ground, if you know what I mean."

"Yes, I do. That's a task Brian Winter and his people would relish, and he's close by. I'll kick that into gear for you, once we've spoken with Schmidt. We should call him now to exchange updates?"

"Let me get my two senior people—they'll be interested in Schmidt's report, and we want to get as much information as possible."

"Schmidt, this is Maeve. I have Linda and two of her analysts. She has an update for you and we'd like a progress report from you, if possible."

"Hi, all. With me, I have Charles, representing the FBI, and some of our team. What do you have for us?"

"Identity of the man who shot Andrew Reeves. His name is Nathan Boyle. Linda will send a detailed file to Chuck and a summary to you. He's got priors and is ex-CIA."

"Indeed."

"Yes. Linda has extra information for you."

Linda said, "We think we've identified the aircraft. We've analyzed two years of flight plans. You can download the file and my team's analysis from our cloud. We've included a table of each flight's start and end points. The results are rewarding. There's a high probability the helicopter is owned or controlled by an AD with NSA, Ken O'Hare."

"Damn."

"That's exactly what Maeve said. There are other links based on the flight plans. One is to Ross Cromarty—you know of him. Another is to a property occupied by a woman, possibly Russian. We're continuing to dig."

"I'll return to Washington. I'll be in my office tomorrow morning. Chuck can handle the troopers. We have a good case to proceed against two or three, in particular, Trevors and Joyce. They'll probably arrange plea deals. There's been some resignations—the State will be looking for a new troop major."

Maeve added, "Good. Final item—we're going to ask Brian Winter if his team will investigate what happened at the airfield where we think the aircraft was refueled. Mark was undoubtedly off-loaded at that time."

"Agree with that. Well done, Linda. Let's keep researching— we need to locate Mark."

Chapter 18

"What do you know about Cromarty?" Schmidt asked. He had reviewed Linda's analysis of the helicopter's flight plans, which included numerous flights to Cromarty's New York State property. "I've encountered him in the past. Your team has details?"

"Yes. He's wealthy, an aggressive takeover and strip them merchant. He tried to buy both the Cerberus and Lifelong genetic research data."

"And failed. RDEz was the only reliable purchaser, at least in the president's opinion," Maeve said. "We had a lot of soft reports in the FBI files, but nothing hard about his dealings. We never discovered anything actionable."

Schmidt didn't mention that he was a substantial shareholder in RDEz, Julian Kelly's company, or that Mark had received a large block of shares in consideration for the sale of all the research files he had rescued from the deadly attack on the Lifelong complex. Maeve and Linda were fully aware of Schmidt's investment, anyway.

Schmidt explained, "We need to know more about Cromarty. Linda, perhaps your team can dig deeper with their research?"

"Yes, I've added that to the list. It's public knowledge that he has substantial interests in shipping, manufacturing, and resources. A lot of foreign investments, mainly in Africa. There's a rumor he has a substantial shareholding in a Russian oil exploration company."

Maeve said, "I remember—we had a suspicion he was using his foreign corporate structures to bypass sanctions against trading with Iran. That's it. His mother—no, his grandmother—was Iranian; she moved to California in the 1970s. She passed away about ten years ago. Also, he has a reputation for being a vindictive business opponent."

"The FBI didn't proceed against him? Breaking sanctions carries severe penalties, I thought?" Schmidt asked.

"We only had vague rumors. Our legal people recommended taking a wait-and-see approach. I don't know what's happened since I retired."

"I'll add that to our list," Linda offered.

"Please do," Schmidt said. "Do we have any idea why Cromarty might be interested in Mark?"

"I'm going to take a leap into the dark. Don't laugh," Linda said. She paused. She was deep in thought, her expression serious.

"Go on," urged Maeve.

"You have to be joking," Schmidt said, looking at Linda.

"No, I'm serious."

"What are you two talking about?"

"It's a 70% probability," Linda offered.

"Might be closer to 75%," Schmidt returned.

"Tell me what you're talking about."

Linda flinched at Maeve's tone of voice.

"Relax, Maeve. Linda and I are building the same set of probabilities. Cromarty wants Mark for leverage to get Lifelong trade secrets. He failed to get them legitimately. He probably blames me for his failure to acquire Cerberus, so he's using Mark to trap me. Julian also may be at risk. Interesting."

Linda nodded her head. "I think there's more. He wants to ensure the sanctions issue is buried."

Maeve said, "I don't think I can cope with both of you. One is bad enough."

"Can your team refine your probability model?" Schmidt asked Linda.

"Yes, I'll put it at the top of the list."

"Aren't you overworking your analysts, based on a vague rumor?"

"No, Maeve. It's obvious, when you think about it. I've read about how he reacts if someone tries to obstruct his business dealings. I recall something about a Russian who tried to take over his oil investment—he was found dead. There was a major article about it in the Sunday Times, the British newspaper. The reporters claimed the Russian hadn't committed suicide, that he was murdered. Cromarty threatened major legal action against the paper and the reporters. There was another case, here in New York. Something about a bid for a property." Schmidt said.

Maeve frowned. "The other bidder disappeared? His body was never been found?"

"Yes, that's the one. With headlines like those, there must be other examples of his business misdealings."

"My research list is long," reminded Linda.

"I agree, the priority is O'Hare. Followed by Cromarty. We need data. Something to help us find and rescue Mark," Schmidt said.

"I can make more Cerberus people available, if you need," Maeve offered.

"Yes, please. Ex-FBI types might be best; they've legal training and investigative experience."

Schmidt said, "If you can, send resumes to both Linda and me."

"Consider it done."

"We'll need to brief the president about Cromarty. I should do that, anyway, to update him on Mark's kidnapping."

Maeve said, "I've arranged a thirty minute session—private—

for you, me, the president, and someone from his National Security team, for tomorrow."

###

The president welcomed Schmidt when he and Maeve were ushered into the small meeting room. It wasn't even a conference room, thought Schmidt, as he settled into a chair. He squirmed, trying to find a comfortable position. This was a working office, not a showroom.

"Schmidt, welcome. We were wondering when you'd be back in business. Missed your insights."

"Thank you, sir. I'm pleased to be back. I'll arrange the medical clearance when I have a moment to spare."

"Ha! I'll bet that will take a while. Maeve, also welcome. What do you have for us? I take it the only good news is Schmidt's return?"

"Yes, sir. I'll cover quick headings." Maeve pushed a file across the desk. "This contains the details. Midway has been kidnapped. Nathan Boyle, ex-CIA, posed as a senior FBI agent and arranged a police blockade to grab Midway. We're searching for his location. We traced the helicopter Boyle used. Identification is based on partials, unfortunately. Once we had that detail, we analyzed the aircraft's flight plans for the last couple of years. There are solid links. Suspects—Ross Cromarty might be involved. Other names include General Grovers, who is on his staff, and Ken O'Hare. He's NSA, an AD managing a foreign affairs resources section. O'Hare's definite and we're gathering evidence. General Grovers is a guess at this point; we're searching for substantive evidence. We're researching Cromarty to find a weak spot. When we're ready we'll probably hit the three of them at the same time. Cromarty's dangerous, also vindictive according to reports, and Mark refused to sell his Lifelong material to him. He was also trying to buy Cerberus intellectual property. Julian Kelly—

well, RDEz—as you know, has both sets of IP. We've arranged additional security for Kelly. Schmidt, of course—"

"Refuses additional security, I suppose?" commented AJ Jenkins, the president's national security advisor, with a smile. He and Schmidt were old friends.

"Reluctantly accepted, in this case. I'm aware this could get heated before long."

"It's disappointing to hear one of our senior NSA people is possibly involved. Let me know when you have enough evidence to act. What are your next steps?"

"We don't know, yet, where Midway is being held, and rescuing him is a priority," said Schmidt. "We know where the helicopter re-fueled and it's likely there was a changeover at that airfield. We'll apply pressure to our three suspects— we need some good pressure points, first."

"Take care. I'm aware of Cromarty and his reputation. What's the certainty of the involvement of the other two?" the President asked.

"Approaching 100% for O'Hare. Grovers—our estimate is 60%," said Schmidt. "We'll ensure we're 100% before we take action. And we'll let you know before we go public with arrests. At least, as long as they don't react in a way that requires immediate action."

"Good. Maeve, what about Midway's partner and their wards—are they safe?"

"Yes, sir. We've increased security. They've added another child—a talented twelve-year old girl. There's a page on her in the file."

"I'm interested in Midway and his—what, extended family? Do what you need to ensure their safety."

"We agree, sir. They're well guarded. If Cromarty got his hands on them, he'd have substantial leverage against Midway and we don't want that to happen. Besides, they're also friends of ours," affirmed Schmidt. He had a reputation for protecting his friends as aggressively as he pursued his enemies, if not more so.

"Report every second day, please. Anything else I should be aware of?"

"No, sir. You have the critical items."

"Thanks, Maeve. Good to see you back in action, Schmidt. We've got too much on our list today to spend more time with you. Schmidt, it's time you took up golf."

The president laughed at the horrified expression on Schmidt's face.

Chapter 19

He twisted and turned. His neck burned. His head ached. His arms were strapped to a metal frame. He tried to move his legs and discovered they, too, were strapped down. He tried to sit up. A strap across his upper body held him down. He was able to lift his head, barely an inch or so. He built up the energy to try to open his eyes. His eyelids were stuck and he struggled until at last he managed to open both eyes. They were full of grit, aggravated, painful.

There was nothing to see—the room was pitch black; there was no light, anywhere. He could hear faint, distant noises, so presumably it was daytime. It might be early—very early—morning.

His nose itched. He couldn't scratch it. His elbow itched. He couldn't reach that, either. The back of his hand stung; it felt like a wasp was drilling into a vein. He could move his head, a mere fraction. That didn't help. He blinked. His eyes felt less gritty. He realized he was wired, he could feel pads on his body—he was being monitored.

He swore. He was back on the zinc autopsy table; he could feel the cold metal on his back. The nurse—no, she said she was a psychologist—had not only avoided his control, she had somehow drugged him again, and strapped him into position. Something in his food, he supposed. He felt totally stupid. That's what comes of being overconfident. His right arm, which he had freed, now was firmly held down. He tested the restraint. This time there was no movement, no give, no weakness, in whatever held him.

Unless, he mused, it had all been a delusion, a dream, a result generated by whatever cocktail mix of drugs they were drip-feeding into his arm. It had been so real. She had brought him a meal. Water. His mouth was dry. So dry. He fought against the natural inclination to dwell on his thirst and succeeded in shutting down, for the moment, the subconscious alarms his body was generating. He knew he needed to escape—he did not need reminding.

A door opened and closed. Voices drifted closer.

"Let's have some light." The man's voice was familiar. He couldn't recall, yet, where he'd heard it before.

Mark squeezed his eyes shut against the painful glare.

"You've eased off the dose?"

"Yes, sir." This speaker, he thought, was Emma. The nurse—no, she was a psychologist, she said. Mark dug into his memories. Yes, she had said she reported to Ken O'Hare, a senior NSA employee. Therefore the other speaker must be O'Hare.

"Clean him up. Give him some water. He can have a meal. Something light. Free his head so he can eat."

"Yes, sir."

"Add a vitamin mix to his IV. We don't want him to die on us. After he's eaten something I'll ask him some questions, see how he's reacting. Let me know. I'll be in the Strawberry Fields building." There was the sound of a door opening and closing. Strawberry Fields struck a chord. If his memory was correct, it was some kind of black site, in Guantánamo Bay. So he was in Cuba—perhaps he was not being delusional.

"Yes, sir. No, sir. We're now a catering service. Wash time."

The flow of water was welcome. It somehow helped to fight his feeling of extreme dehydration. His hose-down was followed by a repeat of the rough towel treatment. At least his face was clean and dry. Again, the towel was draped over the lower part of his body. The table was cold and wet. He wondered if pneumonia was intended to be part of his treatment.

"There." The psychologist released the strap holding his head in place. "Use this straw. You'll have to turn your head to this side—you can do that? Good. Drink slowly, otherwise you'll choke." She held the bottle while he drank the water.

The water was a relief; the body did not care for dehydration.

"That's four ounces, enough for now. If you promise to keep still, I won't strap your head back down. I need to get you some food. I'll be ten to fifteen minutes, okay? It's part of the new catering service."

"Yes," Mark managed after a number of attempts to speak. "Do you have a menu?"

"Smart ass. It's whatever the mess will give me. It will be suitable for someone who hasn't eaten much for days. Soup. Oliver Twist gruel. Who knows?" The door opened and closed with a bang.

Mark, partly refreshed by the small amount of water, tried to think. He needed to stop the flow of drugs into his system. He'd managed that once, he was sure. The nanites had been effective. His thoughts leapt from subject to subject, randomly. He struggled to focus. He lifted his head and dropped it down, hard, onto the metal table. He shuddered with pain—his nerve ends were still affected by whatever pain enhancement pharmaceuticals remained in his nervous system. He cursed. He tried to focus his thoughts. Stop the drug flow. Use nanites to block the needle. Nanites. Yes, they were the answer. He struggled. He visualized the result he required, copying his commands from a day—only a day?—before.

The cell door opened and closed again. It was Emma; he could tell by her lighter footsteps. She was accompanied by the odor of warm food. Mark could not determine what food the odor represented. He turned his head sideways on the table and watched. She set the food containers down on a small table and rolled it across to his bed.

"What is it?"

"Nutritious. The kitchen, when they know it is for a patient, make up a special mix. I have no idea what it is— proteins, carbs, about 2,000 calories. Semi-liquid, to make it easier to eat and digest. It's not what I call human food. I can't release you—you'll have to enjoy Emma's feeding service." She raised a spoon full of a gray, unclassifiable mixture.

Mark opened his mouth and eventually swallowed. He was unable to identify the food category. Emma raised another spoonful. Mark opened his mouth. The feeding process was repeated until the container was empty.

"I brought you a hot drink. It's milky and well-sugared tea. Do you want that?"

"Yes, please."

Emma placed the straw in his mouth and held the container for him. It was, he thought, a form of nectar. Either that or his taste buds had been utterly corrupted. When he was finished, Emma placed the plastic mug back on the small table.

"You're looking better," she said.

"It's the water and the food—although how that —gruel, you called it—could improve anyone is a mystery." It was also, he thought, because he'd managed to reduce the inflow of her pharmaceutical cornucopia.

"Can you ease some of these straps? The pressure is causing too much pain."

"Remember what happened before? No. Ask me again after my boss goes back to Washington. Or wherever he comes from, somewhere hot, I'm sure."

So it hadn't been a dream.

"You don't like him?"

"I need to survive. I also need to let him know you're ready."

It was, Mark estimated, an hour before Emma's mysterious boss re-appeared. In the meantime he had tried to relax, even though he was strapped down to an autopsy table. The nanites had stopped the drug flow. The food had revived him to a degree. His mental state was still affected by the drug intakes.

The door opened and closed. Two sets of footsteps approached. He was facing away from the door to his cell and could not see his visitors.

"Midway, Mark Midway." The speaker was the man who had given Emma instructions earlier. Mark did not respond. His head was lifted up as far as possible and pushed with force back onto the table. The pain was excruciating. He assumed his assailant was O'Hare. He embedded the man's name in permanent memory.

"I said Midway, Mark Midway. I expect a response."

"Yes." Mark blinked through the flashes of lightning.

"Good. As long as you behave, you'll survive. Behave, in this context, means comply with my orders. You're in my world, understand?"

"Yes." The lightning flashes were easing.

"You're Cerberus?"

"No."

His head was lifted and Mark expected another bruising slam into the zinc tabletop. Instead his head was, to his surprise, lowered gently.

"My error. You know of Cerberus?"

"Yes."

"And you work with them?"

"Sometimes."

"Are you Cerberus-engineered?"

"No, I'm not."

"Hmm. I'll follow up that answer, later. You know General Schmidt?"

"Yes."

"Good. How well?"

"We're not close friends. I haven't seen much of him since his accident."

"He'll try to rescue you, though?"

"I believe so."

"Why?"

"I've helped Cerberus. He'll want to help me."

"Good. I want you to record a video message for Schmidt. He needs to see that we have you under our control"

"Why?"

"That response takes you close to another head slam. You will record a message?"

"Y—yes." Mark realized there was no advantage to be gained by refusing to cooperate. His mind leapt into action—there must be a way to take advantage of the intended video.

It was well into the afternoon; at least Mark assumed it was afternoon, when his captor organized the video session. O'Hare suspended the camera on a weighted mechanical arm above the autopsy table and tested the focus.

"Good, it works," the NSA agent said. "Your friend Schmidt is going to get a full image, and I'm sure you realize, with sound effects. I want him to get—what should I say—yes, an unexpurgated message."

There followed what seemed to Mark like hours of electrical torture but which he assumed was only five minutes or so. He did not repress his screams of pain, nor his involuntary movements, when O'Hare or Emma pressed whatever button caused his electric shocks. This time he managed to not bite his tongue. He hoped whoever viewed the video caught on to his coded message, as brief as it was.

O'Hare switched off and removed the camera. "A good performance, far better than I'd expected. Emma will keep you company for the next few days." He waved the SD card from the video camera at Mark. "This will go to Schmidt—with an editorial commentary, of course. I'll leave you now, in Emma's good hands, at least until I need to send Schmidt another message."

Chapter 20

Linda Schöner stopped to chat with the maître d' of Restaurant Placido. She had attended the same college as his daughter, and some years after graduation she had prevailed on Cerberus resources to rescue the slightly older woman from a relationship that was fraught with disaster. As a result, the so-called boyfriend had been sentenced to jail for major drug dealings and Teresa had vowed she would never again be caught up in a similar situation. As far as Linda knew, Teresa had kept her promise.

"Terrie is getting married," Victor said, with a large dose of fatherly pride. "A nice boy. Attorney. I know his father, and we have mutual friends." Victor had a broken nose from his youth and spoke with a subdued Brooklyn-Italian accent.

Linda wondered about the mutual friends. "Please tell her I said congratulations."

"I will, she'll be pleased. I have your table, as you requested. Some of your friends are here already. I seated them not too close."

Victor, Linda knew, was referring to soldiers from the 145th. She had prevailed on Helen Chouan, CO of the MP Battalion, to lend her some resources in case she needed backup for today's effort. She had not informed Schmidt that she was initiating one of the pressure points that would impact

Ross Cromarty and also was taking a leading role in that process. She had, on reflection, considered it necessary to have some protection at hand.

Linda said, "Good. Now, when Senator Fordsby arrives and asks for Thomas Driscoll, show him to my table. He'll have his two men with him; they need to be seated at another table, where they cannot overhear our conversation." She was not sure whether the two men were minders, bodyguards, or simply companions; however, she did know they accompanied the senator everywhere.

"It will be done as you say, Miss Linda. If there's anything else I can do for you?"

"No, Victor. It's good of you to help me. I appreciate it more than I can say."

"No problem. As you know, it's my pleasure to help you. Anytime. May I show you to your table, now?"

Placido was one of Washington's tony restaurants, well regarded for both its cellar and its chef and Linda rarely felt she could justify the expense of dining in such luxury. She smiled to herself at the thought of Schmidt's reaction if she claimed a meal here on her expenses. The table Victor led her to was in a semi-private nook, not too hidden, yet not in the wider, more open section of the restaurant. Three tables along, three fit young men had placed their order. Linda caught the details of how they wanted their steak, something along the lines of break off its horns and slide it onto a large plate. They were, she guessed, from 145th, smartly dressed and on their best manners. The giveaway was their military haircut. There were another couple; they were further away. The man had a similar military-style haircut and the woman, who also looked fit, was smartly dressed; it was possible Helen had provided backup for the backup. She looked around at other tables and to her surprise saw Helen, seated at a far table, with a male companion—she recognized him; he was a captain from the battalion. Linda smiled to herself, without acknowledging either Helen or her soldiers. Well, she thought, I have backup plus.

JOHN HINDMARSH

Twenty minutes later Victor accompanied a middle-aged man to the table. The senator was portly and his suit required regular intervention of a skilled tailor. His weight gains were part of the penalty of his current lifestyle.

"Senator Fordsby," Victor said, "Mr. Driscoll phoned to say he was running late. He also said Miss Schöner would act as hostess until he arrived."

Fordsby's stare as he looked at Linda was borderline impolite. "I don't know you," he said.

Victor interceded. "I have known Miss Schöner for a number of years, Senator. She is a nice lady, with an impeccable background."

The senator looked startled as he recognized the hidden censure in Victor's voice. "Oh, all right. See that my friends are cared for." He accepted the chair that Victor was holding out and sat down at the table. "Thank you."

"Victor, I believe Senator Fordsby's drink of choice is whisky—Scotch—you know his preference. I'll stay with my current drink."

"Yes, Miss Schöner."

Fordsby stared again at Linda. She had exchanged her usual horn-rimmed glasses for a gold-rimmed pair, selected to communicate a strong and luxurious fashion sense. She wore a tailored dark-colored suit paired with a soft peach blouse and her hair, normally straight and unruly, had been blow-dried into temporary submission. She wore a bare minimum of makeup. She did not flinch under his regard. She lifted a thin briefcase onto the table.

"Senator, we have time for a short discussion before Thomas arrives." Thomas Driscoll was the senior strategist of a Super PAC, which was offering funds to the senator in support of his pending re-election bid. Linda had prevailed on Driscoll, using the results of some of her team' research as leverage, and he had promised to delay his arrival for thirty minutes.

"Yes?"

"Indeed," Linda replied. She opened her briefcase. "I've some information that will interest you, in your role as an Opposition member of the Senate Banking Committee." She extracted a dozen or so sheets of paper and slid them across the crisp white tablecloth towards the senator. "Earlier this month you initiated a proposal for the committee to explore the effectiveness of banking sanctions on Iran. While the chairman and some of your fellow committee members are pushing back because this is a retrospective focus, given the current relationship with Iran, we believe there is value to be gained if you pursue your proposal." She tapped the sheets of paper, photocopies of original banking transactions. "These provide details of the money trail for some $500 million of arms transactions in breach of US and international sanctions. The principal is an American citizen. We understand the committee will be able to access the original documents, given the parent banks involved are American."

"Miss—"

"Read them before you reject them. If you wish to create a favorable media situation leading up to your re-election, you would be well-advised to consider following this document trail."

Fordsby, with obvious reluctance, looked down at the first page. After a minute of reading he turned the sheet of paper over and read the second page. He quickly skipped to the third page and the fourth. He riffed the remaining pages although he did not read further. He looked up at Linda, suspicion strong in his reaction. He straightened the sheets of paper into a single block.

"I'm impressed by the details. I'm not sure reality will support the contents." He tapped the papers. "That is, how do I know these are real, that they reflect the truth?"

"Senator, I—we—do thorough research. If I can demonstrate the accuracy of our research activities, will you pursue your proposal, as aggressively as you can, using the material we've provided?'

The senator appeared bemused. He shook his head; it was a sign of disbelief rather than rejection. "How can you convince me of the accuracy of your research?"

Linda withdrew another batch of paper from her briefcase, although this time with fewer pages.

"Let me show you these." She slid a sheet of paper towards the senator. "This is a credit card receipt for a recent hotel stay at a four star hotel. I believe the card is yours?"

The senator looked down at the details. His face paled.

Linda slid the second sheet of paper across the table. "These are some interesting banking transactions. Of course, as member of the Senate Banking Committee, you are aware that transactions in excess of $10,000 should be investigated by your bank—perhaps they overlooked these?" The page contained details of three cash withdrawal transactions of $12,000 each.

The senator remained silent.

Linda slid the third and last page across the table. "This photograph was, I understand, retrieved from one of the hotel's security cameras. I believe other, similar, images can be also retrieved." The senator looked down. The photograph was of two men entering a hotel room, and one of the men was clearly identifiable as Senator Fordsby. The two men were in a somewhat amorous embrace.

Linda said, "I'm sure most people nowadays would find nothing untoward in this apparent situation. The issue would be different if your local selection committee—the members of which I hear are rigid in their beliefs—was to see it. To say nothing of your wife."

"I—" Fear, fight, and flight reflexes were conflicting the senator.

"Senator, I have no desire to publish this material. I have demonstrated the efficiency of our research. I'll do more than that. This man," she pointed at the second person in the photograph, "is on his way to Europe as we speak. He's undertaken to remain there until after the election. We can ensure his whereabouts are untraceable, and, of course, we can arrange for the hotel images to be deleted, if you wish. For no cost. Now, what do you say?"

The senator folded the three sheets of paper and placed them in an inside pocket of his suit.

"You have convinced me of your research capabilities." He shook his head. "Although I must admit, I'm also fearful of them." He straightened his back and looked Linda in the face. "All right. I'll pursue my proposal, even though there's a lot of pressure against me. Your research information will reverse a lot of that pressure."

"Good. Senator, Thomas is due here in a few minutes. He's unaware of the content of our discussion. It's up to you what you tell him. I believe he's in favor of your proposal to the Banking Committee. My suggestion? Remain here, enjoy lunch with Thomas, share your intentions. There's no need to identify the source of your—ah—research material, although he may guess."

Linda pushed her chair back. Before she could stand, Victor was at her side. "You are leaving already?"

"Yes, Victor. No, don't be concerned, I need to run. I believe Senator Fordsby will wait for Thomas—he's looking forward to your chef's special." She smiled at the maître d'. "Remember, tell Terrie I said congratulations." She turned back to the senator. "I enjoyed our discussion. Good luck with your proposal."

The senator stood. He coughed to clear his throat and said, "Thank you."

Linda was already walking towards the double doors leading to the street. She had applied the first pressure point.

Chapter 21

The next day Linda implemented the second phase of her plan to apply pressure on Cromarty. One of her friends, Travis Martin, was a reporter and blogger, and he was always interested in discovering potential scoops. He was, Linda thought, also very good looking—handsome, even—and played on his obvious clean-cut style. She had arranged their meeting in a modest restaurant and this time Linda planned to stay and eat her lunch, even if it wasn't prepared by the chef at the Placido.

Travis was already seated when she arrived—he was early for a change. She went straight to the table. Travis's eyes lit up. They exchanged air kisses, cheek to cheek.

"Hi, Linda. Long time."

"I know. Life's been busy. You?" Linda took her seat, aided by the waiter.

"Same, same. Busy, blogging, trying to discover news, lunching with pretty girls."

"You know—"

"I know. For some reason you don't love me anymore."

Travis and Linda, for a hectic three months, had been lovers. Linda wanted more commitment and Travis wanted less. They'd remained friends after the breakup. Linda took a sip of water from her glass, mainly to avoid a response.

"Still running your research team?" Travis asked.

"Yes. It's getting larger. I liked that exposé you did on the pharmaceutical company—their price increases were ridiculous."

"Thank you. Reader response came close to blowing out my server." He lifted his menu. "Let's order."

The restaurant was efficient and their food was delivered in a surprisingly short time. Linda visualized rows of pre-prepared dishes waiting for someone's selection so that a chef could load them into a red-hot oven. She had chosen a basic hamburger featuring Wagyu beef, and Travis, after a moment of consideration, had chosen likewise. Neither ordered alcohol; Linda wanted to keep her head clear—she was unsure of her companion's motive. She finished her last mouthful of salad as Travis pushed aside his empty plate.

"Aah. It might be only a hamburger—but it's America's staple meal," Travis said. "Now, what do you want to discuss?"

Linda checked her makeup, applying a slight remedial touch of lipstick. She used the opportunity to check whether anyone was interested in their lunch meeting. Apart from the two MPs from the 145th sitting a couple of tables away, apparently enjoying a similar meal, there was no obviously interested diner.

"Travis, this one is serious. It could get you beaten up or worse, understand?" Linda still had a lingering attraction for her ex.

"Now you've made it even more tempting. Tell me more." He pulled a Microsoft Surface out of his briefcase, placing it on the table. At Linda's nod, he opened the cover.

They were interrupted by the waiter. They both declined dessert, although Travis ordered a black coffee.

When the waiter departed with their plates, Linda played with her phone, establishing a secure link to the Surface. Travis had not changed his password; she thought she should warn him about that carelessness. She transferred a zip file.

The process was not fast—the file was large. "It's a zip file—open it later, somewhere private. It's encrypted." She handed a business card across the table. "Use the second line as the key. Include the spaces."

"You sound mysterious, very mysterious. Will it self-destruct?"

"No, you idiot. Well, maybe it should, you never know. Our focus is a wealthy businessman. You will know of him."

"You don't want to mention his name, here?"

"Correct. If when you read the details you decide you're not interested, let me know."

"What's the problem?"

"We think—well, we know—he arranged for one of our friends to be kidnapped. We want to apply pressure to him, undermine his strengths, emphasize his weaknesses. While he's fighting against possible criminal indictments—he'll hate the negative publicity—we'll continue gathering evidence. He may end up charged with serious criminal offenses. His modus operandi is to mount aggressive corporate takeovers, and there are indications he has political aspirations—indirectly. We want to take his focus away from our rescue efforts."

"Ouch—so getting beaten up is really a potential reward, huh? You weren't kidding." Travis closed his computer after checking that the transfer had completed without error. The waiter delivered his coffee. He took a sip. Linda watched his movements.

Linda frowned. She wasn't sure how to convince Travis that her request held danger. "Travis, this is not a joke. Believe me, if you take this on, you'll be in danger." She shrugged. "How much? I don't know. But there is danger, believe me."

"Tell me more."

"The Senate Banking Committee should shortly require this person to attend a hearing—they've been given evidence showing he was involved in illegal arms shipments to Iran. You now have a copy of that evidence."

Travis raised his eyebrows and pursed his lips. He sat up straighter. "Your research is uncovering toads, huh? I'll enjoy the reading material."

"There's more information in the files I sent. The chairman of the committee, Senator Randolph, has received donations from the—er—businessman, so he's not rushing to get this hearing into gear. Instead, he's trying to kill it. Details of the donations—sources, amounts, dates, and recipients with their links to Randolph—are included in the file I gave you. However—" Linda paused and had another sip of water. "The senator is—I don't know whether to call it wooing or screwing—in either case, the girl is only seventeen. She's a Senate page, and somehow he has managed to indulge in definite sexual relations, I believe is the phrase, with her. You now have names and two videos, one taken in his hotel room. We want to protect the girl; she's far too young to be involved in a major scandal. I'll rely on you—do not post her details."

"I can use the knowledge of the affair for—pressuring—the senator?"

"Yes. Wear long, fire-proof gloves, though."

"You like him that much?"

"He's a bastard, to put it bluntly. We'll probably arrange for him to retire."

"Your research team has that much power?" Travis raised his eyebrows, his expression serious.

"Friends. We have friends who use our research services. Travis, I caution you, do not treat the risks lightly. If, at any point, you think that you are in danger—there's a cell number on the card I gave you. Call it. Say—this is Travis and I need help. Give your location in case we can't trace it. Shelter until help arrives. Our people will get to you faster than the police, I guarantee." Linda needed to stress the seriousness of the likely reactions from Ross Cromarty if Travis produced one of his exposés—which, of course, she wanted him to do.

"How will I identify the good guys from the baddies?"

"They'll tell you Linda sent them. And they'll show a

military ID. They'll be military police from an MP Battalion, the 145th."

"MPs? I won't ask. You're swimming in deep waters. Are you safe?" Travis frowned into his coffee. He raised his head far enough to catch Linda's eyes. His concern for her safety was obvious.

She blinked. It was an admission, she realized. Travis knew her too well. "I'll have an escort for a while. Besides, at this stage, he doesn't know me, and I hope it stays that way."

"But you'll use me?" He swallowed a mouthful of coffee.

"Yes. It plays into your ambitions." Linda shrugged, not totally dismissive. "It's what you do. And I'm doing what I do."

Travis laughed and reached across the table for Linda's hand. "I know. I was pushing buttons. So this guy's evil, he's kidnapped one of your people, and you're applying maximum pressure?"

"Oh, yes."

"Can I ask who he kidnapped?"

"No names, Travis. Not this time. He's—well—he's a part of our organization."

"And if I try to discover details, I'll end up with a smacked hand?"

"At least. Amputated, more like."

Toby nodded, keeping eye contact with Linda. "I understand—I'll not explore that path. Why so much pressure—why are you creating this pressure?"

"The person who was kidnapped is at risk of his life. We're doing everything to find and rescue him. No, we don't have any personal relationship—he's one of our VIPs, I suppose you'd say. We even have the support of the president for our rescue efforts."

Travis finished his coffee. "Linda, dear Linda. You are undoubtedly at far greater risk than I'll ever be. I'll help, of course. I'll let you know if I have questions, and I'll report in, occasionally. A good excuse to take you to lunch again."

"I'd like that."

Chapter 22

Schmidt, when he found out, was as angry as Linda had ever seen him. His chastisement was well into fifteen minutes before Linda could get him to stop his tirade and listen to her. She thought most of her team had heard him.

Linda held up her hand, like a stop signal.

"Schmidt. You've been ill. We have been working independently for months. We will continue to be independent, to a degree. You don't think a team of more than a hundred researchers, investigators, and analysts has been sitting still, hands under their bums, waiting for you to return to duty, do you?"

Schmidt appeared stunned. He did not reply.

Linda continued. "We've supported Maeve and a number of Cerberus teams. We liaise closely with Helen and her battalion, providing reciprocal support. We've provided some independent research—sensitive data—to AJ, the President's National Security Advisor. We have other clients, wealthy individuals, plus some corporate. So don't come in here, firing on all cylinders because we've continued to do business as usual."

"You've created a danger for yourself, which might not have been necessary. Likewise for your friend and for that senator—Fordsby."

"Mark deserves every effort we can apply." She closed her lips. She folded her arms.

"Linda, I know and I agree. I don't question your motivation—I'm concerned about your safety."

"The safest thing we can do is neutralize these people, as fast as possible."

"You have a valid point. Okay. Keep me appraised. In future, consult before you climb out on a risky limb, please."

"Assuming you're back and functioning as we need you to be, yes. I reserve the right to climb any limb, if I think it necessary, if you're incapacitated."

"Unfair, Linda."

"No, it's not. As I said, we've been functioning effectively. And profitably. We had to."

Schmidt threw his hands up. "I take your point. Now, let's work together, okay?"

"Yes, sir. I mean that positively. You're our boss—we missed you."

"I know, damn it. I missed you and the team, too. Let's get a round up of actions and statuses. Are you ready?"

"Yes, of course. I've arranged for Winter to report at his favorite time—10:30 a.m. He should have news of any aircraft in the vicinity of the refueling. FBI have questioned the regular pilot; however, he was on vacation in the Bahamas for that week. I believe the DHS team, which was tasked to visit O'Hare's possible girlfriend, should be able to report also by mid-morning. She's European, maybe Ukrainian, and the team was tasked with identifying her. Their focus is her immigration status. Travis sent me a text—he's got a sixty-second spot on CNN through the morning. He fed one of the producers some suggestions and they're interested in the Iranians and whether the Senate Banking Committee is taking action to explore embargo breaches."

"Good. You said Helen has a snatch team ready to extract him, if he needs help?"

"Yes, indeed. She's arranged a team for me, as well."

"That's good to hear. Other reports—what's happening?"

"I have five teams devoted to processing data from all our Cerberus people. We're deluged, although there's a lot of chaff. I have two other teams analyzing their summaries. That's forty people. Another two teams are analyzing official reports, reviewing tapes, statements, you name it."

"Hoping we'll get some grains out of all the chaff, huh?"

"Yes, sir."

"What about Maeve? Does she have anything official from the FBI or other agencies?"

"We're meeting in an hour or so, and she'll expect you to join us for her briefing."

Schmidt was silent for a moment, reflecting on Linda's report. He said, "We're now dependent on whether Brian Winter's teams and your analysts discover something relevant, like details of an aircraft exchange at the airfield south of Boston. Your pressure points should startle up some activities. We'll keep an eye on Cromarty and O'Hare. On Grovers, too. He could prove to be a weak point."

"I've a suggestion for Grovers."

"Yes?" Schmidt was interested.

"Circulate a rumor that the Army is considering a review of his misconduct—you know, if the Army recalls him, charges him with conduct unbecoming to an officer, demotes him, and dishonorably discharges him, his ego damage would be substantial. He is a man alone—no family and few friends—he may decide to come to you or Maeve for help."

"You're getting more devious, young lady. Cruel, as well."

"They kidnapped Mark. I'm prepared to attack anyone who is possibly involved to ensure he is released, unharmed. Besides, you taught me."

"Ha. That excuse won't wash. Work up a plan for Grovers—we'll include him in the pressure program."

###

Three men, clean-shaven, hair trimmed, neatly dressed in dark suits, polished black shoes, with crisp white shirts and carefully tied ties, approached the entrance to the block of apartments. One by one, they pushed though the revolving door into the lobby area, empty of people except for a Winter Security guard who stood behind a high desk. The apparent senior member of the team walked over to the guard, his footsteps muted by the thick pile carpet strip laid across the marble floor.

He said, "I'm Special Agent Fredericks. We have an appointment to interview Ms. Anna Midway." He flashed his badge and FBI identity card and went to return the wallet to his suit jacket's inside pocket.

The guard held his hand out for the wallet. "I'll have to scan your identity card, sir. The same for each of your companions. It's SOP here and agreed to by your office. No exceptions. I'll also clear your presence with Ms. Midway." Anna and the two children—now three children, he corrected himself—had returned late in the previous evening. They were, in his estimation, nice people. He always took special care when he considered the clients were in that category.

"Karl, take care of this," the senior member said as he returned the wallet to his pocket and adjusted his jacket.

Karl, the youngest of the three men, stepped forward and drew a handgun. It was silenced. He snapped off a shot and the guard collapsed, possibly dead or dying, behind the security desk. Neither of the three putative FBI agents noticed the security camera tucked into a high corner, nor were they aware it relayed images and sound on a continuous feed to Winter Security's control room. The monitoring controller's reactions were fast and efficient; she notified the local police and placed a call to the client, advising of the attack and possibly deadly assault on their employee. She also contacted a Winter Security response team and it was only minutes away from the apartment building. Her notification action list required a follow-up call to Cerberus in Washington. That last call generated a major impact: a number of FBI agents and police, all Cerberus and located in Boston, were notified and as a result, an FBI team and a police team were heading to the apartment building.

The three men walked to the elevators only to discover the call button was not functioning; presumably one reaction to their illicit entry was for the elevators to be temporarily disabled. Neither did they know that building tenants, both those in the building and those away from their apartments, had been advised of the lockdown.

"Karl, try the door," ordered the senior member of the small team of intruders. He indicated a door that presumably gave access to the building's stairwell.

Karl pushed and pulled at the door; however, it did not move. "Locked. Nate, this is going bad," he complained.

Nathan Boyle ignored his companion's negative reaction. "Ralph, check if the security guard has keys or a remote control. Quickly, we need to move."

The third member of the group searched the jacket and pants pockets of the security man on the floor, avoiding the flow of blood from his head wound. He checked the desk. He turned to his boss. "No, nothing."

"Blast them to fucking hell," cursed the man in charge. His hastily—now he was prepared to admit to himself—and carelessly thought out plan was unraveling rapidly.

"We should leave—this is going nowhere," advised Karl, moving towards the set of exit doors.

"Shaddup," snapped Boyle. "Let me think. One of these other doors must be unlocked—there are fire laws."

The crescendo of police alarms intruded into the building foyer. Karl and Ralph looked at each other and shrugged. Boyle noticed and reacted angrily. "Okay, okay. I thought this was going to be a simple walk in and walk out. Come on, let's get out of here."

The three men headed to the exit. Despite efforts, none of them could budge the revolving doors. Both Karl and Ralph tried, separately, to push through the heavy doors, without success. As they struggled, Winter Security's team, police officers, and FBI agents, all with weapons ready, gathered on the street outside. Each of the three men inside the lobby drew their weapons and placed them on the marble floor and stepped away. They had no other exit.

Chapter 23

Schmidt, Maeve, and Linda were in the small conference room, their attention focused on the television screen. The channel was CNN. The anchor was introducing their expert for the next sixty-second news snippet.

"Today we were informed the Senate Banking Committee is planning to call a well-known American businessman as a key witness in a banking sanctions hearing. Travis Martin is our expert on the Senate committee and its hearings. Travis, what's happening?"

"Craig, this is very interesting news. The Senate committee is examining the effectiveness of banking sanctions, with a focus on Iran. They are exploring the twelve months prior to Iran signing the latest treaty with us. Sources tell me the committee has received solid evidence that a well-known US businessman breached the banking sanctions last year and illegally sold—via a long chain of shell companies—weapons to Iran."

"Do we know anything about this businessman? Who he is and the extent of his arms dealings?"

"Yes, we do. The evidence apparently identifies him, together with his family ties to Iran. We cannot mention his name at this point. Once the committee formally calls him as a witness, we'll be able to do identify him for you. The

amounts involved exceed half a billion dollars. That's a major breach of sanctions. Craig."

"You'll keep us informed, I'm sure. Is there anything else we should know?"

"Yes, there is. Senator Randolph, the current chairman of the Senate Banking Committee, this morning tendered his resignation, both from the committee and from the Senate, effective immediately. A sexual discretion was rumored to be the cause of the senator's abrupt departure. Interesting times."

"This is a video of the senator announcing his resignation, earlier today. As you said, Travis, these are interesting times. We'll have you back to keep us updated with events, especially when the committee announces the name of the businessman involved."

Schmidt turned to Linda. He said, "Well done."

Maeve frowned. "Your friend, Travis—he'll be at risk for a little while, I think." Linda had briefed Maeve of her efforts minutes before the CNN report. Maeve was not entirely pleased with the risks Linda was running.

"We've arranged protection and a snatch team for him; it will be available on a twenty-four hour basis. Helen's happy to have some support tasks for her soldiers, which allow them to help with our search for Mark," Linda added. "I'm not sure whether Cromarty will attack, but it's good to take precautions." She didn't mention Helen had also arranged a team to protect her.

Schmidt nodded. "Keep your analysts involved. They'll pick up chatter if he or O'Hare reacts. I have a feeling we'll need more than a snatch team from the 145th, before we're finished. Now, did you get feedback on O'Hare's popsy?"

Maeve frowned at Schmidt's choice of noun. She said, "Yes, an ICE team—well, to be precise, it was an HSI team—Homeland Security Investigations—visited the house and interviewed her, to validate her immigration status. There are grounds for further action. She apparently has a green card, approved on the basis she was married to an America citizen. However, her husband wasn't home, she couldn't provide his location, didn't know where he worked, and couldn't describe any of his friends or family. The HSI report states this is one of their classic marriage of convenience scenarios so they'll investigate further."

"Is the HSI team Cerberus?"

"Yes. We made sure of that," Maeve confirmed.

"It will be interesting to see O'Hare's reaction. If his lady friend is at risk of losing her immigration status, he'll try to apply pressure on HSI management. Maeve, you'll need to keep your people protected."

"We've got Cerberus resources in place in the HSI executive associate director's office, and in a number of intermediate domestic operational layers including the New York field office, which provided the team. If any pressure's applied, we'll know within minutes," Maeve said.

"What about the retired general? Anything happening there?" Schmidt asked Linda.

"We've dropped a vague suggestion or two on a couple of military blogs; however, so far they haven't taken up the bait," Linda said. "I don't want to use Travis; the links would be far too blatant if he's running with the banking committee expose."

"Agreed. I'll see if I can use a channel or two. There's an active gossip structure in place; it's used by both retired and active generals—we like to keep in touch. Finally, what about Brian Winter's people? Did they discover anything at the airfield?"

"He's expecting a call from us. We can do that now?" Linda asked. Without waiting for an answer, she dialed Brian Winter on the conference phone and placed it on speaker.

"Winter."

"Brian, good morning. I've got Maeve and Schmidt listening to you."

"Good morning. A couple of items. My team found a

plane-watcher who photographed a small passenger jet at Sissons Airfield, south of Boston, at the same time the so-called FBI helicopter was re-fueling. There was on the ground meeting between crews. We've copies of the photos of the aircraft and yes, the jet's registration numbers are clear. I've uploaded the images and files notes to Linda's cloud. Second item—three men were apprehended at Mark's apartment building earlier today. They claimed to be FBI. Our guard was shot. Fortunately, he's expected to recover; the impact knocked him unconscious and he's currently in hospital, under observation. The three men have been identified—one is Nathan Boyle; he's the perp who shot and killed my man driving Mark back to Boston. The other two are also suspected of involvement in Mark's kidnap. This happened less than half an hour ago so, Maeve, I expect your people will be reporting in soon. We had FBI, police, and one of my response teams in attendance. It was all rather crowded. No one else was hurt."

"Do you know whether the target was Mark's partner or Julian?" Linda asked.

"As far as we know, they were after Anna and the children."

"Your man, the guard—he's going to be okay?" Schmidt asked, reflecting the concern of Maeve and Linda in addition to his own.

"Yes. He has mild concussion according to the doctors."

"Please keep us informed," Maeve said. "Let us know if his family needs support." Cerberus was cash rich and Maeve was prepared to provide all the support the security guard's family required.

""Certainly. Thank you. We're taking care of them at the moment. He has a family, two preschoolers. His wife is upset, of course. How's the search for Mark?"

"We've a good idea of who's behind his kidnap; we're applying pressure while we gather evidence. We hope the details of the aircraft you mentioned will help us locate

Mark," Schmidt explained. "As usual, it's a slow process."

"Understood. Let me know if there's anything else I can do."

"Brian, thank you for your report. If you require assistance, let me or Maeve know. Julian and Anna and, of course, the families—are important to all of us—so maximum security, please."

"Thank you. I've sufficient resources, at least, as far as I know. If your suspect brings in a large number of people, I might accept your offer. Believe me, I'll do whatever's needed."

They ended the call. Maeve stared at the blank television screen for a moment. Schmidt and Linda waited patiently for her comment.

Maeve said, "I think ICE—HSI, that is—should take O'Hare's lady friend into custody within the next twenty-four hours. They can hold her for a week or more, without difficulty."

"You want to increase the pressure on him?" asked Linda.

"Yes. If O'Hare's attempting to add Anna and the children to his victims, we need to be far more aggressive. Linda, find out what you can about the financing of his house and aircraft—let me know which banks are involved. We need to review his and his shell companies' bank statements, to determine whether his expenditures are beyond his legitimate income. Also, trace the origin of his mortgage repayments. I can apply more pressure than he's ever experienced." Maeve's earlier role as director of the FBI, and even prior, had allowed her to develop an enviable depth of business contacts.

"On it, Maeve. I think we've already obtained most of what you need."

Schmidt added, "Maeve, I think I'll move a squad of MPs to Boston. Winter's people are good, but the 145th can provide more, and I daresay, better resources. I'll call Helen. Is there anything more we can do, to pressure Cromarty?"

Linda said, "My team has been exploring—I'll intensify the process. If he's paying O'Hare—or O'Hare's Delaware company—we'll be able to trace the money transfers. We'll let you both know." She stood; she wanted to get back to her team.

Chapter 24

"If some of my people are investigating a green card holder, I can assure you it's for a valid reason," snapped Roy Hoskins, executive assistant director, HSI Domestic Operations. His responsibilities encompassed immigration fraud investigations. Roy had more than thirty years of ICE investigative experience and was not inclined to take nonsense from anyone, whether that person was within Homeland Security or from another government department.

The voice over the phone was equally severe. "I don't give a damn what you say about your people. Stop the investigation—you have no reason to do this, none at all." Roy could hear his caller pounding his desk.

Roy wiped his hand over his face, trying to restrain his exasperation. "Listen, O'Hare, if you've got some little bit on the side, don't expect me to hide her for you. As far as I'm concerned, if Axelton knows you, it doesn't mean squat." Axelton, an executive associate director of DHS, was Roy's boss. Roy had no idea who O'Hare was and didn't care. "I've got hundreds of teams out, and lots of files to go through. So if you're finished—"

"Fucking hell I've finished. I'm an AD and I'll have your balls if you don't stop your team. You won't survive another day if anyone acts against her."

"Listen, buddy. I've recorded this call, and I'm copying it to Axelrod. If you like, I'll copy it to your director, too. As far as I'm concerned, you can shove your threats." He slammed the phone down. He had more to do than get involved in someone's personal issues.

As a precaution, he decided to check with the New York office. He buzzed his PA. "Francine," he said. "Find out why New York is checking out Zarina Glenbrook, maiden name Gorky. She's Russian, here on a green card. Claims to be married to a US citizen. Apparently there are some issues." He read out the details he had noted. "Tell Grecco I'd like to be briefed by whichever team is involved."

The call from the New York office came through an hour later. "Roy, this is Grecco. Whatja want to know?" Robert Grecco was one of the special agents in charge, attached to HSI's New York office, and was responsible for managing a number of teams investigating immigration fraud.

"You've got a team investigating some Russian for submitting false statements for her green card. One Zarina Gorky or Glenbrook?"

"Yeah, the team's one of my best. She's definitely a fraud. No husband in sight, doesn't know where he is, doesn't know his family, yada, yada. Classic. I authorized her detention—they should bring'er in this evening. Clear cut case. Ya wanna talk to the guys?"

"No, your word's good. Send me a summary, keep me informed. Let me know if anyone tries to interfere—there's someone jumping up and down at the NSA—I think she's his bit on the side."

"Yeah, I've heard she's a looka. No worries. I'll let ya know if anyone causes problems."

"Good. Tell Mary I said hi."

"She'll want to know when ya visiting again—she says we owe ya dinna."

"I'll let you know. Too much is hitting my desk at the moment. Keep hard."

"Sure, boss. See ya."

Hoskins copied his recording of the call with O'Hare to Derek Axelrod, his director, with a covering note. He believed in the adage that covering your ass was better than getting it kicked.

O'Hare was furious. First, he'd heard Boyle had totally failed to pick up Midway's partner and their children. Unbelievable. Three men, all cornered and captured, total failures. He'd kill Boyle if the bastard opened his mouth. Fortunately, there were no evidential trails; he'd made sure of that. Even though Boyle was ex-CIA, they had never met, and he'd used a false name when he'd recruited Boyle for what the man thought was a black government operation. Second, an hour or two later, Zarina had called, in a total panic. Two evening ago, a Homeland Security investigative team had knocked on her door asking all kinds of questions. She'd been so unnerved she'd forgotten his briefing and had spent the following day worrying that she was about to be arrested. Any investigation of Zarina's visa had the potential to turn into a disaster and that craphead Hoskins had totally wiped him off. He promised himself he'd kill Hoskins if anything happened to her. He wasn't scheduled to be back in New York State until closer to the weekend, and she was in total meltdown. The danger for him was high. He needed to protect Zarina; otherwise some deadly chickens would come home to roost. Damn.

He paced back and forth across his office. He didn't know whether to call Axelrod or not—he knew Hoskins had told the truth when he said he'd taped their conversation. A copy was probably already with Axelrod. The way things were going, undoubtedly a copy would be with his boss before long. Damn again.

His cell phone buzzed; it was a text. He read the message, anger building. Now Cromarty wanted to have him visit—

urgent and critical, he said. Impossible—the man knew he was in Washington for most of the week. O'Hare raised his cell phone, tempted to throw it against the concrete wall of his office. A soft knock heralded the opening of his door. His PA opened it and peered in.

"What the hell do you want?" he snarled.

She stepped back, totally alarmed at her reception. O'Hare realized his error and walked to the door. He breathed deeply.

"My apologies, Geraldine. I'm under a bit of pressure at the moment. What's the problem?"

The woman took a moment to find her voice. "Sir, there's a meeting. You're wanted. Director's office. You're to bring anything you have relating to someone—a Russian—called Gorky, also Glenbrook. In five minutes, MJ said, and you'd know who she is." MJ was the director's PA and at times seemed to exercise as much power as the director himself.

O'Hare paled. He struggled to rein in his temper. Geraldine moved away, carefully out of reach. She had heard her boss had a ferocious temper although she had never before seen it on display. He shuddered, barely taking control.

"Thank you, Geraldine. Yes, I know the case. Tell MJ I'll be there."

O'Hare returned to his desk and sat in his chair. He drummed his fingers on the polished surface of his desk. A sensible solution continued to evade him. This, he thought, was going to be tough. First he needed to make a phone call.

"Cromarty? Yeah, it's O'Hare. You know I'm in Washington? There's no way I can meet with you until Friday. No, no way at all."

He listened to Cromarty and replied to his question. "No, I didn't see a CNN newscast. So a tame senator has resigned—there's nothing I can do about that. What? No, I have no influence over anyone in the Senate. Look, I have to go. I've been called to an urgent meeting. I'll see you on Friday, all right?" He disconnected before Cromarty could protest. He cursed again. He had planned to be back in Gitmo on Friday—now that plan was shot to hell. Midway would have to wait a couple of days.

Cromarty looked at his cell phone in disbelief. O'Hare had blown him off. That was a first. When he needed the man's assistance, O'Hare dismissed him, without any regard for his crisis. He threw the phone at the potted plant in the corner of his office and stalked out, slamming his door. He walked to the end of the large executive floor lobby, to one of the smaller offices at the end. The title on the door, on two lines, read "Director Public Relations." He pushed open the door without knocking.

The person at the desk raised his head and looked at Cromarty through blurry eyes. "Yes?"

"Where's whatsisname—Threadneedle?"

"Who? Oh, the fucker left last Friday. Resigned, lucky bastard."

"Who are you?" Cromarty didn't know whether to be exasperated or angry. He thought anger would win.

"I'm his temporary replacement. HR said to hold the fort until they told the boss and got him to agree to a replacement."

"The boss?"

"Yes, you know, Old Crome. Oh shit—that's you, isn't it?" The man jumped up and straightened his tie. "Sorry, sir. I'm new and really don't know what I'm supposed to be doing. I'm a media buyer, not a PR person."

"I can tell. Go meet with HR, ask for your severance package. One month in lieu, and that's generous. Tell them Old Crome said so, understand?"

"Yes, sir." He started to collect his personal items from the top of the desk. "What about the CNN request for an interview—you want me to do anything about that?" He lifted his jacket off the back of the chair and looked at Cromarty, obviously waiting for an answer.

The question stunned Cromarty, and he was silent for a moment.

He said, biting the words off, "I think we can both ignore that, for the moment. Get out of my sight. Now!" The last word was a shout.

Cromarty had reached the end of his patience; the mention of CNN was the trigger. Damn. If CNN wanted to interview him, did that mean their news team knew he was the so-called key witness being considered by the Senate Banking Committee? He turned and exited the small office, slamming the door. He ignored the frightened expressions of his employees as he continued back to his office. There had to be a solution. He only needed time.

O'Hare returned to his office in a furious temper. The director had peeled the hide off his back, with that bitch MJ noting it all down. He assumed the meeting had been taped. The director was not interested in his explanations—threatening the employee of another agency was an absolute cause for disciplinary action, irrespective of O'Hare's rank in the NSA. Motive was irrelevant, he had been informed. The director didn't want to hear anything he had to say in his defense. MJ had played the recording of the telephone call, at the director's request, obviously making sure it was included in his disciplinary lecture—and the director had flayed him.

At the end, O'Hare had stormed out, after refusing to use the director's phone to call and apologize to Hoskins.

Apologize be damned. The man was inept, one of those "play by the rules" managers, the kind O'Hare intensely disliked. Well, he thought, that was that; he'd created a brick wall, which would prove impassable, signaling the end to his rise in this agency, or indeed, in any other agency. Well, he had other irons, solid gold, not plated. He only needed another six months.

Of course, that did not solve his immediate problem. He did not yet have a plan for rescuing the situation with Zarina. He'd called. There was no answer. Strange, he thought, she hadn't planned on leaving the house today. Oh well, he'd try later, when he'd calmed down. Maybe then his mind would be more capable of resolving the situation. He kicked a chair out of his way and cursed the pain in his toes.

Chapter 25

Ladder checked his watch. It was 8 p.m. and the library was closing. He had spent most of the afternoon and evening researching Cerberus, with little success. He had learned the name came from Greek mythology, and referred to a multi-headed dog, the guardian of Hades. Sometimes the dog was described as having three heads; in other articles it had hundreds of heads. He found it difficult to reconcile the mythical concept with the twelve-year old Alex, who had been shot, or with her friends, Anna, Niland, and Gabrielle, who had visited her in hospital. Apart from mythological stories, there was nothing of relevance returned in his Internet searches. He sighed. He packed up his notebooks and closed his laptop. It was time he went home.

He was heading, he thought, towards a pending disaster. His mom knew he would be late—he had sent a text, earlier. However, his step-uncle—now that was a relationship to be reckoned with—would be most irate and probably half-drunk. Irate, because he would be, and half-drunk because he couldn't afford to drink enough to reach full inebriation.

Ladder looked forward to when he could afford his own apartment, although he was conflicted—he wanted to leave, yet he did not want to desert his mother. He attended a state college in Redmont, which offered basic courses, while he really wanted to go to college in somewhere like Boston, where he could study broader subject areas that would challenge him.

He swung his backpack over his shoulder and made his way to the street and wondered if he had time to get something to eat before heading home. It depended on the risk—would his step-uncle be drunker and angrier, if he wasn't home for another forty minutes or so? Ladder was about to unlock the driver's side door of his old—very old—pickup when he detected the presence of someone close behind him. He unlocked and opened the car door and swung his pack onto the front seat.

Unencumbered, he spun around, to confront his potential assailant. A man was only feet away. He was taller and possibly heavier than Ladder and better dressed. He was also carrying a handgun, which now was pointed at Ladder's midsection.

"Pray to your god, if you have one. Tonight, though, you are fortunate, because I have questions for you, not death."

Ladder detected an accent, although he could not identify its origin. He balanced himself on the balls of his feet. Dealing with his step-uncle had long ago prompted him to take self-defense classes and, as a result, he had developed a high level of expertise. Not enough to deflect a bullet, but he only needed a minor diversion.

"Who are you?"

"You don't need my name."

"What do you want?"

"A conversation. Some answers."

"A gun is supposed to encourage conversation?"

The man laughed and holstered his weapon. He stepped closer. "My fist'd be more effective, *ya khara*. You are a lightweight, no? Not worth a bullet." He grabbed the front of Ladder's T-shirt. "Now, tell me. You met with some people in the hospital, no? Where did they go?" He ended the question by throwing a punch with his other hand.

Ladder felt the increase of tension in the man's grip and, anticipating the assault, stepped back to avoid the punch, while brushing his attacker's hand away from his shirt. He followed up with a kick to the man's unprotected crotch and a knee to his face when his assailant bent over in a reflexive response to the first explosion of pain.

"*Kess Ommak*," the man moaned.

The stranger fumbled for his weapon and it slipped out of his hand. Ladder grabbed his assailant's right arm in a lock, and brought his knee up and the man's arm down, in a savage and sudden motion. The force of the maneuver dislocated his assailant's elbow and tore tendons. Ladder backed off and kicked as hard and as high as he could, connecting with the side of the man's head. The blow landed with a sickening crunch, and the stranger fell to the ground, silent, not moving.

Ladder stood still, poised, ready to react if his assailant moved. "Shit," he voiced to himself. He bent down to feel the man's pulse. He was still alive. Ladder picked up the dropped handgun and tucked it into the back of his jeans. He used his cell phone to call Kelsi Pierce, his crime team boss.

"Yes, Ladder? What's the problem?" Kelsi sounded sleepy.

"Doc, someone attacked me, here, near the college library, in the parking lot. The guy had a gun and wanted to know about Alex and her friends. He's—he's unconscious—I can feel his pulse, so he's not dead. I don't know what to do."

"Wow. You continue to surprise me. Call base. Harriet could be still on duty, otherwise it's Marion. Tell her— either—you need Lieutenant Harkness. When he calls you, tell him what happened. I'm on my way. Oh, and tell base, you need an ambulance for your attacker."

Harness called him within two or three minutes of Ladder's call to base. "Whassup, Ladder? You just caught me, I'm about to go off duty."

Ladder explained. When he finished, he added, "Doc is on her way. Base is sending an ambulance. Can you get here, too?"

"Can I? Absolutely. I'm on my way. If the guy wakes up, kick him again. Or at least, use his gun to keep him subdued. I'm no more than five minutes away."

Ladder leaned against the side of his pickup for support as his adrenaline rush eased. His knees were shaking. He had often been bullied, taunted, and his step-uncle had often threatened to hit him; however, this was the first time he'd been physically attacked, and the first time he'd used his training for real. He sat on the bottom of the pickup's door sill as his legs gave way. In the distance he could hear sirens. His assailant had not moved.

Kelsi arrived seconds before either Harkness or the ambulance. She slammed her car door and rushed over to Ladder.

"Are you all right?" She looked down at her colleague, still seated on the door rim. She ignored the unconscious body on the ground.

Ladder tried to laugh. "My legs gave way. Apart from that, I'm okay."

"Let me check. Here, stand up." Kelsi helped him to gain his feet. "No pain? No bruises? Some shock?"

"I'm all right, Doc. He tried to hit me. I hit him. Hard. He's probably got sore testicles, a dislocated elbow, and possible concussion, if not a fracture."

Kelsi straightened Ladder's T-shirt and patted his shoulder. "When you break out, you really do it, huh? I'm pleased it's not you on the ground. You can walk?"

"Sure. I think."

"Here's the lieutenant and the ambulance." She waved and the two vehicles edged closer, their lights adding to the parking lot illumination.

Harkness reached them first. "Well, Ladder, what have you been up to?"

"I told you. Oh, here's his gun. He hasn't moved." He handed over his assailant's weapon.

The police lieutenant squatted beside the unconscious

body. "He has a pulse. It's weak. Ladder, you must have whacked him really good."

Ladder looked at Harkness. "I—I'm not in trouble, am I?"

"No, he attacked you, and you defended. He had a handgun. You were unarmed, in fear of your life. We'll charge him once he recovers. We'll get a statement from you, of course. Remind me not to tangle with you in future, though." The lieutenant's smile took the sting out of his words.

Kelsi and Ladder watched as the two paramedics rolled the gurney with their patient to the ambulance. Harkness accompanied the paramedics; he would follow their vehicle to the hospital. He told Ladder he would organize a police guard until the assailant was recovered enough to move to the Redmont jail. Ladder would have to return to the police station where Harkness would take his statement.

"What now, Ladder?" asked Kelsi, after the others had departed.

"First, I'll go give my statement. I need to eat. After that, home. Although—" He stopped. Half-formed plans to drive to Boston drifted into his mind. He'd first need to collect some clothes from his home. He had to find Alex and tell Anna and possibly General Schmidt about this attack. The words his assailant had used—he thought they might be Arabic. Perhaps the men who had attacked Alex were not Russian, but instead, had ties to the Middle East.

"Although?"

"Ah, nothing. I was thinking aloud." Perhaps he could learn more about Cerberus if he went to Boston.

When Ladder reached Boston, he parked around the corner in a side street next to the apartment building where he knew he'd find Alex and her friends. He checked his watch and decided 4:00 a.m. was far too early to visit. He curled up on the worn seat of the pickup and tried to relax. His mind was full, jumping from the assault, concerns about the condition of his assailant, worries about his new friends and their safety, Cerberus, and back again until finally he drifted off into a restless sleep.

Chapter 26

Alex stirred and raised her head off her pillow, listening. She was sharing a bed with Gabrielle.

"Go back to sleep," her friend muttered. "You're safe with us."

"Listen—can't you hear?"

Gabrielle sat up. "Hear what." She yawned.

"I think it's Ladder. He's here in Boston. He's worried about me—us."

The two girls were silent for a minute, intent, focused.

"Let me get Niland. He might know—" Gabrielle padded out of their bedroom in her PJs and extra large socks and returned with a yawning Niland.

"Problem?"

"Alex thinks she can hear Ladder, that he's come to Boston because he's concerned about us."

"Be quiet, and we'll see."

Silence fell on the three children. A minute later Niland said, "We'd better get dressed. I think he's in danger. Gab, go wake Anna, we need her advice."

Anna joined them a few minutes later; she was trying to suppress a yawn. She looked at the group of children, all dressed in their day clothes and with worried expressions.

"Niles said you think Ladder's in danger?" Anna yawned again. "It's only four-thirty."

Gabrielle said, "Alex thought she heard Ladder. Now we all think we can hear him. He's nearby. We want your advice. What should we do?"

"It could be your imagination."

"That's why we woke you."

"Hmm. Very well. Join hands. Let's see what we can hear."

The three children and Anna joined hands, forming a small circle. The formation was more for comfort than necessity. The children followed Anna's lead, relaxing, focusing on the lab technician. After five minutes Anna released her grip and shook her arms.

"Alex, you're correct. I'll phone Schmidt. Niland, call our FBI contact. Gabrielle, you call Winter Security's control room. Ladder definitely is nearby. He was involved in some kind of altercation in Redmont and he was followed here, to Boston, by people trying to locate us."

Alex watched and listened as the calls were made. Schmidt apparently was awake and working. He instructed Anna that no one should leave the apartment until additional security was in place. He added that he would be in Boston by late morning, accompanied by a team from the 145th. Niland had to make a series of phone calls to contact the FBI agent; he had been on late shift and was not at all pleased to be woken until he realized who was calling. He promised to have a small Cerberus team at the apartment within half an hour. Winter Security promised a similar response and also would alert their security guard in the building lobby.

Alex hugged Anna after the phone calls had been made. Anna held her close. She placed her hands on the girl's shoulders and looked into her eyes. She asked, "What was that for?"

"It's so nice to be with family."

Anna wrapped her arms around Alex. "We all agree about that. Now, either back to bed or have an early breakfast—what's the vote?"

"None of us would be able to go back to sleep," said Gabrielle.

"Breakfast," said Niland and Alex, together.

"I agree. Come on, you can all help me."

Schmidt called Maeve Donnelly. He knew she was an early morning person and probably would be working on her ever-present and growing collection of Cerberus files. He'd told her she needed to delegate and her response was that she would, once she was familiar with all of the Cerberus operations, which she had informed him, apparently ranged from marine piracy protection contracts to US embassy protection assignments to parental care teams for Cerberus children plus possibly as yet unknown espionage or surveillance activities. She'd said she hoped all the Cerberus activities were legal; at least she had uncovered nothing to suggest people were engaged otherwise. She had added she also needed to find someone capable.

"Morning, Maeve," Schmidt said.

"What are you doing, calling at this hour and sounding so cheerful?"

"I'm always cheerful." He ignored the response. "I had a call from Anna. A lab technician they met in Redmont apparently has traveled to Boston. As far as they can determine, he was involved in an assault of some kind and decided he should warn Anna and the children they were in danger. The children say he was followed to Boston. They are all are concerned for his safety and think the assault on Ladder was an attempt to discover their location. They've contacted the FBI—one of your Cerberus people—and also alerted Winter Security. I'm heading to Boston, too, with a team from the 145th."

"Any idea who the people are?"

"I suspect they're involved with the men who killed Leary, that Redmont police officer."

Maeve said, "You're probably correct. I'm surprised Linda hasn't picked up social traffic on this."

"Likewise. I'll brief her while I'm traveling. I'll keep you informed. I'll be in Boston for a day or two, if you need anything."

"If you need more Cerberus resources to help, let me know."

"Good. Anything more on Mark?" Schmidt was growing more and more concerned; they had not yet established the flight plan of the aircraft they suspected had been used to fly Mark on to his final destination. He wanted that location.

"I'm meeting the team at eight this morning to see if we have any new data. I'll send you an update."

Schmidt ended the call. He had arranged a car and driver to take him to Dulles International where he and his MP team could catch a scheduled commercial flight to Boston, and it was time for him to leave. He flinched at the recollection triggered by the thought of the flight—one exploding aircraft was enough for any sensible person.

Linda Schöner's internal danger alarm did not alert her until she realized the Uber driver was not following her normal route to the office. Her departure was an hour earlier than she normally scheduled, and the driver had told her that her usual driver was not available because he had an early booking. It seemed a valid reason. She was reviewing overnight emails and messages and looked up as the car halted abruptly at a traffic intersection.

"This is the wrong way," she said to the driver. She felt her pulse start to race. The lights turned green and the car moved forward.

"Short cut." He was Asian, she thought, possibly Indian, and he spoke with a heavy accent.

Her alarm bells were now ringing loudly. Linda folded her

Microsoft Surface and opened her briefcase. She carefully stowed the computer, and as she did, she pressed the panic button on the small communication device stitched into the side of the briefcase. Her rescue team would be with her within a minute or two. She reached for the door handle. The door was locked. She pressed the button to lower the window. Nothing happened. Apparently it was locked, too.

"Stop here," she instructed the driver. "I need to get my coffee."

"Cannot stop. No parking here."

The traffic lights at the next intersection turned red and the driver again braked abruptly. As the Uber vehicle stopped, a man dashed from a vehicle in the adjacent lane, opened the front passenger side door and sat in the seat. He turned and smiled at Linda. His expression sent a shiver down her spine. She did not recognize the man and realized he was not from her protection team.

"Driver," she said, raising her voice. "Unlock my door, now."

The front passenger said. "Sorry, ma'am. Someone wants to speak to you. I think he has a complaint to make."

The driver accelerated when the lights changed and other vehicles moved forward. Two hundred yards or so past the intersection a vehicle suddenly changed lanes to take a position in front of the Uber car. She sensed another vehicle making a similar move in the rear.

The driver cursed. "Fucking rude drivers. No signals, and they're far too close—"

His sentence was cut off as the front vehicle braked suddenly. The second vehicle made soft contact with the rear of the car. The Uber driver cursed again as he was forced to stop. The passenger drew a weapon from under his jacket; however, before he could complete the maneuver, Linda had her weapon out and pressed against the back of his head.

"I don't know who you are and I don't care if I spread your brains across the front of the car. Drop your gun."

Two men exited the vehicle in front and two came from the vehicle behind. They had weapons drawn. One man opened the driver side door and grabbed the driver and pulled him out onto the road. Another man did the same for the front passenger. They stood over their victims, their attitude threatening. A third man opened Linda's rear-side door, leaned in, and said, "Miss Schöner, 145th to the rescue." He had a broad smile on his face. "I'm Sergeant Vendel—we were at the restaurant—"

"Thank you." She returned her handgun to her briefcase. "Yes, I recognize you, Sergeant." She indicated the men on the road. "They definitely were abducting me. If someone could drive me to the office?" She was surprised her hands were steady. She took a deep breath.

"Certainly, Miss Schöner. I'll drive you. My team will continue as your escort, in case these guys have a back-up plan. Our guys will find out more; these two are now our prisoners and we've got a van for them. I'll be interested to hear what they have to say when we get them to Camp Brewer."

A police car, apparently alerted by the traffic build-up caused by her rescue team's efforts, stopped alongside the front vehicle. A policeman got out of his car and cautiously approached.

Sergeant Vendel straightened and said, "Officer, we're MPs from the 1145th Battalion, based at Camp Brewer. This is an Army matter. We'll clean up here and be on our way in two minutes." He held his Army ID for the police officer to examine.

The officer looked dubious. "You guys don't normally get involved in civilian activities."

"These men are deserters. We were escorting Miss Schöner and they attempted to abduct her. Clear cut task for us."

The officer was not inclined to argue. The two prisoners were already handcuffed. An Army van had pulled alongside, and uniformed MPs had the rear door open and were boarding the prisoners as he watched. The escort team members had returned to their vehicles and were ready to leave. He looked at Vendel and said, "All right, Sergeant. Try not to stop traffic next time. Get out of here." He returned to his vehicle, signaling for the convoy to move.

Vendel climbed into the driver's seat and said, "We're fortunate he didn't ask for vehicle details. I've no idea who's the owner of this. We'll sort that out after we get you to your office."

Linda leaned back. She'd had enough excitement for the day. She sent a message to Maeve Donnelly that she was running late.

Chapter 27

Ladder woke from a deep although dream-disturbed sleep when a police officer tapped on his driver side window. He wound the window down. The officer had parked his motorcycle two yards away. Ladder tried to hide his nervousness.

"Yes, officer?"

"This parking lane is designated no parking after 6:00 a.m. It becomes a full-flowing traffic lane. You have ten minutes to leave. However, as a special favor, there's no ticket, not even a warning, this morning. By the way, your FBI friends said to make your way to this address—turn left, left again, and then right. It's a tall apartment building called Essington Towers, about a hundred yards after that last turn. You'll be allowed to enter the underground parking section; this is your entry authority. Someone will be waiting for you. Park your pickup when you're on the second level. Understand? If anyone's watching you here, they'll think I handed you a ticket, so pretend to sign your acknowledgment on this form; it contains the address. You'll be safe. A security firm is also watching out for you."

Ladder's hand shook as he pretended to sign a form. He folded the sheet of paper that the police officer handed to him. He waited until the officer mounted his motorcycle and rode off. He started the pickup's engine. Ladder carefully drove down the narrow street, following the directions he'd been given. He tried to stop his hands from shaking. He checked; however, no one appeared to be tracking him.

Perhaps he should have stayed in Redmont. If his attacker from the evening before had friends, and they followed him, perhaps he had placed Alex and Anna and her two children at risk. It would be better if he simply returned home. Too many what ifs, he decided, and pushed away his panic-driven worries. He continued to follow the directions.

The parking attendant raised the barrier at the entrance to the parking levels of Essington Towers, and Ladder drove down to the second level. He parked in a far corner of the area marked for visitor parking and exited his pickup. He debated silently with himself for a moment and then grabbed his backpack and closed and locked the vehicle door. There was an arrow pointing to the elevators and he headed in that direction.

A woman stepped out from beside a large SUV, a Suburban. Ladder jumped in fright and was tempted to head the other way. The woman smiled and said. "Ladder—or should I say Oxley? There's no need to be concerned. I'm an FBI agent—my name's Renshaw. Here's my ID and badge." She held out her wallet, open, with her badge displayed.

Ladder examined the ID card, giving it the same degree of attention he'd given to the ID submitted by Agent Prentice. He said, "Thank you, Agent Renshaw."

"Good. Come with me." She returned to the SUV and opened the rear door. The windows were heavily tinted. The agent said, "Hop in."

"We're not going here?" Ladder indicated the elevator bank, fifty yards away.

Agent Renshaw laughed. "No, we still don't know if you were followed or whether there is a tracking device on your car. We'll get it checked for you and make sure it's clean. We're close to Anna and the children. They're only a few blocks away. Come on, hop in."

The FBI agent climbed into the front passenger seat and once Ladder was settled in the back, she instructed her driver. "Let's go." She made a phone call. "Winter? We have Ladder. Someone should check his pickup—yes, it's on the second floor—and make sure there are no trackers on it. You can handle that? We're heading to the Midway apartment. Your escort vehicle is right behind us. He's OK. He's tired and worried, I suspect. Let your people know we're coming in. Less than five minutes. Indeed." She disconnected and turned to Ladder.

"People are cooperating to make sure you're okay. We called Harkness, told him you'd be with us for a few days."

"He wasn't annoyed?"

The FBI agent laughed at Ladder's concern. "He's a professional. He said he'd be in contact to make sure you're safe and not suffering after effects from the assault last night."

Ladder settled back in the seat, too worried to really understand what was happening. He only wanted to visit Anna and the children to warn them, and he now had the police, the FBI, and someone called Winter on his case. They'd probably involved that general—what was his name? Oh yes, Schmidt. He wished he could go back to sleep.

"Ladder, you must have breakfast," instructed Alex. Gabrielle stood beside her, equally adamant. He suspected the noise coming from what he thought was the kitchen indicated Anna had not accepted his refusal, either. He gave in.

"I didn't have much to eat last night, I'll admit. I don't want to be—"

Someone cuffed the side of his head; it was a soft blow. He turned to see who it was.

Anna said, "You're not a nuisance. There's a healthy meal for you on the table. When it's family, we eat breakfast in the kitchen. Come on."

Ladder followed Anna and Alex and Gabrielle followed him. Niland was already seated at the table.

Gabrielle said, "You're not eating another breakfast, surely?"

"I thought I'd keep Ladder company."

Anna tugged out a chair and indicated Ladder should sit. "Eat. We all want to hear what happened, so you'll need lots of energy."

Ladder concluded his story as he ate the last portion of scrambled eggs. "So, I thought I should come and let you know."

Alex and Gabrielle were wide-eyed, and Niland looked shocked. Anna said, "You beat the hell out of some stranger who pulled a gun on you?"

"Well, he put it away, first."

"Why did you think we were at risk?"

"It was the way he asked about you—he wanted to know where you went. He didn't have positive vibes. Also he had a foreign accent. No, I don't mean I hit him because he was foreign. He grabbed me after he put his gun away and I reacted to his attack. He used some words—I think they were Arabic. I—I wondered if there might be a link between him and those two—dead—people. The ones the police think were Russian."

The two girls were about to ask more questions when Anna intervened. "No, that's enough. Schmidt will be here later and he'll ask all the questions in the world. I think Ladder should have a rest." She turned to Ladder. "We have a bed you can use. No PJs, though. Curl up, have a rest. I'll keep these would-be inquisitors away from you. Niland, take Ladder to the spare room, show him how the shower works. Children—let Ladder have a rest."

Anna's prediction proved to be correct. The first words from Schmidt, when he entered the apartment, were, "Where's Ladder?"

"We fed him and he went to bed to catch up on his sleep," Anna explained.

"Can you wake him?"

Alex said, "Yes, but he'll need to shower and change before you question him. He'll want to be awake and alert."

Schmidt looked at the girl. He wasn't accustomed to being ambushed by a twelve-year old. He said, "Can someone wake him, please?"

Alex said, "Niland, will you do that? Ladder has a backpack, so I assume he has a change of clothes. We'll wait in the—what—study?"

Anna agreed and led the way to the room she and Mark used as their office. It was larger than some apartments, and one wall was floor to ceiling windows, providing a view of Boston's skyline that Schmidt always enjoyed. His friend and business partner, Julian Kelly, had an identical apartment on the floor above, and Schmidt was seriously inclined to purchase an apartment in the same building.

"Can we talk about Mark?" Anna asked as she sat down in one of the comfortable chairs.

"Of course, my dear," Schmidt replied. He pulled Anna out of her chair and enveloped her in a bear hug. "I apologize. It was remiss of me not to update you first. We don't have new information on Mark, I'm sorry to say. Maeve briefed me this morning, while I was in transit. Brian Winter is still trying to track the aircraft that might have taken Mark." He sat Anna back down in the large chair. "There's been a lot happening. There was an attempt to abduct Linda Schöner this morning; she was rescued by a snatch team from the 145th. We'll hand her abductors over to the FBI once we finish questioning them." There was an element of savagery in his voice.

"She's all right? Did they harm her?" Anna asked.

"The snatch team got to her fast enough to prevent anything happening." He did not mention that he thought the team's response had been far too slow, that Linda had been at risk for too long. Unfortunately, she refused to travel in a military

SUV. "Her escort will be closer and quicker in future."

"Was this related to Mark, do you think?"

Schmidt, for a moment, wondered how to answer. He decided truth was the only valid approach and said, "Possibly. Linda has been applying extreme pressure to people who might be involved."

Further discussion was halted when Schmidt's cell phone rang. "It's Maeve," he said, checking the caller ID. "Let me speak to her."

"Yes, Maeve?" Schmidt listened. "What?" he shouted in shock.

"Can you get a copy to me? On Linda's cloud? I'll use one of the computers here—yes, Anna's. Good. Yes, once we see it."

He disconnected and said to Anna. "Someone has posted a video of Mark on YouTube. Maeve asked them to take it down. She's sending a link to our research cloud, where she stored a copy of the file." As Anna was about to hurry to her computer, Schmidt added. "Maeve said he's alive and the video is not nice. You should let me watch it first."

"No," said Anna, firmly. 'We want to see what they've done to Mark." A chorus joined in as Niland and Gabrielle agreed with her.

Schmidt shrugged. "Let me log into the cloud and I'll download it." He hid his concern that the contents of the video might be more than Anna and the children could cope with. He wondered about his own reactions, too.

Chapter 28

Zarina pressed the switch of the door monitor video display. Two men and a woman stood at the front gate. She recognized the two men; they had called on her earlier in the week and after presenting their Homeland Security Investigations credentials, had questioned her for what seemed like hours. She had not seen the woman before. She considered, for a brief moment, ignoring her callers. She even thought about leaving by the back door and switched on the monitor to check if the rear of the house was clear. She was not surprised to see a man, a stranger but presumably from Homeland Security, waiting at the gate at the end of the garden. She sent a message to O'Hare and hid the phone in a small recess behind books in the study's large bookcase. It would not be good for her if these agents examined calls and message details on that phone. She picked up a second cell phone from the desk and slipped it into the hip pocket of her jeans.

She pressed the audio button on the security system. "Yes? Can I help you?"

"Mrs. Glenbrook. I'm Agent Roberts, Homeland Security. We met earlier this week. Could you open the gate, please?"

"One moment." Zarina pressed the release button for the front gate and took her time to meet with her unwanted visitors. Someone knocked on the door while she was still stepping down the stairs. He sounded impatient, she thought. She edged open the door without removing the security chain and spoke through the three-inch gap.

She said, "What do you want?" She pronounced each w as a v, adding color to her speech. She'd heard that Americans underestimated their opponents if they didn't speak English correctly. As a result, the agents outside heard her say. "Vot do you vant?"

"We have reason to believe your application for permanent residence contains false information. You are to accompany us to our New York office to help us resolve our questions." The agent held out a folded document, pushing it into the gap between the door and the door jamb. "I'm serving this notice on you. Please unchain and open the door."

Zarina allowed the document to drop to the floor. She said, "Why are you attacking me like this?"

"As I said, we have reason to believe your application contains false or misleading details. We will question you at our New York office. If you don't open this door, we will force it open."

"You—you can't do that?"

"I have served the necessary document—you now belong to us until we're satisfied." Roberts signaled to someone standing behind him. "You can break down the door—"

"No. No, I'll open it." Zarina closed the door over, half inclined to slam it shut and run. She realized an escape attempt would not aid her cause and instead slipped the security chain from its slot and opened the door wide.

"I'm not inviting you inside," she said. "I want to call an attorney before this goes any further."

Agent Roberts retrieved the summons and handed it to Zarina; this time she reluctantly took it. One of the other agents used his cell phone to photograph the action, which showed her accepting the document. She crumpled the paper and dropped it on the floor. It was a futile gesture, she knew.

Zarina retrieved her cell phone and searched through her

contacts. She stopped at a name and before she actioned the call, said, "This is my attorney. I'm calling him now."

"It's not normal to allow this until we have you in our office. However, I daresay it won't do harm," Roberts said.

The agents, three men and a woman—the third man had joined the group at her front door—listened to the phone conversation. She thought they probably were recording it.

"David Attwell, please," she said when the call was answered.

"Please tell him Zarina Glenbrook called. I'm being detained by an HSI team led by Agent Roberts from the New York office."

She reached down and straightened out the document she had earlier crumpled. "Their case reference is AAR3061. I'd like Attwell to arrange for my release as quickly as possible. Tell him it's extremely urgent. There's no fee limit." Her English was impeccable; she'd forgotten her intention to appear uneducated. She concluded the call when her instructions were confirmed.

As she returned the phone to her hip pocket, Roberts held out his hand and said, "I'll take that. You'll get a receipt when we check you in. This is Agent Thornton." He indicated the woman standing next to him. "She will search you. You are not allowed to have a weapon or anything that could be used as a weapon; the penalty is high for any breach. Tell me now, if you are carrying?" She shook her head and Roberts continued. "You can bring a change of clothes, some minor items. Agent Thornton will supervise and check the things you've packed. If you promise to behave, we won't handcuff you. Understand?"

"Yes. Please wait here. Agent Thornton, come with me." She stared at the three men in the entranceway. "I do not give permission to anyone else to enter my house, understood?"

She did not speak as she headed up the stairs to her bedroom. Agent Thornton followed, also silent.

"What can I take?" Zarina asked when they reached her bedroom.

"Personal documents—passport, driver's license. A change of clothes. Toothbrush, toothpaste. Minimal makeup, comb and brush. Of course, we'll hold them for you. If you want to change, I'll wait."

Zarina did not reply. She was trying to restrain her anger, anger at herself, anger at O'Hare; he was her late father's US contact. This was never supposed to happen. O'Hare was supposed to ensure she was safe and comfortably established. She suspected he had done something, made a mistake, perhaps, which had drawn attention to her, and she could see no way out of her predicament. She had compounded her difficulties, she realized, with her responses earlier in the week. The agents' visit had caught her unawares and she had panicked.

She finished changing into more formal clothes and turned to Agent Thornton. "I need to get some toiletries from my bathroom. Also a change of clothes, my wallet, my passport. Okay?"

"Sure. If you don't mind, I'll check before you pack them into your case."

Ten minutes later they rejoined the waiting agents at the front door. Agent Roberts led the way to the waiting SUVs and opened the rear door of the lead vehicle. "Mrs. Glenbrook, if you give me an undertaking to behave, I will not restrain you. Okay?"

"Yes. I won't do anything to escape or cause you trouble. Thank you."

The HSI interrogation room was dismal. A bare table, situated in the center of the room, appeared to be bolted to the floor. Four steel chairs, paint chipped, were distributed around the table. There was a large mirror along one wall; Zarina thought it was for observation purposes and wondered who was watching from the other side.

"Please sit here," directed Agent Roberts.

When they arrived, people had taken her photograph and fingerprints, and Agent Thornton searched her again. It was a thorough and undignified process. Roberts led her to this room, on the way offering her a paper cup of water, which she had accepted. She had dropped the empty cup, crumpled, into a waste bin before entering the room.

"We're recording this meeting," Roberts said, "It's both video and sound. Anything you say will be available to us for future reference, and we may use the recording in any action we decide to take against you, understand?"

Zarina sat on the cold, hard chair. "Yes." She shivered, whether from cold or fear she was uncertain. She tried to tell herself this was not the KGB.

Roberts stated the time and date, and the names of the people in the room—himself, Zarina and two other agents. He asked his first question.

"Mrs Glenbrook, you arrived in the United States using a permanent visa, a green card, which you applied for at our embassy in Moscow, correct?"

"Yes."

"You produced various supporting documents, including a marriage certificate, claiming you were married to an American citizen, Thomas Jefferson Glenbrook, and that your marriage had taken place a year before making your application?"

"Yes."

"Where is Mr. Glenbrook today?"

"He travels a lot for his clients. I don't know his precise whereabouts."

"You have his phone number?"

"It's in my cell phone. I can call him."

"Later. Tell me what your husband does for a living."

"He works with various clients, advising them on utilization of social networks in support of their business activities."

"Describe your husband for me."

This, thought Zarina, was where she was on thin ice. She knew a call to the number in her cell phone would go to voice mail; however, she couldn't recall the precise details of Glenbrook's appearance. She'd only met the man once, and that was two years ago. She decided she could only do her best.

"He's six feet tall. Weighs about 200 pounds. Blue eyes. Brown hair, slightly receding."

"That's so general it could apply to probably twenty percent of males in America. What are his distinguishing features—scars, for example?"

"I don't think he has any. Oh, wait. He has a scar on his left hand. It's across the back of his hand. He said it was from a knife fight."

"Did your husband serve in any branch of the US Military?"

A knock on the door interrupted her reply. An agent opened the door, entered and handed Roberts a folder. The agent checked the contents and nodded his head. The agent left the room, closing the door softly.

"Please answer," prompted Roberts.

"I—I don't recall him mentioning any military service."

"You don't know your husband all that well, do you?"

"Why, what do you mean?"

"Your husband, Thomas Jefferson Glenbrook, served two tours in Iraq. He was shot in the leg. That, I believe, would leave a scar. Oh, he was balding and what hair remained was blond. His eyes are green."

Roberts opened the folder he'd been given, extracted a photograph, and slid it across the table. "Is this your husband?"

The image prompted her memory and matched what she remembered of the man she'd married in Moscow. She flicked the photograph back across the table and it spun to finish its journey in front of Roberts.

Zarina said, "Yes. It looks like him."

"That's unfortunate. I would, in other circumstances, offer my sympathies. We've traced Thomas Jefferson Glenbrook, the man whom you claim you married and who we've identified from the details in your visa application. Sadly, he died six months ago as the result of an auto accident. He was in France at the time. Near Paris. With his wife."

Her heart sank. She had no idea what to say or what her options were. She wondered when her attorney would take action.

Agent Roberts continued. "You should expect to be with us for a few days while we explore your situation. At least, your visa will be rescinded; your application was clearly false, which gives us grounds to hold you for further questioning."

Chapter 29

Ken O'Hare straightened the collar of his short-sleeved shirt. He was slightly nervous. There was an exceptionally large sum of money at stake. He checked his reflection in a window and quickly hurried on when he realized he had chosen a Victoria Secrets store window. He admonished himself. This was not the time for inefficient thinking. He checked his watch. He was early. Perhaps if he had a coffee and sat for a while, he could bring his nerves under control.

He'd been sloppy, he had to admit, reflecting on the last week as he sipped his coffee. Perhaps he'd been too confident—but he'd always succeeded before. He knew he'd been excessively aggressive with Midway. Emma had voiced her doubt that his captive would recover from the videoed torture, and she wanted to consult with an Army medical officer. The US Army had a number of doctors on duty; probably because of the treatment meted out to prisoners. He was loath to agree and had eventually persuaded the psychologist to wait until after the weekend. He'd promised that if Midway was still in a coma, he would consider her request. He didn't want to use a local Army doctor; it was far too risky to have the military nosing around NSA business or indeed, around his private activities. He needed Midway as bait for Schmidt, so he might have to arrange a visit by one of

NSA's tame doctors. That was a Monday decision, O'Hare concluded, and put the issue out of his mind.

He had other problems. Zarina.

He checked his watch. Still thirty minutes before his meeting. It was a sunny Saturday afternoon and normally he'd be more than willing to sit and watch the attractive young ladies promenading past as they went about their fashion shopping ventures. Today he was sitting at one of the pavement tables, but without noticing any of the passersby. That was careless, perhaps dangerous, he decided, and tried to focus.

His mind was running the same concerns over and over again. Homeland Security had taken Zarina, and she had disappeared into the jaws of their New York office, captive of a team investigating possible immigration fraud. The problem he faced was how to retrieve her. He'd tried forceful persuasion to get her released and hoped that did not end up backfiring. Oh, he was confident she would keep silent, at least if the only issue against her related to her green card. Other matters—he had major issues.

O'Hare swore to himself, a little more savagely than was warranted either by the coffee or the location, and customers at a nearby table looked alarmed. He took back his self-control and half-smiled an apology that was ignored. He wondered if Schmidt and his team had arranged for Zarina's arrest; he'd tried to run that thread back to its spool—another failure. The two men he'd sent to grab one of Schmidt's people had failed totally. He knew only they'd been taken by a team of MPs—the scary thing was that they were now held by Schmidt's own battalion. There were cutouts with no direct link back to him. He did have doubts about the effectiveness of the cutouts, though.

He check his watch again. He had another fifteen minutes, He sipped his coffee. His next worry were the deaths at Midway's New Hampshire property, which had been followed by a failed assault on one the local crime team technicians. The same people, he was certain. His Saudi contact had offered him the use of some of their Chechen resources, which he had declined. While his people had not fared well with the tasks he had given them, refugees, no matter how dedicated, were not people he wanted to use. Their Sunni background and wahhabi fundamentalism defined a street down which he was not willing to walk. Those links, he had decided long ago, if exposed, would not only endanger his life but also counter the longer term strategy he was pursuing.

O'Hare chuckled softly to himself; apparently he had been correct about the poor quality of the resources, if the reports he had received were anywhere near accurate. Somehow a twelve-year old girl had defeated the attempt by a two-man team to kill her, and later, a nineteen-year old technician had severely injured a third Chechen, who now was in a critical condition in the local Redmont hospital. He placed his coffee cup back on the table. If the opposition was so much better than he and others expected, perhaps he, too, would have to up his game.

He checked his watch—it was time to head to his meeting. His local contact, a senior officer in the Saudi General Intelligence Directorate, was a stickler for punctuality. He stood and edged past the neighboring tables and set off down the street, ignoring the feeling that his short collar was folded the wrong way. O'Hare did not notice the man on the other side of the street, who, looking totally bored with the world, had stood in the same place for thirty minutes. Now the man moved off and coincidentally was going in the same direction, trailing thirty yards or so behind.

O'Hare's destination was Airyaman Persian Rugs, a well-established importer and retailer of expensive new and sometimes antique, carpets, silk rugs, and prayer mats. It appealed to O'Hare, in a quirky sense, that his fellow Americans were totally anti anything Iranian, yet Persian rug outlets flourished. Perhaps they did not realize Persia and Iran were the one and the same. He did not want to consider how purchase moneys for new stock was transferred to Iran. It appealed even more that a Saudi espionage mission was utilizing a Persian carpet warehouse to shield its activities.

He entered the store, waved a casual greeting to the senior salesman, ignored the two young carpet handlers and the handful of wandering customers, and continued through to the back office, avoiding the large piles of rugs that burdened the storage area. When O'Hare reached the small office, he picked up the furthest telephone and dialed nine. He listened for a moment and carefully set the handset back in its cradle. He left the office and walked further towards the rear of the building. He ignored the washrooms. He stopped at a door marked "Janitor," tapped once, and opened the door. He ignored the buckets and mops, and, after closing the door, walked to the far wall. He tapped again and after a minute had passed, a section of the wall slid open, revealing a one-person elevator. He stepped into the elevator; the door closed and the sensation indicated the elevator was descending. It always seemed it traveled a long way, far more than one floor. He never inquired. Perhaps, after so many years of NSA experience, such hidden features were normal, not to be wondered at.

The elevator jerked to a stop and O'Hare waited patiently for the door to open. A long corridor stretched out in front of him, dimly lit and poorly ventilated. He followed the twists and turns of the passageway, covering at least, he estimated, forty yards. Last time it had seemed like sixty yards or more. The design was impressively devious, in his opinion. He suspected explosives were planted behind the walls and ceiling, and the passageway could be destroyed at the press of a button.

He reached a door and tapped a random pattern. The door opened and he stepped into a small office. A man was waiting for him, standing inside the office. Ignoring the hiss of the door as it closed behind him, O'Hare smiled inwardly when he noticed the clock on the wall had reached the hour. Impeccable timing, he thought.

"Dr. Chaborz," he said, reaching out to shake the other man's hand. "*Assalam alaykum.*"

"*Wa alaykum a salaam,*" came the reply. "You're on time. Good."

O'Hare nodded his head.

The doctor continued, "There is tea, freshly made. Come. We'll sit and share our reports."

It was going to be a long afternoon, thought O'Hare, as he sat at the small table where the tea making equipment and cups were set out. The first ten minutes, at least, would be used to discuss the weather and other general courtesy subjects. After they completed the courtesies, the real business of the meeting would commence. He sighed silently.

At last O'Hare thought it was time to take the lead in the conversation. He said, "Dr. Chaborz, we should commence. You can advise Prince Khalid the plan for delivery of the software programs and hardware details developed by Project ForeSight is on target. I'll deliver the first tranche at the end of the month—that's only a week away—and in return, I'll expect to see a deposit of ten million dollars to the Lichtenstein account, details of which I've already provided." He didn't mention the deposit would automatically trigger a transfer out to accounts in British, Swiss and, Luxembourg jurisdictions.

"The prince will be extremely happy," acknowledged Dr. Chaborz, his eyes twinkling. "I am certain the transfer will be made as you requested, *inshallah.*"

O'Hare considered the deposit of ten million dollars to be crucial, if nothing else, as a sign of Saudi goodwill. He had agreed with the Saudi prince to make technology deliveries each month over the next six months. Sixty million dollars was the total fee and he had ten million to pay out, a net of fifty million dollars, which would be a comfortable bonus. The General Intelligence Directorate, of course, in turn would receive a complete picture of NSA's foreign satellite interception activities, including big data collection and analysis, satellite hacking, tracking, and control software, and even the detailed specifications and design of their new satellite killer.

He said, "Good. Sometime over the next few days, I'd like to have a teleconference with Prince Khalid to discuss again how we validate the contents of this and subsequent technology transfers. His Directorate people may not have the skills required. We have this and a further five transfers scheduled, and the details will become progressively more technical in content and structure."

"That is a valid concern." Dr. Chaborz bowed his head. "I understand the prince is recruiting senior experienced personnel, but whether he will be successful in time to review your transfers is not known."

"That's all I have to report," O'Hare concluded, leaving the floor for the doctor to raise any items for discussion.

"I have some minor items, if you're not too busy?"

"Of course, Dr. Chaborz. I am here to listen."

"How is your campaign proceeding against Cromarty?"

"The pace is slow. There is progress, though."

"You should accelerate your plans."

"I may not need to." O'Hare didn't bother to defend his activities; for once he was able to deflect the doctor's focus. "The Senate is threatening to investigate how Iran was able to purchase arms when there were stringent sanctions in place— it seems Cromarty is their target."

"Aah. That is good to hear. You will keep me informed?"

"Of course," O'Hare said.

Dr. Chaborz continued, "We discovered the whereabouts of some of Satan's creatures, these genetically modified Devil's spawn. We lost two men. They attacked a young child, a girl, yet they were both killed. How can this be?"

It's not my problem if your resources are inept, O'Hare thought.

He said, "That's difficult for me to assess. I don't know if others were involved, or if the men you sent were—possibly—not highly skilled." He shrugged. "It may have been a simple accident. I don't have enough data."

"Yes, I understand. We sent a more skilled man—at least, so we thought—to track down this child, and if the opportunity arose, to kill her. Our man was bested by a youth and is in hospital with severe concussion. I admit, we are disappointed with our failures. I suspect it is God's will, yet we are trying to do what we believe is His will. Do you have any suggestions?"

O'Hare shook his head. "I had heard of the misadventures and wondered about the skill level of the team you sent."

"That too, is our concern. We now have two men, exceptionally skilled; they are assassins who have worked in Europe and America. They are now tasked with finding this girl and her companions, whoever is protecting her. They are to terminate all. We hope for better results."

"Dr. Chaborz, may I suggest caution?"

"Certainly. If you have advice, I welcome it."

"The girl is undoubtedly genetically engineered. I have no idea about the youth; however, I suspect your experts may experience difficulties. There are over five thousand of these Cerberus people, all capable. You may not be able to field enough people here in the United States to overwhelm their defenses."

"I understand. We could utilize resources that are more—dedicated—to do the job."

O'Hare understood the reference was to Chechen jihadists, fundamentalist wahhabis, who had fled Chechnya and settled in America as refugees. He hoped the Saudis were not seriously considering the doctor's idea.

"Americans may not appreciate your necessity for waging a jihad in this country," he said.

"We might be able to form an alliance with one or more of your fundamental Christian groups?"

"Very dangerous, very dangerous." O'Hare inwardly shuddered at the thought of mixing Muslim jihadis and extreme Christian groups. It was one thing for NSA to train members of the Saudi intelligence community, but it was another to see Saudi-sponsored jihadists working with American extremists.

Dr. Chaborz smiled, his eyes twinkling. He said, *"Inshallah."*

Chapter 30

Schmidt was extremely reluctant to permit the children to watch the video he'd downloaded from the Cerberus cloud. He was in two minds about allowing Anna and Ladder to see it; he suspected the contents would be traumatic. The debate was loud and aggressive until at last he surrendered.

"Okay. If you all have nightmares for the next year, don't ask me to come and hold your hands," he said. "This is going to be unpleasant. It will be the worst thing you've ever experienced." He overlooked the experiences of Camp Brewer, when assassins had calmly poisoned and shot their Cerberus siblings, and Anna had taken a weapon and killed the murderers.

Anna and the children, pale and anxious, gripped each other's hands. Ladder was in the middle, with Alex on one side and Gabrielle on the other. Niland sat next to Anna, holding her hand. Schmidt sat at the computer and clicked on the video file. The beginning of the tape was blank, except for a metallic-sounding voice, electronically disguised.

"General Schmidt, I hope you don't have anyone else watching this video, 'cos it's not pretty. I have your friend Midway and he's completely at my mercy. Oh, and remember, he's at your mercy, too. I'm willing to consider an exchange, you for this man. The offer ends of course, if

Midway dies—this is a stressful experience for him. Now watch while I show you what he's been experiencing for the last week." The voice faded out.

So, thought Schmidt, *part of the motivation for the video is to put me under pressure, by suggesting to others who view the recording that Mark's torture can be eased—no, stopped—by swapping me for him. He's trying to drive a wedge between me and my team or between me and Anna and her family; that's something I need to stop as quickly as possible.*

An image slowly took shape on the screen to reveal Mark strapped to a metal table. Schmidt recognized it as an autopsy table and fervently hoped no one else made the connection. The view was from directly overhead. Mark was naked and straps across his arms and legs held him down. Additional straps restrained his body so that his ability to move was completely restricted. An IV was attached to the back of his right hand. Round pads—Schmidt estimated there were twenty leads and assumed they were electrical contacts— were attached to his body. Mark's arms were stretched alongside his body and his hands were visible. His eyes were open. His face, unshaven, was gaunt.

A white-coated attendant moved into view and stood next to Mark. Schmidt thought the person was female, although her face was covered and shielded from the overhead camera.

She was checking the electrical contacts. Apparently satisfied, she stepped back out of camera view.

The voice over said, "As you can see, we have Midway wired. Four of the contacts allow us to monitor his heartbeat, so we can tell if his heart stops beating. The other fifteen, no, sixteen, deliver electrical currents. We can select the connections or deliver voltage to all. See."

Mark's body spasmed and he appeared to hold back a scream. Anna hid her face. The two girls were crying. Niland had his hands across his eyes, reluctantly watching. Ladder was staring, entranced, focused on the screen.

"We can shut the power off and apply it again, at an even higher voltage. Let me show you. Watch."

This time Mark screamed and his body locked into an arc, straining against his restraints. Schmidt checked. Ladder was still entranced. He wondered how the young man could watch—it was difficult for him to see Mark tortured.

"Oh, dear. That's so shocking." The tone was glib. Schmidt thought the man had no empathy and indeed, was psychopathic.

The speaker paused as though checking notes. After a few seconds, he said, "We've been medicating your friend. We have a particularly helpful hyperalgesic mix. What's a hyperalgesic? Let me see. Think of it as a pain enhancer. This one is derived from a refined mixture containing opioids and platypus venom and enhances pain to an excruciating level. It's a helpful medication for my purposes, as I'm sure you'll appreciate. My assistant is adding some to Midway's medication, and this time we'll use a low voltage."

Schmidt was intent on the screen—and so was Ladder, he noted—as the attendant adjusted the IV and stepped back out of camera view.

"Now watch. This is a far lower voltage. Saves power and helps the planet, don't you think? I'll cycle through the connections on a random basis to demonstrate the benefits."

Mark's body jerked and jumped, twitching and straining at the straps. The restraints were cutting into his limbs and he was bleeding onto the table. He screamed and moaned as the voltages were applied.

"I'll stop for a minute to allow Midway to recover. He promised to say a few words to you. Well, he said he would, after I thumped his head on the table a few times. My attendant will give him some water otherwise his throat will be far too dry for him to speak. We'll probably use a hose after we've completed the video, to wash him down. Or we may leave him."

Schmidt and Ladder watched as the attendant presented a

paper cup and straw to Mark, who sucked down the liquid.

"I forgot to mention his drink contains a hallucinogen. It will take—oh, a couple of minutes to hit—and he'll think he's flying or covered in insects or something. It's entirely unpredictable. We'll let you watch the beginning of his trip while I tell you, General Schmidt, what you need to do."

Anna moaned. "I don't think I can listen to any more," she sobbed. She fled the room, followed by the three children. They were trying to comfort Anna while coping with their own emotional reactions.

Schmidt hit the stop command for the video file. "What about you, Ladder?"

Ladder turned to Schmidt. "But didn't you see? He's acting. He said so. He's in control of the medication and of the electrical pads."

Schmidt was totally taken aback. "What the hell are you talking about?"

"But he told us," protested Ladder.

"I don't understand you. He was screaming; he didn't say anything—at least, not yet."

"No, of course he didn't speak. Didn't you see? He was signaling."

"You saw him signal? He was strapped down and whoever was torturing him was watching. How could he signal?" Schmidt did not hide his perplexity and growing frustration.

Ladder looked worried. He closed his eyes for a moment, opened them, and said. "Hold out your hands. Tuck your thumb away. You've got eight fingers showing, right?"

Now Schmidt looked worried.

"Go on, do what I said," instructed Ladder.

Totally bewildered, Schmidt held out his hands and folded his thumbs into his palms. "Okay."

"Extend your fingers."

Schmidt did as Ladder instructed.

"Fold them back."

Schmidt folded his fingers back.

"Now on your left hand, extend your second last finger and on your right hand extend your last finger."

"What the hell?" Schmidt barely hid his impatience as he struggled to move his fingers.

Ladder demonstrated. He folded back all his fingers and then extended all his fingers. He folded them all again and extended his second last finger on his left hand and his last finger on his right hand. He said "Upper case A."

He kept his left hand steady, focused on his right hand and first folded his fingers and then extended the second last finger. "Upper case B."

Schmidt stared at Ladder, his eyes round. "You didn't— he didn't—"

"Binary code. Eight-bit. Used by computers. Logically, a bit can be true or false, on or off, or one and zero. His extended fingers represent numeric ones and the others, those he's folded, represent zeroes. He's using ones and zeroes. Each finger is equivalent to a bit. That gives him an 8-bit binary code, as I said. Understand?"

Schmidt nodded his head; the light was beginning to dawn.

"So 01000001 is upper case A. 01000010 is upper case B. He really doesn't have to move fingers on his left hand—the changes for the upper case alphabet are all on the right. I followed most of his message. He flicked his fingers back and forth, all zeros and all ones, a number of times, coinciding with the electric shocks. He went through the vowels. After that he started to signal. His words are in upper case. The message portion I saw was something like GITMO OHARE NSA IM OK HVE CTRL BLKING PAIN. There were other words but he was fast and I missed them. We'll have to replay the tape and watch it through to the finish to get his full message."

"You're a bloody genius, Ladder. Get Anna back. I'll call my office."

While Ladder was persuading Anna and the children to return to the study, Schmidt phoned Maeve. When she answered, he said, "Stop watching the tape. Connect Linda. You both need to hear this. It's critical." He waited until Maeve connected Linda Schöner into the call and continued, "Mark is signaling in 8-bit binary code. Watch how his fingers move. He's in Gitmo. As we suspected, the guy who has him is O'Hare. Mark says he's controlling the pain. Ignore the apparent torture and degradation—watch his hands. Get someone on this immediately—he's fast. No, it wasn't me, it was Ladder. He's a damn genius. Go, go!" he disconnected the call.

He looked at Anna and the children who had returned to the study. They were wide-eyed. "Mark is signaling us using a binary code. Ladder recognized it. He says Mark is controlling the pain, he's in Gitmo, and we know who kidnapped him. Linda will have the entire message for us within fifteen minutes. You don't have to watch that horrible video."

Anna grabbed Ladder and hugged him, her tears flowing. "Oh, Ladder. Thank you so much." The children stared at their visitor, their expressions wondering.

Alex shrieked and said, "You're ours now. You've helped save Mark." She wrapped her arms around as much of Ladder and Anna as she could reach. She was copied by Gabrielle and Niland.

When eventually they released each other, Schmidt said, "Ladder, congratulations. I don't know whether my team would have recognized Mark's code or not. You did. I'm impressed. You're resigning from the Redmont crime team and coming to work for me. Okay?"

Ladder smiled, not sure what to say. He was overwhelmed by the outpourings of emotions and uncertain why he was the only person who had seen the signals and understood the code.

In a follow-up call to Maeve and Linda, Schmidt said, "As I said, the boy's a genius and I'm adamant he's going to work for us. We'll subsidize his college fees. I don't care what it costs."

Linda said, "I don't know if we would have caught it. If we did, it would have been after we'd played the video through a dozen times, looking for clues. I agree, he will add value to our team."

"And he's not Cerberus," Maeve commented. "Well, I assume—"

"You're correct; he's not, as far as anyone knows. He's a young man with an alert mind. Linda, I'll arrange for him to meet with you—interview him, introduce him to some of your senior analysts. I'd like your team's feedback. Your's too, Maeve."

Both Maeve and Linda assented to Schmidt's request. He continued, "So we have confirmation it's O'Hare. Not enough evidence yet to arrest him, but close. We believe it was his helicopter, and the victim has identified him even if in unusual circumstances. I'm not sure we can use the torture video as proof enough for an arrest warrant. We've enough, though, to launch a rescue mission and I'll start Helen thinking about how we use the 145th once we finish this call. Linda, I want you to focus your experts on O'Hare. I want his life history, whatever you can discover. I want him trailed everywhere he goes until we recover Mark. I believe ICE has his lady friend?"

"Confirmed. She is not being co-operative, apparently," Maeve said.

"Can we get her transferred to Camp Brewer? I'd like to question her. While she may stonewall ICE, I'm confident there's more to her than a green card fraud. If we place her in a military environment with a threat of sending her to Gitmo, we may open some floodgates. We could let O'Hare know she's in our hands—that would add more pressure."

"Yes, I agree," Linda said. "Also, I'd like to arrange for the banks that advanced funds for his house and aircraft purchases to call in their loans. I'm sure my team can find breaches or flaws in the documentation."

"I know people in Compliance in both the banks that wrote

the initial mortgages," said Maeve. "They'll work with us. They also tell us if the loans have been sold on to other investors."

"We could buy them out; that might be a way to apply more pressure. Imagine O'Hare's reaction when he receives a communication to make his repayments to General Schmidt," Linda said.

Schmidt did not smile. "I'm struggling with motive—why does he want to swap Mark for me? It's been bugging me ever since I heard his demand. Maeve, can you present a summary of all this to the president? Show him excerpts from the torture tape. He'll give his go ahead for us to use the 145th, I'm sure."

Chapter 31

O'Hare was on the list of attendees for three meetings, two of which were categorized as critical business. He ignored the third meeting; it had been called by another department and he had no interest in the subject matter. The two critical meetings were providing a challenge; while he could watch the presentations on his computer because his desk monitor was large enough to cope with two sets of PowerPoint graphics and whiteboard displays, he had to take care which of his two cell phones was connected to which presentation. He cursed whoever had set up the meetings. He had accepted neither invitation; however, an instruction from his boss, relayed via MJ, had made it mandatory for him to be involved in both. He shrugged. Next time he would protest vigorously if someone set two meetings to run simultaneously and he was required to attend both.

He had managed to improve his meeting-switching expertise and routine when his office phone rang. He checked the caller ID. It was Roy Hoskins. That was the idiot from DHS who refused to help him with Zarina's green card problem. He hoped the man burned in hell. He was tempted to ignore the call. Eventually curiosity got the better of him. He reached for the phone.

"O'Hare."

"Hoskins. I thought you'd like an update. Your little Russian piece is no longer in our hands. She was transferred today to Army jurisdiction. They want to question her for spying or something. So don't call us again, okay?"

"What?" O'Hare's shout echoed off the walls of his office. "What shit are you trying to pull? The fucking Army has no jurisdiction over civilians."

"I'm afraid they do if they're illegal Russians who are suspected of criminal involvement with Army personnel. She has terrorist links, I hear. Your problem, not mine. Enjoy."

Hoskins disconnected.

O'Hare stared at the now silent handset in total disbelief. The bastard Hoskins had stiffed him completely. He ignored the in-progress meetings, both of which had gone quiet except for the two meeting leaders each repeating his name. He had more to deal with than the safety of NSA resources in Kyrgyzstan and Uzbekistan. He hadn't agreed to locate teams there—it was up to their project managers to sort it out. He shut down the laptop and disconnected it from all cables. He locked the NSA computer in its security cabinet and stormed out of his office. He didn't know where he was going, he only knew he wanted out. He ignored his open-mouthed PA who watched him head towards the elevator bank.

Linda Schöner knocked softly on Maeve's office door and entered at the silent invitation.

Maeve said as she removed her earbuds, "I was listening to a recording. We received an interesting tape of a conversation between Cromarty and a third party—we're trying to identify the other person. What can I do for you?"

"I want to make a quick report. We had a good response from the banks involved in lending to O'Hare's Delaware companies. The compliance manager for"—Linda checked her papers—"Barto Aviation Funding LLC, in particular, has provided copies of all their documentation. He's had his team sifting through the fine print, and he thinks he's found a breach for us to use."

"Good to hear. Details?" Maeve sat back in her chair. She brushed a wave of hair back from her face.

Linda explained, "The loan conditions require a copy of the maintenance log and airworthiness certificate of the subject aircraft to be provided to the lender within ten days of the date of the granting of the certificate. That's an annual requirement. The latest documents are two months overdue, so either the helicopter is out of airworthiness or O'Hare has forgotten to send the paperwork. We bought the loan thirty minutes ago, with the assistance of Barto, and we're about to issue a default notice to the company, and O'Hare will receive a copy as guarantor. The notice will request repayment of the mortgage because of a breach of conditions. If the aircraft has not been certified airworthy, the failure is fatal to the loan. He'll have seven days to repay. We're also advising the FAA the aircraft may not be airworthy."

"You are an evil player of the game," Maeve said. "Will we be adding a helicopter to our assets?"

"You never know," Linda replied. She handed Maeve some of the pages she was carrying. "A summary for you— the rest is available in our cloud, reference O'Hare. We're using our attorneys' address and they're issuing the notice. We're checking his house mortgage next; the mortgage on that is over a million dollars—that's a lot of money, even for a senior NSA employee."

"You still have your escort from the 145th?"

Linda frowned. She disliked the idea of having a team of MPs trailing her, especially after Schmidt had hauled them over the coals for their slow response to her attempted abduction.

She replied, "Yes, they follow me all the time. They are totally on tenterhooks—Schmidt must have ripped them."

"Good. I have a feeling you'll need them."

###

O'Hare had barely reached his SUV when his cell phone buzzed. He checked and opened the message. He couldn't believe his eyes. Someone—he'd find out who and ream them a new one—was claiming his chopper was not certified airworthy, and the current holder of the mortgage was demanding repayment of the loan. He had seven days to remedy the situation. He checked again. No, the notice required payment; it was the only remedy offered. He sat in the driver's seat and fought to restrain the explosion of his temper. If his pilot—no, he couldn't blame Ferguson, the responsibility was his alone. He'd arranged the annual inspection, he was certain. He'd have to check the documents when he got to his apartment. Or were the documents at his home in New York State?

His cell phone buzzed. It was Ferguson, his pilot.

"Yes, Fergo?"

"I've been informed by my buddy at the FAA that the chopper is out of certification. Did you forget? I thought Brown Aviation handled that?"

"Don't you have the log book?"

"No, I handed it off to you—it must have been ages ago. Remember, you wanted to check with Browns about some requirement or other. I'm not sure what you were chasing— maybe a new transponder."

"Damn. I'll have to check with them. I thought it was done. The paperwork's probably sitting on their desks somewhere. Take it easy, I'll get back to you."

O'Hare paced back and forth beside his SUV as he thumbed through his contacts to find the number for the aviation company. He made the call. He entered the extension for the sales engineer. The call went to voice mail. He disconnected and re-dialed. He pressed the required numbers for the front desk. That too went to voice mail. At this point he was ready to throw bricks. He returned to the driver's seat and tried to force himself to relax. He re-dialed the number for sales engineer and left a message, hoping the man would return his call before the day was out. He could feel his fury building. He tried to swallow the bile that had forced its way into his mouth. Someone was going to pay and he was starting to suspect where the pressure was coming from.

Schmidt.

He punched the door of his SUV and cursed the surge of pain.

This was not part of the plan.

This was war.

Chapter 32

The helicopter touched down precisely on the center of the H landing pad at Camp Brewer. Schmidt signaled his thanks to the pilot after he removed his headphones. He exited the aircraft as the blades whined to a stop. Helen Chouan and her aide were waiting for him.

"General, welcome." They exchanged salutes and Helen led the way to her office.

"Thank you. You received a report from Linda?"

"Yes, I did. That tape was difficult to watch."

"She explained the code?"

"Yes. Her report was detailed. So we're going on a trip?"

"Donnelly is meeting with the president, probably as we speak. She managed to get an urgent session for fifteen minutes. It should be enough time to get his authorization. Once I hear from Donnelly that the president has given us approval, I'll meet with NSA, SECDEF, and SECARMY. These are tentatively scheduled for today if possible, otherwise tomorrow. Once everyone's in the loop, I'll talk to USSOUTHCOM to confirm plans with them. Local command, JTF-GTMO, is under the control of a rear admiral, so it's a jurisdictional mess. We have to be cautious—O'Hare will have listeners who'll report back to him if they hear about our proposals. I'm hoping we can cause him enough grief to keep him distracted. What's your status?"

"I'll have half the battalion available and ready to move within six hours. Oh, I know we're not planning to leave quite that soon; however, it's good training. It's not enemy action, so we'll travel light. The other half of my battalion is on duties I can't defer; protective details, for example. What will you do if we don't get a go-ahead?"

"Resign, look for volunteers and mount my own raid." He had to go through with the rescue.

"You'd be overwhelmed with volunteers. My people would step forward, to a man—and woman. Me included."

"Thank you. I hope we don't need to exercise that option."

Helen laughed. "There's a few thousand non-military Cerberus people with law enforcement experience who'd jump into a fire for Midway. I've heard we have over a thousand in police and FBI, and as many in other federal agencies. We can add military and ex-military—we've a couple of thousand ex-military on private security contracts, according to Maeve's last status report. You'd have no shortage of resources to draw from."

Helen stood at her office door and Schmidt indicated she should enter first. She sat behind her desk and Schmidt sat in one of her visitor's chairs. It was passably comfortable.

"We'd be declaring some kind of war—that's not the way to go. At least, as long as we can rescue Mark with the president's approval for action."

"I've arranged for three of my captains to join us in thirty minutes. One had a posting in Guantánamo for a couple of years so has good local knowledge. What do you want to cover first?"

"Transport?"

"We've two new Hercules C-130Js based here. The pilots have been eager for a long flight. We're supposed to be testing an enhanced model for HALO action, using the wings RDEz developed. We've room for up to a hundred men in one aircraft, more than we need. We can use the second aircraft to carry vehicles. It would be prudent to bring our own. The aircraft will be ready when we are, guaranteed. The pilots tell me flight time will be closer to three hours and thirty minutes. They expect a headwind for the first half of the trip and the edge of a hurricane might hit as we get closer to our destination. They'll confirm details when you lock in our departure time."

"Departure time?" He shrugged. "I'm waiting on approvals. I think fifty or so men will suffice, so we'll keep it to two platoons plus officers. You and I will go, plus platoon officers. We need the most level-headed. The remainder can remain here or we can set them additional protection duties until we settle this. Maeve, Linda, Julian, and Anna, and their families, are all at risk."

"Agreed."

"We need to file dummy flight plans. A flight from our base of operations to Gitmo will raise all kinds of alarms for O'Hare."

"The word is we're heading to Fort Bragg. We can file a variation while we're in flight. We might have some please explains when we return. I'll let you resolve those."

"I'll do that with pleasure," agreed Schmidt.

A knock on the door signaled the arrival of the three captains Helen had scheduled to meet with Schmidt. Planning was about to enter the intensive stage.

After the flight plans and strategy were agreed with Helen and her team, Schmidt arranged to question the Russian illegal, Zarina Gorky. He had an hour or so to spare before he was scheduled to return to Washington. He waited in another room adjacent to the interview room where the Russian woman was delivered by a guard. Schmidt had instructed the guard to not to tell the Russian of his presence. He let her wait for twenty minutes before he entered the room. The room was wired for sound and video.

He opened the door and sat down at the interview table opposite the Russian. She was—he agreed with the file note made by a member of the ICE team—an attractive woman. He wondered for a moment if that was O'Hare's motive. However, that did not align with what appeared to be a regular monthly visit. She was blond, fit, and her smooth complexion and trim figure were all the attributes to make a man forget his objectives, if he was careless. Her face was showing strain and fatigue. He dropped his file on the table and flipped through the pages, stopping every so often to read details. He'd already read the papers in the folder and could probably repeat the contents verbatim. At last he allowed himself to look at the prisoner.

"Well, Ms. Gorky, what do you have to say for yourself?"

"What do you mean? Who are you? Why hasn't my attorney made contact? Why are you keeping me in isolation? What are you, a general?" She had examined his shoulder badges and for a moment seemed alarmed.

"Isolation? This is a military base and we don't have facilities for many prisoners. Conditions on Guantánamo may be more to your liking, perhaps?"

"Gitmo? That American embarrassment? Why would you threaten to send me there?"

"I don't threaten. We're preparing an aircraft to go there; you could be a passenger."

"Who the fuck do you think you are? I want to contact my attorney—you can't hold me like this." Her face was not so pretty when she snarled.

"Ms. Gorky, our investigations have been rewarding. While your grandmother—that is, your maternal grandmother—has been difficult to trace." He tapped the file folder. "I don't believe this nonsense for an instant. We think there is a Saudi link—there was a Saudi presence at her funeral, we know that much. Your paternal grandmother— your father's mother—was Chechen. Killed by a Russian hit team when they tried to assassinate your father. He continued his terrorist activities and eventually was killed in Syria, a year ago, no?"

Zarina cursed, both in Russian and English. Schmidt's expression did not change. He was impressed by her vocabulary. He ignored the outburst and continued, "According to our records your father was advising Daesh. His involvement with terrorists makes you a candidate for questioning at Gitmo and for you to be held in isolation. Also, without an attorney. Understand?" Schmidt was sailing close to the wind on this, he knew.

"Your constitution doesn't allow—"

He shrugged. "Our constitution applies to Americans. It provides no relief for foreign terrorists." He did not wait for a response. He opened the file and silently re-read a report. He looked back up at the prisoner and said, "It seems you were in Syria last year, visiting with your father. You departed only minutes before an explosion destroyed the house where he was hiding. You went to Turkey. Perhaps the authorities there would be interested in talking to you about an Iraqi who was murdered in Diyarbakir—in the Hilton, of all places. Assuming, that is, we make such a suggestion."

Zarina's face was pale except for a pink spot on each cheek. She spat out her words. "You American terrorists fired missiles that killed my father and his friend. Now you want to kill me, is that it?"

"What I want is simple enough. Some truth and honesty, for a start. I have two questions and I want answers. What are you doing in this country? What is your relationship to O'Hare?"

Her eyes brightened as she solved the puzzle. "Aah. So you're the infamous General Schmidt." She sat back in her chair, a satisfied expression on her face.

Schmidt wondered whether he should turn off the camera and sound recorder. After a moment's reflection he decided that would be imprudent. "Yes. I could be even more infamous, I assure you. Now my questions. Let's start with the first one. What are you doing in this country?"

"It's such a lovely country—anyone would wish to be here. Isn't that why you have so many illegal immigrants?"

"You're one of millions. So you had no particular reason for coming here? Not, for example, to avoid Russian authorities? FSB, your infamous Russian internal secret police, for example, who might be interested in your activities—or more likely, in your father's activities?"

"Bastards. They are bastards. They have even less decency than you and your Gitmo. You should know."

Schmidt didn't comment. He thought the woman was well-informed. He had encountered the Russian secret police and the experience had not endeared them to him. "So your presence here is entirely innocent? Nothing to do with Dr. Chaborz and his intelligence operation?"

"How—?" She shook herself. "I don't know how you could link me with Saudi operations of any kind. I have been living quietly in this country for a year, and once you release me, I'll continue to do so."

"Zarina." Schmidt's voice was soft. "I didn't mention a Saudi operation. You had better rethink what you wish to tell me, and quickly. Our aircraft will leave for Guantánamo in the next day or so. It could be unpleasant for you, there."

"Bastard." Her eyes filled with tears.

"I'm immune to crying. Help me, and I'll prevent your transfer. Talk to me, about O'Hare, about his Saudi connection."

"He'll kill me," she sobbed. "It's a devil's choice—Gitmo for torture or O'Hare for my death." She wiped away a tear.

"We can protect you. I can offer you indemnity and even obtain approval of a new green card for you." He reached out and touched Zarina's wrist. "Talk to me." Schmidt's voice was soft, his gaze intense.

He was learning.

"You'll be safe, you have my word."

Her expression troubled, Zarina started to speak. Her voice was low, nearly out of Schmidt's auditory range. She seemed conflicted, as though she was saying things against her will. "They—the Saudis—have a video of him. Compromising. With Daesh leaders. There's more. I don't know what. They blackmailed him to help with my visa and to protect me— he's being paid large sums of money. He's firmly in the grip of the Saudis."

Later, in his telephone conversation discussion with Maeve, Schmidt said, "I think I experienced one of the more subtle effects of my Cerberus change. I've noticed how Mark can influence people, same for Anna, and the children. Well, I touched the Russian's wrist when I was trying to convince her to talk. Up until I did that she had been totally bulletproof. She changed completely after that, told me more. I doubt she revealed all that she knows—she's a strong-willed woman. Of course, Linda's team can do their research. I've uploaded the tape to her cloud environment; you can watch it at your leisure. O'Hare has interesting friends. He's working some project with Saudi intelligence. Perhaps because NSA has had links with the royal family dating from when they originally trained their intelligence people, the Saudi General Intelligence Directorate."

"What's her relationship with O'Hare?" asked Maeve.

"Nothing personal, as far as I can determine. He was hired by her father or Daesh to provide protection in addition to arranging her green card. She's inherited her father's wealth—he controlled a lot of the oil flow managed by the terrorists. There's probably more. I'll arrange further interviews and some of Helen's people can take part."

"A worthwhile interview."

"Yes. I've promised we'll release her back to Homeland Security if she continues to help us."

"I agree. Next subject. I've confirmed your other meetings now the president has approved your flight. It's SECDEF, followed by ARMY and after that you have Angus Jensen, the new director of the NSA. Before I forget—there's a meeting also with the admiral heading up the Gitmo Joint Task Force. I'll send you the schedule; tomorrow is all meetings, I'm afraid."

"Thanks. I'm waiting on the chopper. Do you have an update on O'Hare?"

"He was with Brown Aviation, according to the last report. That was an hour or so ago. I understand he's trying to sort out his missing FAA certificates."

"O'Hare has to arrange re-financing. He's receiving Saudi funds; he could use some of that money. They'd be offshore, of course," Schmidt said.

"He could still surprise us," Maeve added.

Schmidt muttered under his breath. O'Hare was starting to more than annoy him. The man was a criminal and possibly a traitor.

He said, "Please tell Linda to continue the search for pressure points. Ask her to backtrack the origin of the funds he used for his own home purchase and for his deposit on the helicopter. If we keep digging, something might show."

Chapter 33

Mark was conscious. He was intrigued. O'Hare's tame psychologist had stopped the shock treatment and reduced the drugs. He wondered if the change was a prelude to a new battery of attacks, although he could not imagine what would be worse. His body ached, his muscles felt as though they'd been beaten incessantly for days, and he was fighting against the effects of various drugs in order to regain coherent thought. He did not know whether it was night or day. He didn't even know what day it was. He was hungry. He was thirsty. He was in dire need of a proper wash. He wanted to get off this autopsy table. He wanted to be with Anna and the children.

For the moment, his problems had no obvious resolution.

A clatter of noise disturbed his worries.

"Aah, it's clean-up time, again."

The soft, feminine voice was totally in conflict with the torture the psychologist regularly inflicted. The splash of cold water was welcome. She hosed him from head to toe. The water flow cut off abruptly and—he forced himself to recall the woman's name—ah, yes, Emma. She threw a towel over his body.

Emma said, "I'd say dry yourself but even I can see the difficulties with that." She rubbed some of the water off his face and chest and draped the damp towel across his lower body. "There. I'll bring you some water to drink and a cup of the gruel you love so much."

She was gone for what seemed an age but which was probably only fifteen or twenty minutes. He'd managed to open his eyes and keep them open. They had adjusted to the soft light and were now relatively pain free.

Emma held a straw to Mark's mouth. "Drink this. It's warm tea with some vitamins added."

Mark clenched his teeth tight against the possibility of more drugs.

She hastened to reassure him. "No, I promise. I only added some vitamins. I've stopped your—ah—other medications; they weren't having any effect, anyway."

Mark drank deeply through the straw and choked.

"I've told you before, drink it slowly."

Chastened, he followed her instruction and sipped more sedately. The paper cup gurgled as he drained it.

"Good. Now the Oliver Twist soup. Here, it's thin enough for a straw, so I don't need to spoon-feed you. Take. It. Slowly."

Again, Mark followed instructions and soon emptied the larger container of warm soup and other small items, the identities of which he preferred to remain in ignorance. His stomach protested.

"Can you let me get up? I need to go—" His voice was croaky and strained. While he needed the washroom, he did not know if he could walk.

"We'll try. Promise first you won't attempt to attack me."

Mark said, "Yes, I promise." He considered his promise meaningless; it was given under duress and he'd do anything to escape this prison.

Emma released the straps holding him in place on the zinc table. He tried to raise his head. She placed her hand at the back of his neck and supported his effort. He lifted his body off the table and swung his legs over the side. His world spun.

His eyes closed and he fell back onto the metal surface.

"Here, let me help more."

The psychologist was surprisingly strong although, on reflection, Mark thought, it might be that he was surprisingly weak. He opened his eyes and tried to concentrate on his task. Feet onto the floor. Stand. Ignore the fierce piercing flames of pain streaming up his legs as they supported his weight. He focused, taking control of his pain receptors. Damp towel around his waist. He moved a foot forward, along the floor. He hoped it was in the direction of the washroom.

"This way," Emma directed.

He moved his other foot, followed by the first one again, establishing a hesitant, sliding gait. He held onto Emma's shoulder. He could feel the warmth of her body and a memory surfaced. He had tried to influence her once before and seemingly had failed. He moved his hand closer to her neck, to touch bare flesh. He didn't speak; his mind had two chores and he didn't want to risk a third. He shuffled his feet, blocking out the pain. He leaned on Emma, trying to silently establish control. After more shuffling, she stopped and Mark glanced up; the washroom door was only a foot away.

"I'll wait here. Yell for help only if you really need it."

He released his handhold and gripped the door for transitory support. He collapsed onto the toilet seat.

"Are you all right?" Emma inquired through the half open door.

"Yes." His voice was still hoarse. Mark was washing his face a degree more thoroughly than Emma had managed with her hose. He dried his hair and face and checked the mirror. A gaunt, unshaven, and unkempt reflection peered back at him through bloodshot eyes. He had not realized his whiskers would grow that much in—what, a week? Ten days? He had lost count. Mark closed his eyes momentarily and turned away. He hung the towel back on the rail and set out on a shuffling journey back to the other room.

Emma was waiting outside the door and grabbed his arm

to steady him. She said, "I won't ask you to climb back onto the table. I think we're past that, for now."

Mark did not respond to her words, but his mind raced. What was happening? He fumbled his way and reached out again for support. He used his contact on her bare skin to continue his attempt to establish control.

"Where do you want me to go?" he asked, as he shuffled past the table and appeared to be heading towards the exit door into the office area.

"There's a comfortable chair in the next room. You can sit there for a little while and build up your energy. I'll get some more food for you, which will help."

He uttered words, matching the sequence of his shuffling steps. "Why? Why have you released me?"

"I'm not really sure. I've been worried ever since Ken did that video. I'm not sure he intends to keep you alive. I decided I'm not going to be party to anyone's murder."

Mark thought, *I could murder a couple of people, if I had more energy.*

"Here, sit in this chair. While I'm getting some more food for you, I'll try to find your clothes, too."

The second meal was more substantial although still not far removed from some kind of basic gruel. Emma spoon-fed him, slowly and patiently. She was sitting in a chair beside Mark. When she finished, she said, "That's about two thousand calories so far. You'll have to wait for a few hours before I give you any more."

"Thank you." Mark's voice was stronger. He was sure he could feel the reaction of his nanites and knew he'd need more sustenance in less than four hours. A steak, he thought, in about two hours, was more to his inclination.

Emma had found his clothes; they had been laundered and stuffed away in the bottom drawer of a spare desk. Mark planned to shower and change, as soon as he was confident of his strength.

"Tell me again, why you released me from the table."

"I—I told you. Ken's attitude on his last visit frightened me. I've tried to speak with him since and he's been short-tempered. That is, when he does answer my calls. He's not his usual self."

"Perhaps Schmidt has been pressuring him. He—and my friends—know who he is, you realize?"

"How could they? He wasn't in the video and his voice was altered. There's no way your friends could know."

Mark reached out and took hold of Emma's hand. She had discarded her medical gloves and he could feel the warmth of her skin. He added to the control links he had established earlier.

"Emma, I assure you they know about O'Hare's involvement. They know he is NSA. They don't know your name; however, your anonymity won't last. The penalties for kidnap and torture are severe. You are involved, right up to your pretty neck."

"But it's Ken—I'm working for NSA and following his directions."

"I think we might have touched on this issue before. I'm not a terrorist. O'Hare has his own personal agenda that he's following."

"I think you might be correct. I—I'm afraid. That's why I released you from the table."

Mark did not state his opinion of someone who followed orders to torture an illegal prisoner. He hid his anger, as fierce as it was; he wanted to escape his prison and needed a cooperative jailer to help him.

"Emma, listen to me. I showed you before how much pain you were inflicting. Do I need to remind you?"

"No—no, you don't. I remember. I know how it felt."

Mark was inclined to refresh Emma's memory, notwithstanding her claim. He relented. "Good. You will obey me until I'm free of this prison and free of Gitmo. Understand?"

"Yes. But—"

"But nothing. You will help me escape—no, not just help—you will do what you can to insure my freedom. Agreed?"

"Yes, Mark."

"What weapons can you get? Do you still have the handgun you showed me before?"

"Ken took it. He said it was too dangerous to leave here."

"Cell phone? Do you still have yours here?"

"No. Ken took it off me. He was worried you might get hold of it."

"So how do you call him?"

"I have to go to a central office."

"Damn. Can you get hold of a cheap cell phone?"

"I—I'm not sure I should."

"It's a risk you have to take. Get me one as soon as you can."

"Yes, Mark. On the weekend when I'm away from here."

Chapter 34

Two men, probably in their mid-twenties, causally dressed in jeans and sweatshirts, dark-haired and of medium height, strolled along the Boston street, pretending to search for a non-existent address. If checked, they would claim it was the address for Said's cousin, a relation he had promised to contact. They had left their vehicle three blocks away, carefully parked to avoid either attention or parking tickets.

"Sos," said Said, "I don't see how we can get close to this family."

His companion frowned. He hated being addressed by the diminutive of his name. "Soslanbek. That's my name." They both spoke Arabic, albeit with a Russian accent typical of Chechens. "I agree. We've been past the apartment building three times and I cannot see how we can overcome the security."

There was a security desk inside the lobby of the building that had drawn their interest, and a doorman was stationed outside, sheltered by an awning reaching to the edge of the pavement. Said had detected a vehicle nearby with a driver and two passengers and suspected they were there to provide additional security. Probably private guards, Soslanbek had suggested, when he noted the vehicle had private plates.

"So should we continue circling like lost vultures or do something else?" queried Said.

"No, let's return to our vehicle. We should talk with the doctor, unless you can think of a better idea."

"He will criticize us."

Soslanbek shrugged. "As Allah wills. The security is extensive. We cannot fly to the roof. We cannot enter by the front door. Perhaps we could pretend to be delivering something from a store."

"Or we could set a car bomb along the street, either in front of the apartment building, or park it outside the restaurant where they refused to serve us unless we wore suits." Said was still angry at what he saw as an infidel plot to demean and belittle him. He had shaved off his beard because of this assignment, and the restaurant added insult to injury. He rubbed his chin, in memory.

"A good idea for revenge. Perhaps not so good for our objective."

They both turned at the corner and headed off in the general direction to where they had parked their vehicle. Neither man noticed the motorcyclist that passed them nor the small Smart car, both of which leap-frogged them as they walked. Nor did they notice that a furiously pedaling messenger cyclist crossed the road as they unlocked their vehicle, close enough for his Go-Pro to capture details of their license plate.

Brian Winter's team reported to Linda Schöner and provided a description of the two men plus details of their vehicle, including the owner's name and address.

"We checked as thoroughly as we could," said the team lead to Linda. "The owner's address appears to be a Chechen fitness club of some kind. I had someone drive by; they said there's a gym, small and scruffy looking, at that location. My guy took a photograph and my people here think some of the signs are in the Chechen Cyrillic alphabet. We'll upload our files and a copy of our log. You might be able to make sense of it all."

After the call ended, Linda sat back in her chair and rested her feet on the corner of her desk. She'd kicked off her shoes earlier. Her claim was that her thinking improved when she felt relaxed—there were few on her team who would argue with her, given the evidence of her successes.

Perhaps, she thought, these two men were tied somehow to the man who attacked Ladder. She'd been impressed by the young friend of Anna and the children and had agreed with Schmidt that he would be an excellent recruit to her team. Unfortunately, Maeve Donnelly had matched her assessment and wanted to also recruit him. The tug of war should be interesting.

She checked her files for the copy of the police report on Ladder's assailant and reread the details. His passport details identified him as a refugee, it seemed, from Russia. She checked his DHS file. No, she corrected herself, he was from Chechnya. Well, she was close—Chechnya was a republic of Russia.

The link was worrisome. Linda downloaded the Winter team's files—the team leader had said they had taken videos of the two men, which included some audio. She ran the files marked with audio and listened carefully. Her knowledge of Arabic was moderate. It seemed they were looking for someone and were concerned about the amount of security. She tagged the file for review by two of her specialists who had a far more fluent ability with the language.

So, if she was correct, the three men were somehow linked. They were Chechen. Possibly seeking Mark and his family; she doubted the two men in the street were looking for Ladder—that seemed a touch extreme.

After she organized her people, Linda called Maeve and detailed her concerns. When Linda finished, Maeve said, "You want me to free up a team? I have ten people with in-depth investigatory experience, mainly FBI. Do you want to brief them?"

Linda said, "Yes, please. I've asked my people to tap into all cell phone calls from the gym. There's a couple of towers nearby and they're collecting call details from our—er—government sources." She meant they were digging into NSA database files. "We'll need people to help match cell phone numbers to faces and to track likely suspects. There's a couple of coffee bars nearby, and it's possible our targets frequent those."

Linda's people had designed, programmed, and manufactured their own devices that could electronically reach into a cell phone within twenty feet or so of the user and strip out the data it contained, including its number, messages, images, calls made and received, and emails—the last only if the person was amateurish enough to use their phone for sending and receiving mail. The final step in the identification process was to photograph the owner of the cell phone in order to feed images to their facial recognition software. Her team would work with the resources Maeve supplied to combine efforts and data. Within days they would know more about the people frequenting the gym than their targets knew about themselves. All the information they gathered would be off the record, of course; certainly nothing they collected would be admissible evidence—there were no warrants involved.

Later that day Linda sat with members of her team plus the additional Cerberus people provided by Maeve and defined the tasks required. Once the team agreed the scope, she left them to define the working details—she did not want to interfere in the granular details. As she closed the door on the conference room, two of her senior people rushed towards her; their expressions were so concerned, she could feel the anxiety.

"Linda, we need you—"

"Urgently. This is—"

"Critical."

Linda threw her hands up in a pretend defensive move. "All right, you have my attention."

"Your office—"

"With the door closed and—"

"All phones left outside."

"We have information—"

"That could be dangerous."

"You two have been working together for far too long. Remind me to give you separate offices. And maybe some Valium. Come with me."

Linda listened intently to the two analysts, gradually growing as concerned as her two team members.

Finally she said, "You've told no one?"

"No one at all."

"The source files are—"

"Under double security."

"I'll contact Archimedes. Continue to regard this as more than secret. If you see or hear anything more, inform me immediately. Understood?"

Their reply was a chorused, "Yes, Linda. We'll bury it deep."

###

Linda contacted Schmidt; he had not left yet for Camp Brewer.

"Don't you have time off work?" Schmidt asked. He was wide awake, fully alert, and sounded eager for action.

"Not when it's something as urgent as getting Mark back," Linda replied. "My teams work in shifts, and I check their research at eight-hourly intervals. Well, kinda." She didn't mention that sometimes checking research meant she worked far more hours than her researchers. She had also spent hours double-checking the data her team provided earlier that afternoon.

"What can I do for you?" Schmidt asked when the silence dragged out.

"Did you know O'Hare has—well, had—a stepsister?"

"No, I don't know much about him, at all."

"She died last year. She was an FBI agent."

Schmidt recognized the karma cycle. "Her name?"

"It's someone you knew." For once Linda wanted to not deliver this item of research. She finally said, "MayAnn Freewell."

The world held its breath and paused for a long moment. Schmidt did not say anything. Linda did not add any details. She knew Freewell and Schmidt had been an item until Freewell had died in a fire. The coroner's report had stated the fire was accidental.

Linda heard noises while Schmidt was silent and suspected he was moving around in apartment.

"So—he blames me for what? Her death?" Schmidt was breathing in short gasps, as though he was struggling with a heavy weight.

"It seems it could be the basis for his attacks. My team states the probability is high, approaching 95%."

"Brief Maeve in your 9:00 a.m. call. I'll may be in the office—perhaps late tomorrow—depending on what happens with Gitmo."

Linda heard the initial roar of an explosion, suddenly terminated as Schmidt's phone disconnected. She didn't hesitate and immediately called 911. When she finished her call she contacted Helen Chouan who quickly agreed to send one of her best teams to investigate. Neither Linda nor Helen voiced their innermost concerns.

Chapter 35

Schmidt staggered for a moment and then stood tall. The explosion had damaged some of the interior of his living room in addition to taking out the window. There was no sign of fire, at least not yet. He assumed emergency services were on their way—the shock wave of the bomb had deafened him and he hoped it was only temporary. He shook his head. The bomb caused more damage than he would expect. The explosion had driven glass splinters into furniture across the room. The evening was not proceeding quite as he had planned.

He sat down, sighing. He had splinters in his arm and something had creased his forehead; something sharp, he suspected, because blood was flooding his eyebrow and dripping down onto his cheek. He closed his eyes momentarily, jerking back into full-consciousness when a mental prompt reminded him that if he was concussed, he should try to remain awake. He stood up. He did not know how long he had sat on the settee. He wondered if it was damaged. Perhaps he had bled onto the cushions. Pain was starting to make its presence known as the shock wore off. He looked down at himself. His clothes were torn. Blood from wounds he hoped were minor was leaking out onto his floor and his ears were ringing. Perhaps his hearing was returning, he thought, and staggered to the door in case firemen were planning on knocking it down to gain access.

He cautiously opened the door. A fireman grabbed him as his knees gave out. He could see more firemen grouped outside.

"Come in," he croaked. "I don't think there's a fire."

The fire chief looked over Schmidt's shoulder. "Damn, that was one hell of a blast. Sir, you were fortunate—here, sit down. Our paramedics are on the way. Is there anyone else in the apartment? Sir, I said—"

Schmidt raised his hand in acknowledgment. He was shocked by the tremors in his arm. "I—I heard you. No—no, there is no one else."

"Good. Now sit still, you shouldn't move until—"

"My cell phone," Schmidt said, carefully forming the words.

"Sir, I don't think you should get up—ah, here's our man. Thomas, we have one victim. Conscious. Possible concussion. Able to respond."

The paramedic dropped his bag beside the settee the fireman had chosen for Schmidt to use. "I'll take over from here, chief," he said.

Schmidt tried to remain focused. The room was not co-operating with him and it danced around, spinning him. "I—I feel dizzy."

"Sir, can I have your name, please?"

"Arch—Archimedes. Schmidt."

"Can you tell me what happened?" Two paramedics stood beside him, one asking questions while the other began to strip off his jacket and shirt.

"Someone tried to blow me up."

"Do you know who it was?"

"No." His answer was not as truthful as it could have been.

Further questions were halted when another group entered the apartment. They were MPs from the 145th. Schmidt recognized the sergeant although he couldn't remember his name.

"Sergeant, come on in." His voice was scarcely above a whisper.

"General, we got here as quickly as we could. Do you know—?

"No. Lots of possibilities, no one in particular."

The paramedics continued their triage. One was wiping blood from Schmidt's face. "Sir, we recommend we take you to the local emergency—"

"I'm cut in places. I have mild concussion. I've lost a modest amount of blood. Not sure there's much the hospital can do."

"Sir, your forehead needs stitching. You should be checked over, x-rayed, in case there's anything more serious."

The sergeant addressed the senior of the two paramedics. "I'm Sergeant Bresler. Schmidt is our general. He's only recently recovered from a month or so in hospital—aircraft accident." The sergeant didn't think it necessary to go into details. "I'll have our medics take over, if you don't mind. We have a doctor with us."

"Okay—sure, we don't need a territorial dispute. Thomas, the Army'll take over. I'll let the chief know."

Schmidt surrendered himself to the medics from the 145th. He had no idea how they had arrived so quickly and his mind could not focus on the problem. He struggled to remain conscious and he felt his eyes close.

"General, stay awake, Focus. What can you tell us about the bomb and explosion?"

"Damned if I know. It went bang. It knocked me out, I think. Cell phone—I need to call Major Chouan—"

"Sir, she knows. So does Ms. Donnelly. And Ms. Schöner."

"Whole bloody world—"

"Yes, sir. Probably even the president, by now."

Schmidt struggled to sit up straight. He'd started to slouch against the soft cushions.

"Gently, sir. I'll stitch this cut, otherwise it will leave an

224

ugly scar. There's some blood on your leg; we'll need to see where that's coming from. Keep still, the injection might sting for a moment."

Schmidt could hear his cell phone ringing. He was surprised it still worked. He half-heartedly raised his hand to point in the direction of the sound. "Could someone—?"

The phone was placed in his hand. Schmidt held it up high, trying to see the caller ID while not wishing to make the medic's task more difficult. He did not recognize the number. He shrugged and pressed the answer button and held the phone to his ear.

"Schmidt. I hear something went bang. I hope you weren't hurt too badly. I have a lot more in store for you."

"Who the hell—" Realization struck. "O'Hare. You bastard. I'll have your balls for this."

The caller laughed. "O'who? I have no idea who you mean. Enjoy the pain. There'll be more."

The call disconnected. Schmidt looked at his cell phone and debated throwing it through the large hole in the wall where a window used to be. He didn't have the strength. He sighed and placed the phone beside him on the settee. He'd get Linda to trace the number, although he expected it would not lead anywhere. It was O'Hare, he knew, without doubt.

"Sir, please stand. I need to get your clothes off; there are glass fragments everywhere." The medic turned to the sergeant. "Bresler, have a look for a change of clothes. I'd suggest pajamas, the general is going to need a day or two of bed rest. There's glass—and blood, of course—all over. I'll help him walk to the bedroom. He also needs a wash, to clean up the blood. Come on, General, I think you can stand."

Maeve Donnelly organized a meeting with Linda Schöner and Helen Chouan. She included each of their three senior people. The meeting was face to face in the Cerberus offices. Maeve taped her small collection of papers to attract the attention of the attendees.

"The x-ray results are clean. Schmidt wouldn't agree to an MRI; he said his concussion was mild. However, the medical consensus is to take him off the active list for five to seven days; perhaps longer if he has any adverse reactions."

"I daresay he's had enough of in-depth medical examinations—I don't know how he coped after that helicopter crash," Linda said. Helen Chouan simply nodded.

Maeve continued, "Suggestions welcome regarding Mark and the rescue Schmidt was preparing with you, Helen."

The major replied, "I'm conflicted. I want to rescue Mark, of course. My team is more than prepared to go. We're missing Schmidt and the authority he carries, though."

"I want to meet with the president later this afternoon to gauge his reaction to all this," Maeve said. 'We'd need fresh authorities if we want to take action without Schmidt."

"I haven't seen enough data to make an assessment, but do you think Mark will survive another week or so?" Linda's deputy asked. He was Cerberus, one of her brightest analysts.

"Aaron, we don't know. He was far more alert than he should have been in the torture video. Every day we delay is likely to reduce the probability of his survival."

A knock on the door provided an unexpected interruption. A hesitant PA opened the door and said, "Maeve, I have a call from Anna. I think you should take it."

Maeve reached out for the cell phone. She waited for her PA to leave.

"Yes, Anna?"

She listened for a few seconds. "Hold on, I'll put you on speaker. I have Helen and Linda, plus our three senior deputies in the room. Go ahead."

"Something happened? What was it? Niland said it was Schmidt. Is he okay?"

Maeve said, "It was a bomb of some kind. Schmidt's out of action for possibly a week. Someone attacked his apartment. We're meeting now to determine what we should do. I have to report to the president later."

There was silence for half a minute. "Damn."

"That's our reaction, too."

"Please—please let us know when Schmidt recovers," Anna said.

Maeve said, "Yes, we will, I promise. We'll carry on with our meeting. I'll call you after I've spoken with the president."

"Thank you. All of you, thanks. Mark will appreciate your efforts, as will we."

Maeve disconnected and turned her attention to the other attendees. "The questions now are whether we think we should delay Mark's rescue and whether there are alternative actions we can recommend to the president. Will Mark survive for another week, if it takes that long for Schmidt to recover? Do we recommend that the president appoints another general to take Schmidt's role, or do we think it's sensible to wait until he is well enough to lead the rescue efforts? What do you say?"

"What if O'Hare discovers we know he's holding Mark?" questioned Helen.

Maeve said, "I think we will be here for a while, trying to examine what ifs. Keep them sensible. Let's see where it goes. I'll go around the table. Linda?"

Chapter 36

O'Hare cursed. He cursed Schmidt, he cursed the apartment building, he cursed the drone pilot, and he cursed himself. Schmidt, he was willing to curse anytime. The apartment building because he'd wanted to do more damage, to remind Schmidt who was in control. The drone pilot, just because. And himself, likewise—he wasn't certain this venture was heading down the path he'd planned. O'Hare knew, without doing any research, that the finance issue with the helicopter could be laid directly at Schmidt's door. Also, while he didn't know how the man had achieved it, Zarina's arrest and disappearance into the bowels of DHS and subsequent transfer to some MP outfit could only be attributed to Schmidt.

O'Hare fumed. He paced the floor of his study, back and forth, back and forth. He was so close. His dreams of a fortune were only weeks away. His dreams of revenge on Schmidt seemed more difficult to realize. Also, Cromarty was chasing him. He'd committed to visit the man at his home in New York State. He missed his regular transport method. He could rent, ask Cromarty to send his chopper, or he could drive. He decided to drive; it was only an hour or so to travel. He was not looking forward to the meeting.

Cromarty frowned at O'Hare as he opened his door. "What

the hell is wrong with you?" he snarled. "I'm in more trouble than you realize and you're missing. What do you think I pay you for?"

O'Hare raised his hand. "Don't. You think you have problems?"

Cromarty threw his cheroot out the door and pulled it closed. "Come."

O'Hare followed him to the grandiose room Cromarty called a study. It was large enough to house two families, he thought. He sat in the chair nearest the door. It was a subconscious seeking of an emergency exit. He watched Cromarty select another cheroot and carefully light it. The puff of smoke did not reach him.

"So what's your story?" Cromarty blew another puff of smoke. It also failed to reach O'Hare.

"Disasters. Chopper's off—waiting on its annual checkup." He decided not to mention the mortgage repayment notice.

"I saw a news item on cable news. Someone tried to assassinate an army general. Schmidt, I think his name is. Know anything about that?"

"No, not a thing. Did they say what happened? How badly he was hurt?"

"Not a mention of any details. The authorities apparently suspect it was a terrorist attack. I'm not sure where the news anchors get their information from. So it wasn't you?"

O'Hare shook his head. "No."

Cromarty stubbed out his half-smoked cheroot. "What else is happening?"

"Nothing. Where's Grovers?"

"Home, I suspect. I thought this meeting should be only you and me. I'm disappointed in you."

"I've had some critical calls on my time." He wasn't going to give details; that would weaken his position.

"Same here. We could help each other, co-operate. It could ease our mutual problems."

"Not sure you can assist with Agency issues."

"What about your missing Russian lady friend?"

Shit, thought O'Hare, how did he connect those dots? "Not sure I'm following you."

The expression on Cromarty's face was triumphant. "Zarina—Zarina Gorky? Doesn't the name ring a bell? She has a green card, obtained, it seems, under false pretenses."

O'Hare shrugged. "I've heard about her. Where did you dig up that snippet of data?"

"I have my contacts. Now what can you do to help me with my issues?"

"You need to be more precise."

Cromarty thumped the top of his desk. "I'm about to be investigated for breaching banking sanctions! I understand the Senate Banking Committee has been given a complete paper trail. It's a bloody mess and you're not fucking helping."

"Ross, calm down. How can I disrupt a Senate inquiry? Think it through—work out how to soften the results." He knew he was treading on thin ice. "Come clean, plead insanity or something." As soon as the words left his lips, he cursed himself. Stress was undermining his caution. Normally he would never had said that to Cromarty.

The man exploded. O'Hare had never seen such a display of unrestrained temper. Or, he thought, perhaps it was fear of what would happen to him when the Committee's decision was published. Cromarty threw his pen set including its glass inkwell, apparently full, across the room. Ink blotched the white patterned wallpaper and ran down the wall in fine black streams. He picked up the brass reading lamp, pulled out the power plug and threw it. His aim was off—it missed O'Hare by three or four feet.

O'Hare protested. "Ross, stop it. You need to relax, think this through." He stood, undecided whether to leave or move towards Cromarty, perhaps to restrain the man. His natural inclination was fight, not flight.

Cromarty shouted, "Relax? Relax? How can I bloody relax? This is why I employed you and that useless general." He drew a deep breath. "To help me resolve embarrasing issues. You're both bloody hopeless. You can't even deal with Schmidt, let alone Chaborz." He looked around, possibly seeking something else to throw.

O'Hare now was extremely worried. Cromarty was not supposed to know anything about Dr. Chaborz. He cursed under his breath. Cromarty snatched a sword off the wall behind his desk and waved it, his temper unabated. He stumbled over a chair beside his desk and headed for O'Hare. The weapon was a Japanese Katana, the blade about two feet long, and O'Hare was unable to determine whether it had a decorative edge or was fully sharpened.

He rushed Cromarty, blocking the man's wild swing of the sword. He grabbed his wrist and bent his arm back, forcing Cromarty to drop the sword. Cromarty backed off and went back to his desk. He snapped open a drawer and pulled out a handgun. He fumbled as he released the safety catch and tried to aim it. O'Hare jumped over the chair between them and grabbed the man's fist. He was stronger than Cromarty even though the man was fueled by rage. He forced Cromarty's fist backwards while avoiding ill-aimed kicks and ignoring wild, one-handed blows.

When the pistol was pointed towards Cromarty's temple—he guessed it was seven inches or so away—he forced Cromarty to pull the trigger. The explosion, close to his own ear, temporarily deafened him. Cromarty fell to the floor, dropping the weapon. O'Hare bent down and checked for a pulse. As far as he could determine, Cromarty was dead. He stood, his face pale, his hands trembling. It took him a moment or two to steady his nerves. He had touched barely anything in the room. Cromarty hadn't even offered him a drink. He wiped the chair arms where he had sat. He used his handkerchief to prevent fingerprints and picked up the Katana, wiped it, and hung it back on the wall. He left the pen stand and the brass desk lamp where they had fallen.

He had visited this house a number of times in the past so he did not need to wipe away all possible fingerprints; a room totally devoid of fingerprints in itself would generate questions.

The blowback of the shot fired into Cromarty's skull had left powder burns on his hand and jacket. He was certain he could feel blood, bone fragments, and brains splattered on his face and there was something in his eye. He shuddered. He could not afford the time to wash before he left. Using the bathroom would create the risk of leaving some thread of evidence that would undo the suicide scenario he had established.

It was time he left. The house, he hoped, was empty; at least no one had come to investigate the sound of the shot. Cromarty would not have so openly allowed his temper to display if any family members were in residence. He was thankful he had not arrived in his helicopter—the noise of its arrival and departure would have alerted neighbors, which he could ill afford. He headed out of the house, closing the front doors.

He sat in his car realizing he had a two-hour drive in front of him, during which he could not afford to be stopped for any traffic offense. Not for any reason at all. He could imagine a police officer shining a flashlight onto his face and asking "Sir, why is there blood on your face?"

He could not cease his incessant worrying all the way to his home.

He would need to arrange an alibi.

General Grovers hit the replay button on the security camera. Cromarty had wanted to meet with him after his discussion with O'Hare and had told him to park his vehicle, an SUV, around the side of the house and to wait in the security control room located at the rear of the house. Intrigued, Grovers had turned on the security camera in Cromarty's study. After O'Hare's arrival, he had watched the unfolding drama with total disbelief. He knew nothing about the Senate inquiry. He had flinched when Cromarty threw his pen and inkwell set. Likewise the brass lamp. He had jumped up when Cromarty grabbed the Katana and wildly attacked O'Hare. He eased back into his chair when the NSA agent disarmed their angry boss. He started to move towards the door when Cromarty pulled out his handgun. He sat slowly back down when O'Hare struggled with Cromarty and—as far as Grovers could determine—forced Cromarty to shoot himself in the head. He watched in utter disbelief as O'Hare cleaned possible fingerprints off the chair he had been sitting in. He began to breathe again when O'Hare left Cromarty's office, only to stop breathing as he wondered if O'Hare was aware of the security room. He waited, his handgun pointed at the door. No one came to the room. After ten minutes, he holstered the weapon. His hands were shaking.

Grovers pulled the tape cassette from the deck and weighed it in his hand. It felt light, given its contents. He slotted the cassette into a separate player and pressed play. He skimmed the tape forward. Satisfied, he ejected the cassette and dropped it into his briefcase. He unconsciously emulated O'Hare and wiped the chair and equipment clean of his fingerprints.

Life suddenly was both interesting and of extremely high risk. He had not felt his pulse race as fast since Iraq.

Chapter 37

Harry, Maeve's PA, knocked tentatively on her office door. She was reading reports and he was always reluctant to interrupt her when she had that frown on her face.

"Yes, Harry?"

"Ma'am, I have a strange situation."

"Go on."

"Someone from the British Embassy—that is, he says he's their Assistant Defence Attaché. He wants to speak with whoever is in charge. Colonel Davis, Colin Davis."

"Put the call though to me."

Harry disappeared and a moment later Maeve's desk phone chimed. "Yes?"

"Colonel Davis, ma'am." The phone clicked as the connection activated.

"This is Maeve Donnelly."

"Aah—Ms Donnelly. I'm Colonel Davis—that is, I'm Colonel Colin Davis, Assistant Defence Attaché at the British Embassy."

The caller had a strong English accent; it sounded theatrical, thought Maeve. She said, "Yes, Colonel?"

"Ma'am, would you care to call back and request you be connected to me? To verify I'm with the embassy."

Intrigued, Maeve said, "I'll do that. Give me a minute or two."

The colonel disconnected and Maeve looked at the telephone handset, frowning. Why would the Brits want to talk to her?

"Harry," she called.

"Yes ma'am?"

"I want the—"

"I have it here." He handed Maeve a Post-It with the British Embassy's telephone number.

Maeve used her cell phone and called the number Harry had provided. Eventually, after coping with inadequate messages and instructions, she succeeded in connecting to the earlier caller.

"Colonel Davis."

"Maeve Donnelly."

"Ah, good. Please accept my apologies, Ms. Donnelly, for the roundabout contact. However, I thought if you called back, at least you would know I was located at the embassy."

"Indeed. What can I do for you?"

"We've been informed, in the last hour, that six of our citizens are about to arrive in Washington to visit with you. Three are serving Army officers and three are civilians."

Maeve frowned. She did not know any British Army officers.

The Assistant Defence Attaché, apparently not expecting a reply, continued, "My call is because of the three officers, a Colonel Evelyn Hudson and Lieutenants Thomas Young and Laura Allen. The three civilians—I only have their first names—Owen, Lewis and Carys. I believe they're Welsh." His tone was disdainful. He continued, "The Army personnel are on official leave from their posting in Germany."

"I think I know who the three civilians are, and I have an idea about the three officers. They haven't contacted me, though."

"The only data I've received is a couple of words. Cerberus and Midway. Do they mean anything to you?"

Maeve laughed. "Yes, you've confirmed why they are

visiting me. I assume you know of my involvement in Cerberus US?"

"Yes, Ms. Donnelly, our embassy is aware of your organization."

Maeve thought that was probably an understatement. "Midway is the chief executive for Cerberus UK."

"We were not aware of that. I must say, Colonel Hudson has an extraordinarily positive record and her soldiers are well regarded. We'd appreciate you informing us if you experience any issues."

"Colonel, if the people are who I think they are—and I'm confident I'm correct—I do not expect any difficulties. We have common interests and welcome their visit."

Maeve could detect the sense of relief from the British officer. "Excellent. My boss, Brigadier Crichton, was uncertain as to their reception. When fellow officers unexpectedly travel into our areas of responsibilities, we like to be aware of the wheres and whyfores, you understand."

"Yes. Now, do you have arrival times, any travel details?"

"We understand they're arriving this evening. Their flight—it's a private jet—is expected to land at nineteen hundred hours."

"If you can email details, we'll arrange to meet the aircraft."

"Excellent. Thank you, Ms. Donnelly." He provided his contact details including his direct line and cell phone numbers. Maeve did likewise, including her email address.

After the call ended, she phoned Schmidt. While he was under doctor's orders, he was mobile and working. She provided details of her discussion with the British colonel.

"Red carpet welcome?" Schmidt questioned.

"Oh, definitely. I have some ICE contacts and they'll help our visitors clear Immigration and Customs. Can Helen provide transport and an escort?"

"I'll contact her. Do you know—okay, I'll arrange their hotel and we'll meet them there. I'll move to the same hotel;

that will make transport easier to arrange. Be prepared for a late night."

"What about you? Are you well enough? Perhaps the Brits can help?" Maeve continued to worry that Mark was still undergoing the torture regime portrayed in the video.

"Of course I'm capable, even if I'm not on duty. I expect it will be a day or two more before I get my clearance." Schmidt's proposal to lead the flight to Gitmo was suspended until he received a full medical clearance. He needed to be on that flight.

Maeve met Schmidt at the Four Seasons Hotel on Pennsylvania Avenue, where their visitors had checked in forty or so minutes prior. Schmidt was still shaky from the injuries he'd received in the explosion; according to his medical report he should still be in bed, recovering. He had earlier reserved a small meeting room and he asked the concierge for directions. The man led them to the room, which was guarded by a small team of MPs in plain clothes. Refreshments were set out on a table and sideboard, and six people were already in the room, waiting for them.

Maeve looked at the person she assumed was Colonel Hudson. "Colonel?"

"Maeve? Call me Evelyn. It's a pleasure to meet you."

"Likewise. This is Archimedes Schmidt."

The British colonel turned to Schmidt and said, "General. It's also a pleasure to meet you. Let me introduce everyone. Lieutenant Laura Allen, Lieutenant Thomas Young, and Owen, Lewis and Carys—all friends of Mark Midway."

The following five minutes were a mix of accents and introductions and welcomes.

"Did you have a good flight?" Maeve asked.

"Oh, yes," Owen said. "We had a Cerberus company jet. It was marvelous."

Evelyn Hunter agreed, "It was comfortable. I was fortunate; the captain on the flight over is instructor-rated and he let me add some hours on type, including two takeoffs and landings." She explained when she saw Schmidt's expression. "I'm a pilot. Bit of a varied career. I went to Sandhurst with a Masters in Aeronautical Engineering, and the Army lent me to the RAF for a while."

"Evelyn's a good pilot," added Carys. "We didn't feel any bumps when we landed."

"I didn't know UK had a corporate jet?" Schmidt was curious.

Colonel Hunter explained, "It was originally purchased for the late Chairman. No one else has used it. Lewis, Owen, and Carys created quite a fuss with Cerberus UK management. The Board was also concerned at the lack of communication from Mark. I think—to keep our three Welsh friends quiet—Cerberus UK offered to fly them to Germany where we are based. I'd previously agreed with Owen that something was wrong. They arrived in Stuttgart ready to travel and convinced me of the urgency. It's an experience, dealing with these three."

Owen looked as though he was about to object and sat back when Carys tugged his arm.

Maeve asked, "Let's get down to the burning question— why are you here in the US?"

Colonel Hudson looked towards the three Welsh siblings. "Owen? Do you want to answer?"

"Yes, Colonel. Maeve, we're here because of Mark. We know he's in danger somewhere and no one has informed us—Cerberus UK or anyone—what's going on. So, we want to know, we want to see Anna, and we want to ensure Mark is safe; rescue him if need be."

Maeve wondered at the lack of communication. Schmidt had taken on the task of informing Cerberus UK, and she thought he had done that.

Schmidt said, "Well, you're welcome to join in with us.

Yes, you're correct. He was kidnapped. Please accept my apologies for my communication failure. We've been totally focused on finding Mark. We believe we know where he is. We're planning his rescue. There is some confusion; we seem to be making enemies as we go."

"I knew it," exclaimed Lewis. He turned to his two companions. "I said it was dangerous, that someone was out to capture or kill Mark."

Evelyn Hunter said, "Enemies?"

"In addition to Mark's kidnapper, we've traces of foreign terrorists showing an interest. Either Russians or Chechens," Schmidt replied. "The kidnapper—at least we think it was the kidnapper—tried to blow up my apartment two days ago, with me in it."

"We're mounting an operation to rescue him. The terrorists are compounding our issues," Maeve added. "We think two Chechens, refugees, were checking out Mark's apartment a few days ago. We've additional security protecting Anna and the children."

Evelyn nodded her head, "I understand."

"What details do you have of Mark's kidnapping?" the British colonel asked.

Everyone looked at Schmidt. He said, "We have videos. Too many videos. Maeve brought files and her computer. We'll run them through for you. It will take up to an hour."

Schmidt's estimate was optimistic. The related discussions added another thirty minutes.

Schmidt concluded, "That's why we believe he's being held somewhere in Gitmo. I should be cleared tomorrow for active duty. The 145th is preparing to mount a rescue operation—I'll lead it." He looked around at the travel weary visitors. "We've probably done all we can, tonight. Tomorrow morning we'll take you to meet with Anna and the children."

"Yes, please," agreed Colonel Hudson. "An early start?"

"We can leave at any time you wish," Schmidt said.

"It'd be more efficient if we fly to Boston? Our plane's available; we've a relief crew."

Schmidt asked, "Do you have room for additional passengers?"

"We can manage three or four."

"I'll join you and bring two MPs. We may need extra security. Maeve, do you want to join us?"

"I'll stay. Report in when you have news."

Schmidt ended the meeting, aware the three Welsh teenagers—at least he thought they were teenagers—wanted to phone Anna and the children. He had not asked how these members of the small delegation had known of Mark's kidnap and danger; that was a topic he intended to explore during the flight to Boston.

"There's something wrong, here," said Owen later, as they sat in his hotel room after a long phone discussion with Anna, Gabrielle, and Niland. The latter two had scarcely constrained their excitement on hearing from the visitors. Owen's brother and sister waited for him to continue.

"Mark's not in Guantánamo. He's somewhere north of here, not south. We know—we—all of us—can sense him. Mark's coded message was wrong. The kidnapper has tricked him somehow. Schmidt was meant to get a false message. He and his MPs are being set up—Gitmo is a trap."

"When we get together with Niland and Gabrielle, we'll be stronger," said Carys. "We'll know."

"Yes. The five of us—with perhaps the addition of the Army types—Thomas and Laura's talents are strong—we'll soon confirm Mark's location," Lewis said.

"Don't discount Evelyn. While she's post-Cerberus, she has a lot of power, too."

"Plus Anna. With all of us working together, we'll find Mark," concluded Owen.

Chapter 38

Mark was feeling stronger. His repeated intakes of food—far more than Emma had proposed—were providing fuel for the nanites working to repair his body. He had checked after his shower; he was still gaunt-looking, his eyes were not near as bloodshot, and he was in dire need of a shave. He was recovering.

Emma commented when he returned to her small office. "Your recovery rate is impressive."

Mark shrugged. She had not permitted him to exit the CHU, and he persevered with the two rooms and this long hallway she now was using as an office. As a result, there was little he could do to increase his range of exercises. He was not yet ready to challenge and overcome the guards who she said were on duty outside the unit.

"There are always guards on duty; they're stationed within ten or twenty yards. There are more further away. If they see you outside, they'll sound an alarm and possibly shoot you."

Realizing he wasn't bulletproof, Mark didn't push the issue. Emma brought him hot food as and when he required. There was no way she could make him return to the autopsy table; that would require weapons and muscle, lots of both. Or drugs. He was confident he could cope with the latter. His body was now aware and conditioned against the various chemicals that she had used in his torture. He was in waiting mode as the nanites rebuilt his body.

Another day would see him far more restless and willing to take risks. Surely, at night for example, there would be times when the guards would be less alert, their attention not as focused? Lack of a weapon was an issue, though. Emma no longer had her handgun, or so she said. He planned on searching the office in its entirety when she left for the evening, to discover what he could utilize for attack or defense. In the meantime he exercised; it was the only way he could think of to help the nanites with their repair tasks.

Emma left the small facility at five o'clock. She kept regular office hours and would be back precisely at nine in the morning. She had earlier returned with three meals from what she called the mess facility, enough to last him until breakfast, which she would bring when she returned in the morning. He filled in an hour, watching the news channel on the small office television set with the volume low. If anyone outside heard the sound they should assume Emma had neglected to turn it off before departing for the day. The external telephone did not work—he had tested it a number of times while Emma was outside. His search had revealed nothing he could use as a serious weapon. Scissors, drugs, and needles were the most effective items on hand; however, it would be difficult to inject a guard with drugs. Eventually, he managed to sleep.

Mark suffered another day of boredom and eating. Emma visited only to deliver meals, with little discussion. She appeared fearful, as though she was worried about either releasing him or some requirement of O'Hare's. She would not explain or clarify, no matter how much influence Mark brought to bear. She was surprisingly able to withstand his pressure. He wondered whether she was naturally immune or perhaps her training allowed her to devise defensive routines.

Emma returned late in the day, well after her normal time for closing down her office. She was pale and shaking. When she closed the heavy metal door, she checked that it was securely locked.

"There's something happening," she said in response to Mark's question. "I—I don't know what it is. There seems to be a pending threat of some kind."

"You're being vague," Mark suspected some trap of O'Hare's making. He suggested, "Probably your boss."

"No, I haven't heard from him for a couple of days, which is odd."

"He might've found another girlfriend."

"No—don't try to agitate me. He has dozens of girlfriends; it's how he operates."

At least, thought Mark, she had no false illusions about her boss. "Tell me why you are afraid."

"Afraid? No. Yes. I suppose."

"Tell me."

"I can't put it into words."

Their discussion was interrupted by a vigorous hammering on the steel door that provided entry into the modified CHU. Emma jumped. Mark was certain she had grown paler.

She said, "No one's ever done that before."

"Are you certain there's no telephone facility here?"

"Yes. I don't have my cell phone. The landline's been disconnected for a few days. I don't know why."

The hammering resumed, louder, longer. Mark could hear voices. Neither he nor Emma spoke until after the hammering ceased.

Finally Mark said, "Do you have any idea why someone should be hammering on the door? Is O'Hare up to something?"

Emma shook her head. She was biting her bottom lip. Mark thought if she clenched her mouth any tighter, she'd start to bleed. He estimated five minutes had passed since the first hammering session. Emma began to say something, and Mark held up his hand, stopping her before the words formed. Another five minutes passed, straining his patience. Of course, this CHU didn't have windows. It had heavy metal doors. Two of them. He was staring at one.

"Where's the other door?" Mark spoke softly.

Emma pointed over his shoulder. Mark, as silently as he could, turned around. The corridor, narrow and long, stretched most of the length of the CHU; about forty feet, he estimated. He walked quietly to the far end. There was another door; it apparently provided egress from the housing unit. He checked the door. As far as he could determine, it was controlled by a single handle that was locked by two levered bars inserted into slots at floor and ceiling level. There was also a Yale-type lock. It would require a major effort to overcome the lock mechanism from the outside. He returned to where Emma was waiting. He checked that door. It too had a levered locking system, which was in the closed position. He looked at Emma and shrugged.

"Are there any windows? Other access?"

She shook her head. "No."

Mark considered the situation. Emma did not know who was trying to attract their attention or gain entry to the CHU. He doubted it was O'Hare. He also doubted it was someone coming to his rescue. Conclusion: whoever, they implied danger. At least, for him. He had two doors. If there were only two people, one on each door, he could exit and overpower that person. Perhaps. If there were two people at the door when he exited, the overpowering result might be reversed. It was like playing chess blindfolded, without knowing the moves permitted by the pieces.

He drew Emma away from the door. "What made you afraid, earlier, when you came back here?"

She was still biting her lip. "I—I don't know. I think— there were guards, but they weren't the regular guards."

Mark frowned. This was Gitmo, a military base. Guards were guards. Navy, Army, whatever. "How could the guards be different—they're all military?"

She drew blood.

"I asked—how could the guards be different?"

"I—It was the way they looked at me."

"How many were there? Hundreds? One? Two?"

"Here, at this CHU?"

"Yes." He was starting to lose patience.

"Only two."

"And in the rest of the NSA section of the facility?"

"Only two."

Mark examined his torturer with intense curiosity. He held her hand, the one without the knotted handkerchief. "Where are we?"

He saw a mental image of a sign—it read Gitmo. "No, tell me where we are?"

'He'll kill me, he really will."

Mark thought, that makes two of us with the same intent. He stared into Emma's eyes as he fed a memory of the pain he had endured on the autopsy table. She screamed and her knees buckled. He held her up by the elbow.

"No, don't. Don't. I'm sorry. So sorry." She wept, tears running unheeded down her face.

"Again, tell me where we are."

"This unit is called Gitmo."

"Where?" He grabbed her shoulders and shook her. "Where are we?"

"I can't tell you."

Mark shook her again. "Can't or won't?" He was not gentle.

"He'll kill me."

She collapsed to the floor, sobbing hysterically.

Outside, the hammering resumed.

Chapter 39

Schmidt, before he managed to get to bed, called Julian Kelly, the majority stockholder in RDEz. It did not take long for him to persuade Julian to purchase the empty apartment in the building where he and Mark had their apartments. There was an empty floor on the level below Mark and Anna.

"It's a good investment," Schmidt said. "I'll be able to use it when I visit. For now, we've got six people arriving in the morning and they'll want to be near Anna and the children. Tell your realtor friend we want it and hand him a bank draft for immediate possession. We can find someone to furnish it. We'll add some temporary bunks and sleeping bags.Three of the visitors are British Army; they won't mind roughing it. The teenagers should be able cope with temporary accommodation—they're triplets—engaging, with hidden depths, I'd say. Yes, genetically modified, but not Cerberus. Same people who designed Mark and his sister, I suspect, or at least the same process. I'll call you when we touch down—well before midday, I expect."

That night he slept fitfully. His dreams were elusive and foreboding. He could not focus on the details and woke the next morning with a headache and an increasing awareness of danger that appeared to be threatening him and somehow it included Mark. He cursed. He was still unfit and, being realistic, knew it would be at least a week before he would be medically cleared for duty. He shook his head. He couldn't send Bravo Company and Major Chouan off on what was effectively a major military raid without his presence. It was not that he lacked confidence in the major; rather, he needed to be the officer in charge. SECDEF would not agree to anything else.

Schmidt joined the visitors in the hotel lobby; two MPs had arrived earlier, and everyone was ready to travel. Drivers and vehicles—three SUVs—were waiting and in less than five minutes the small convoy was on the way to Dulles International airport. It was 8:00 a.m. and the visitors, apparently suffering from jet lag, sat quietly. Schmidt was traveling with the three British officers while the three Welsh teenagers were in the second SUV. Their MP escorts were in the third vehicle. Fortunately, the road trip was uneventful.

He watched with humor as Owen and his younger siblings settled into the comfortably cushioned aircraft seats and fastened their seatbelts. They were obviously enjoying the luxury of flying in a private jet. They ordered coffee from the cabin attendant and after a minute or so, it seemed the caffeine worked; there was a buzz of conversation, although in soft tones. Schmidt was seated across the aisle and next to Colonel Hudson. The two lieutenants were seated in the block behind the teenagers.

"Swmpus," said Lewis. "We need to do this more often."

"You'll need plenty of dosh," chided Calrys.

"I can write some more apps," volunteered Owen.

Schmidt turned his attention to Colonel Hudson. "I suspect they'll provide a challenge as they get older."

"It's already happening. They have survived a difficult upbringing; I'm impressed with their abilities and behavior. They applied strong pressure on Cerberus management and on me. They weren't accepting a refusal from anyone. It was like facing a battering ram. They were extremely concerned about Mark and were worried that no one knew anything. I wanted to contact Donnelly before we left; however, they were worried that the problem might have been at the Cerberus US level. They can be suspicious, at times. The welcome treatment when we arrived helped allay that concern."

Schmidt said, "It was my oversight. I called the directors last night to apologize. I should've informed the UK organization, I admit. It's been hectic. You've seen our videos. O'Hare is our candidate; however, we only have circumstantial evidence. We've reviewed Mark's message with attorneys and the consensus is we need evidence that's more specific. A series of finger movements in a video is not enough, they say."

"Pity. You haven't uncovered other links?"

"We think it was O'Hare's helicopter that was used to take Mark from the highway. Only part of the aircraft registration was visible and we don't have enough evidence for solid identification. His pilot was somewhere in the Caribbean and the flight log for the aircraft shows it was unused during the week he was away. The shooter—the person who is being charged with Mark's kidnap—is under arrest. He claims it was an FBI black op. He didn't meet the pilot, says he doesn't know who it was—he wore a helmet and it covered most of his face. Again, it's that lack of certainty." Schmidt's hand shook as he reached for the glass of orange juice delivered by the cabin attendant. He cursed at his apparent weakness; the shock of the explosion should've worn off by now.

Evelyn Hudson didn't seem to notice. She sipped her juice.

"What are your next steps?"

"After we arrange accommodation for you and your lieutenants? You can visit with Anna and the children— you've met them before?"

"Oh yes. Some of my soldiers wanted to guard them against the Chairman, when he was trying to kill Mark. That was awkward. The Chairman grabbed me, held me hostage, and forced my people to retreat. I don't think they've forgiven themselves."

"Well motivated, it seems."

"Yes." She sipped again.

"There's something wrong—we've changed course. This isn't the direction for Boston," Schmidt said, an element of tension in his voice. The jet had banked and was heading more easterly, towards New York

He pressed the call button. The cabin attendant was at his side in seconds. "Yes, sir?" She had a Scottish lilt to her voice, Schmidt noted. Her name tag read Heather Jones.

"We've changed our direction. Can you find out why?"

"Certainly. I won't be a moment."

She disappeared forward of the passenger area. All conversation had stopped in the cabin. After a couple of minutes one of the pilots walked down the cabin; the three rings on his jacket sleeve identified him as the co-pilot. He stopped beside Schmidt.

"General? You have a question?" He had a strong English accent. He did not appear to be aware of the hush in the cabin.

"Yes. You've changed course? Can you tell me what's happening?"

The co-pilot laughed. "Sir, Boston is still fogged in. ATC is holding back private flights in order to give priority to commercial flights, so we'll be in this pattern for a while. It could be twenty minutes or so before they allow us to continue." He addressed the avid listeners in the seats on either side of the aisle. "You'll have an opportunity to see some good views of New York. We'll probably stay five or ten miles north, to keep out of the way of the busier flight paths." He looked back at Schmidt. "General, is there anything else I can do for you?"

Schmidt acknowledged the details with a half salute. "No, thanks. You've covered what I wanted to know."

The co-pilot smiled and made his way back to the cockpit, stopping on the way to talk to the cabin attendant.

"He was one of your pilots on the trip from Europe?" Schmidt asked Colonel Hudson.

"No." She shook her head. "I didn't see him. We had a captain and a co-pilot on the flight deck and another two in the cabin, so as not to have issues with hours and rest time. The two spares sat in the back, behind curtains, and slept. Both were Kiwis—New Zealanders. The two pilots on duty— we met them briefly when we boarded in Stuttgart—were Aussies. This Heather Jones—the cabin attendant—is also new." She frowned.

Schmidt said. "So we've departed from our course and have at least one pilot not on your flight. I need to make some calls."

The conversations in the cabin had resumed, although at a noticeably subdued level. Schmidt called Linda Schöner. He listened to her latest reports and made minor suggestions. He said, "You've been managing the team for months, and I agree, I don't need to micro-manage you. These are minor issues and I fully delegate the decision-making to you." He listened. "Yes, refer the major items—you know, if someone has declared war and you think I should know. Now, I have a small task for one of your team. Contact the pilots who flew in yesterday—the Cerberus UK people. They're staying at the Marriott. Yes, that's the one. See if they are comfortable, all accounted for and so forth. I have a twitch and could be totally in error. Yes, we're in the aircraft now, on our way to Boston. Yes, you've got it. Strangers. Call me back as soon as you have an answer."

Colonel Hudson had listened intently to the call. "We do tend to over-react, once we encounter enough adverse events." She raised her hand. "No, I don't disagree. It's worth checking, given the current circumstances. All our crew coming over were Cerberus—the two people we've seen so far have no Cerberus structure that I can discern."

"My two can get ready, in case we need a safety factor." Schmidt made his way towards the rear of the cabin to talk to the two soldiers from the 145th. He knew them both and sat in the opposite rear-facing seat.

"Good morning, General," said Corporal Winton.

"Sophie," acknowledged Schmidt. He thought the private was slightly nervous, confronted by the top brass. He looked at the soldier.

"Sir, General. I'm sorry—uff." The corporal nudged him ungently in the ribs. "Sorry. Good morning, General."

"Good morning. Mike, isn't it?"

"Y-Yes, sir. Michael Perez."

"We're still training him, General. Although in his defense, he's one of our best unarmed combat people; he regularly defeats even Sergeant Rodriguez, and I think he is good."

"Praise indeed, Sophie. You both brought weapons?"

"Yes, sir. Handguns in our briefcases; something heavier packed away in the hold."

"Still expert marksman status?"

"Oh yes, sir. You have something for us?"

"I don't know, yet. I want you both to get your weapons. Be inconspicuous. When you're armed, go forward to the door into the flight deck. Wait there. No one is to exit or enter the cockpit. Sophie, I'd like you to check out the cabin attendant. All three—pilot, co-pilot, and attendant—are new, and they're not Cerberus. We weren't expecting strangers. No fuss, now. Use your best crowd control technique—don't let them realize they're being controlled. Understood?"

Both replied in unison. "Yes, sir."

"Good. I'm waiting on a call from the office—our concerns may be unwarranted. I'll stand you both down if that's the case. Let me get back to my seat and then you can proceed."

Schmidt returned to his seat next to Colonel Hudson. He smiled at the two British lieutenants as he made his way back. "Relax. Business as usual," he said, loud enough for both them and the three teenagers to hear. "Prudent precautions, is all."

Three minutes after Schmidt sat back down, the two MPs made their way to the front of the cabin. Schmidt waited patiently for Linda's phone call. The chatter behind him resumed at a normal level; however, Schmidt could discern a lack of focus in the conversations. Everyone waited.

Chapter 40

General Grovers had utilized a favor owed for a past deed. As a result, a Defense Courier Division courier was standing at his door, waiting for a small package. The DCD's mission included the provision of secure and timely delivery of sensitive military material, and he considered the security camera tape of O'Hare and Cromarty's struggle represented exactly that, although it had required an extra favor to obtain door-to-door service. He slid the cassette into the courier-provided envelope. It was addressed to Maeve Donnelly. The documents contained the sender and recipient details; there was no hiding that he was the sender. He sealed the envelope and handed it and the signed forms to the courier and, in turn, was handed a time-stamped copy in receipt. The tape would reach Maeve some time through the day. His contact had arranged a One Time Authorization for Maeve, which undoubtedly had bemused her when she had received the letter. The courier would validate her identity and the existence of the letter as part of his process to authorize delivery. He could imagine the reactions of both Maeve and her team, and of Schmidt, when she communicated the contents of the tape to him.

Today, one way or another, was going to be memorable for a number of people, for a number of reasons. He waited for the courier to return to his vehicle and as the soldier drove off, closed his front door. He changed out of his uniform into a scruffy pair of jeans and a causal shirt. He added loafers, a light jacket and a Redskins cap. He checked his cash; he didn't need to visit a cash machine—there was enough for his needs for the next few hours. His cell phone was in an inside pocket. He checked himself in the hall mirror. The image reflected a casual, non-official, and seemingly harmless appearance. He lifted the backpack that had taken him a couple of days to prepare. Its weight was more than he had estimated; however, it was necessary for the furtherance of his plan. He tucked his SIG SAUER P238 Desert into its holster and checked it was secure and hidden by his jacket. Finally, he dropped two seven-round magazines into his jacket pockets, one in each, and zipped them up.

The second taxi, following his short journey by MetroRail, left him half a block or so from the coffee shop usually frequented by O'Hare when he was intending to meet with the Saudi spymaster. Although he thought the Saudi was more a terrorist-master, or perhaps he was both. He planned to wait in a coffee shop further along the street until O'Hare was on his way to the carpet emporium.

He bought a coffee and sat down at a table with a window view. He turned on his cell phone, linked to the coffee shop's WiFi and checked his messages. O'Hare, according to the leader of the tracking team he had organized, was drinking his coffee. Based on his usual pattern, he would leave in fifteen minutes. Grovers sat back to wait for an update.

To the second, Grovers received a message that O'Hare was about to pass his coffee shop. Grovers lifted the newspaper he was reading in order to partially hide his face, on the off-chance O'Hare looked into the shop's interior. After O'Hare passed, he gathered his papers into a tidy pile, lifted the backpack onto his back, made some adjustments, and headed out the door. His tracker was a hundred yards or so in front; he had slowed his pace.

He murmured as Grovers caught up and passed him, "Usual place, usual time, as far as we can determine. Henry is in position."

"Good. I'll follow him, now," Grovers instructed.

The tracker half saluted and turned back, away from the direction O'Hare was heading. Grovers increased his pace until he managed to catch sight of his target. He slowed; he did not want O'Hare to realize he was being followed. Grovers paced along, occasionally stopping to check a shop window or look at messages on his cell phone. He saw O'Hare turn into the carpet emporium, Airyaman Persian Rugs. Grovers had a good idea of the layout and access into the area where O'Hare had his meetings with the Saudi doctor. His small team had done some valuable research.

He waited on the pavement a few yards away from the windows and entrance of the rug store, giving his target enough time to reach the elevator at the far end of the building. The subterranean walkway from the basement led into a building on the other side of the block. His small team had checked for an access from the other building and their recommendation was to enter the same way as O'Hare. He had listened to their reasoning and agreed. He entered the store.

The salesman and his two carpet handlers were showing carpets to a customer, unfolding and refolding large items as the customer at first showed interest and then disinterest. The customer was one of his team and his task was to distract the salesman and his helpers. Grovers slipped past the sales area, through the stockrooms, and headed to the back of the building. Old architectural plans had shown him and his team where an elevator had been installed; they assumed this was still in use, although a casual examination had not revealed its existence. The best guess—and Grovers hated guesses—was that the elevator was now disguised as a janitor's room.

He opened the door marked "Janitor," entered, and closed the door behind him. He stepped to the back wall. There was no door, no seam, no split in the wall structure that he could see. He tapped on the wall. After a moment, and to his utter surprise, a section of the wall slid open to reveal the interior of a small elevator. Ignoring the possibility of a trap, while aware that it was highly probable, he accepted the invitation. The door closed and without obvious command, the elevator began its descent.

Dr. Chaborz, when he heard the buzzing alarm, checked his security monitor. He smiled. He was going to enjoy this meeting with O'Hare, especially when Grovers also entered the office. He lifted the handset to the internal phone and spoke to one of his guards. The conversation was in Arabic

"Khasan, our friend O'Hare has a follower. Let him enter. Watch carefully in case he makes a move against me. I'm not worried about O'Hare. Understand?"

"Yes, Doctor. It shall be as you require."

"*Inshallah.*"

Chabortz sat back in his large comfortable office chair. He checked his handgun was in easy reach, under the desktop. He waited for the American agent.

Chabortz estimated he did not have enough time to go through the elaborate tea greeting before Grovers' arrival and decided to forego it. He was confident the American would not understand the insult. When O'Hare entered, he indicated one of the visitors' chairs that faced away from the door.

"Please sit. I apologize for my abruptness; however, I need to monitor my messages on the screen. Important things are happening." He waited for his visitor to seat himself. They exchanged small pleasantries for a few minutes.

Chabortz took the lead and asked, "What do you have to report?"

O'Hare shrugged. Chabortz thought the man appeared distracted. The American said, "Nothing further in regard to Schmidt, unfortunately."

"No? I thought you had that all under control?"

"So did I. The men with the drones were useless. Oh, the first drone, when they detonated the explosive, blew out Schmidt's window. That was okay. However, the second drone was far too close. It was caught in the shock wave and crashed. Fortunately, without detonating the explosives it carried. My—operatives—gathered up the wreckage and left before law enforcement arrived to check for the source of the attack."

Remembering a comment from their previous meeting, the doctor said, "Ah. I understand. Possibly the men were not highly skilled."

O'Hare ignored the jibe. Perhaps, thought Chabortz, he did not even recognize the source of his comment: O'Hare's own words now used against him.

His visitor continued, "In regard to Project ForeSight, I understand the first tranche is with the prince."

"Indeed, yes. Prince Khalid confirmed receipt with me, earlier this morning. He has a validation process underway. Its success or failure is one of the messages I'm waiting on."

"If his people know what they're doing, the process will be positive. I have arranged movement of the second tranche as agreed. I expect the next payment to be remitted, within the week." The next ten million dollars would flow in the same directions as the first payment.

"Of course, my dear friend, of course." Chabortz was watching the security display in the top right hand section of his computer screen. Grovers was approaching the office door. He waited for a moment to build the result he sought.

"What happened with Cromarty—how did you kill him?"

"No, of course I didn't—"

Grovers pushed open the door, interrupting O'Hare's attempt to claim innocence. Chabortz decided he did not understand Americans. The man should have claimed victory—the prince would have been generous.

Chabortz looked at the intruder and said, "General

Grovers, welcome. What can we do for you?" He watched as O'Hare looked to see who had entered the office. The man's face turned white, whether in anger or fear, Chabortz couldn't tell. He decided it was anger.

The doctor continued, "I should make some tea. Would you care to sit and join us?"

Grovers replied in Arabic. "Thank you for the courtesy, Dr. Chabortz, but not this time. The man I really wanted to see is here."

The general pointed at O'Hare, who was now standing, his body obviously tense. He backed away from Grovers, unknowingly, the doctor thought, towards his personal emergency exit.

By this time O'Hare had drawn a weapon; he held it ready although not yet aimed at Grovers.

The general said, "You did a good job with Cromarty. I congratulate you. The authorities are accepting the implied suicide."

"Don't be an idiot. I was miles away."

"I have a security video showing your actions. I liked the way you grappled with Cromarty and forced his pistol towards his head. The shot must have covered you in gore; I suspect blood and some of the man's brains splattered onto your face."

If it was possible, O'Hare's anger grew. He aimed his weapon at Grovers.

"You lie," he claimed. His voice was shrill.

Chabortz was experiencing total delight at the exchange. Then everything seemed to happen at once. O'Hare fired his weapon, the bullet striking Grovers in the chest. O'Hare turned and to Chabortz' surprise, rushed to the emergency exit. He forced the door open. Neither O'Hare nor the Saudi noticed that after Grovers fell, he seemed to struggle with a strap to his backpack.

The explosion forever stopped Chabortz from further enjoyment of the exchange. It ignited other charges set to destroy all records and evidence possibly related to the Saudi spymaster's activities. The result was total destruction of the office and most of the building. Bodies, unidentified and some unidentifiable, were recovered only when the building was declared safe.

Chapter 41

Schmidt's cell phone intruded into his thoughts.

"Schmidt."

It was Linda. "We checked. The crew who flew out from Europe are in hospital. They ate or drank something last night that might have been poisoned or at least drugged. They're recovering. We're waiting on toxicology for details. Looks like you need to take action."

"Planning for it. I'll contact you once we're in control. See if you can find anything about the replacements. Not sure where you'd start—maybe the operator who serviced the Cessna has details."

"Already on it. We'll let you know when we have more details. Good luck."

"Thanks. I think we're going to need it."

Schmidt turned his attention back to the front of the cabin. Corporal Sophie Winton eased the unconscious cabin attendant into a seat at the front of the cabin. Schmidt met her halfway; he had watched the confrontation as the corporal had held the attendant's hand. It was, he thought, a subtle form of questioning, with the victim falling unconscious when the intensity of the interrogation increased.

"What did you discover?"

"She isn't fully aware of their plans. She doesn't know

where they intend to land, although she has major concerns that they don't intend to take us to Boston. In other words—"

"A suicide flight."

The corporal nodded. "Yes, sir."

"Can you get access to the cockpit?"

"Three clicks on the intercom and the same number of knocks on the door."

"Let me brief the colonel and then we'll go ahead."

"Yes, sir." The soldier resumed her position at the front of the cabin and Schmidt returned to his seat.

"It may be a suicide flight—90% probability. My corporal has the code to gain entrance to the cockpit. We can take out the two pilots—leaves us in a jam, though, without pilots."

"Not altogether. I mentioned to you last night that I'm a pilot. I have over two thousand hours from my RAF service and my commercial license is current. I have three hundred as co-pilot on Hercules and the same on Gulfstreams. I landed this little beast on the way over; at Keflavik— Iceland's international airport where we stopped to refuel—and at Dulles. Under guidance of the captain, I'll admit. However, I'm confident I can handle the landing, once we find out where to go."

"Welcome news. Come with me, we'll have to do this quickly."

Entry to the cockpit was straightforward and fast. The co-pilot opened the door and when he saw the two MPs he grabbed for a weapon. Sophie shot him. She stepped forward and held her pistol to the neck of the captain. Evelyn followed, stepping over the body of the dead terrorist. She dropped into the co-pilot seat and said, "I have control."

The man sitting in the captain's seat had frozen when he heard the shot and saw the co-pilot's body fall. He held up his hands. Schmidt stood in the doorway and instructed the corporal, "If he twitches or looks sideways, shoot him."

"With pleasure, sir." Corporal Winton addressed the pilot. "You'll get out of your seat, very carefully. Don't even think about attacking me—there are two other pistols aimed at your head." One was in Perez' steady hand and the other was held by Schmidt. She stepped back, out of what she thought would be the pilot's reach even if he lunged at her, and monitored his moves with a total focus, forgetting to breath. The pilot appeared to have given up his objective, although Sophie was not convinced.

"Mike, get your ties out, quickly. You, put your hands behind your back. That's the only move you can make—anything else and it'll be your last. Mike, come on, tie his wrists together. Good. Pilot—whatever your name—walk into the cabin. Don't make any sudden moves. Stand next to the second seat on the left." Schmidt had moved backwards into the cabin, keeping a yard or so in front of the pilot. He held his handgun ready as the pilot followed the corporal's directions.

Sophie directed the private. "Mike, search him first. Empty his pockets, remove his belt." She watched as the soldier followed her instructions. She continued, "You, now sit down. Mike, tie his arms to the seat armrests." She looked at the pilot and smiled. "I know, it'll be uncomfortable with your hands behind your back. Hey, sue me. Now tie his feet together—as tight as you can; we're not worried about blood circulation. Good. Now tie his feet to the seat fittings, where they're bolted to the floor. When you're finished, take the seat behind him. Hold your weapon at his head level. If he moves, shoot him."

The pilot looked like a trussed chicken. Perez grinned at the corporal and muttered, loud enough for her to hear, "Bossy woman."

Schmidt said, "Well done, both of you. I agree with the corporal's instruction: if our prisoner moves, shoot him. Sophie, you'd better tie the cabin attendant; even though she's unconscious now, that condition won't last."

"Yes, sir. That task was next on my list." The corporal holstered her handgun and lifted the woman into the seat across the aisle from the pilot. It took her seconds to restrain the cabin attendant in the same manner; it would be uncomfortable, but it was secure.

"There you are, sir," Corporal Winton said to Schmidt. "Should I help the colonel?"

"Don't tell me you're also a pilot?"

"Yes, sir. Not as many hours as the colonel, though. I can press buttons or use the radio, if she needs to stay focused."

"Go, go. Why are you wasting time here?"

The corporal was in the cockpit before Schmidt had finished speaking.

"Colonel, I've got about four hundred hours. Nothing too sophisticated. Twin engine, props, no jet time."

"Sit, make yourself comfortable. Do you know how to talk to that fighter—the Raptor—out there? I think we're in the wrong airspace."

"Wow. Yes, sir. What's our rego?"

"We're GOLF ALFA ONE XRAY OSCAR. Use 121.5; they'll tell you to change if they want."

"Yes, sir." Sophie donned the headset, selected the emergency channel, listened for a few seconds, and pressed the mike button.

She said, "This is Cessna GOLF ALFA ONE XRAY OSCAR. Over."

The reply sounded in both headsets. "This is Texas Hat to Cessna GOLF ALFA ONE XRAY OSCAR. You're in the wrong place. Follow me. I hope you've got a good story. Out."

The Raptor pilot turned his aircraft and Colonel Hudson followed.

"Texas Hat to Cessna. Confirm fuel for thirty minutes plus. Over."

Sophie said to the colonel. "Sir, do you know?"

"I think we have enough for a couple of hours. So confirm one hour."

"Cessna to Texas Hat. Confirm one hour. Over."

"Texas Hat to Cessna. Advise pilot experience. Over."

Colonel Hunter laughed. She said, "My turn was a little unsteady. Let them know enough detail so they are aware of what our needs might be."

"Cessna to Texas Hat. We've had problems. Current pilot in command is British Army Colonel Evelyn Hunter, limited hours on this aircraft type. US Army Corporal Sophie Winton is co-pilot. Note co-pilot has nil hours on type. Original co-pilot is deceased, original pilot in command is under restraint. We suspect they are terrorists. Passengers include US Army General Archimedes Schmidt plus others, British and US military, and civilians. Over."

"Texas Hat to Cessna. I said you needed a good story. I think you might have one. We'll escort you to a suitable Air National Guard Base. Emergency services will be on full alert. Let me know if you have a problem or need assistance. Over."

Sophie by-passed correct protocol. "Thank you, Texas Hat."

They followed the fighter jet for another fifteen minutes.

"Texas Hat to Cessna. We're going to land you at Stratton Air National Guard Base. We'll handle all communications. Stay on 121.5. The base shares Schenectady County Airport. We'll land you on runway 22, which runs north to south. Towards the southern end as you complete your landing run, you'll divert to the National Guard Base. Understood? Over."

Sophie looked at the colonel. "You okay with all of that?"

"Tell them acknowledge. I'm not sure of the buttons to press for cabin announcements so tell our passengers to strap in and come back to your seat."

"Cessna to Texas Hat. Acknowledged. We're landing at Stratton Air National Guard Base. We'll remain on 121.5. We're using runway 22, north to south. We'll divert to the National Guard Base on completion of landing run. Over."

"Well done. Now follow me. I'll lead you in. Don't forget to drop and lock your landing gear." There was a touch of laughter in the reminder.

"Cheeky sod," said Colonel Hunter. "He owes me a beer for that."

"I think if he leads us in safely, we'll be the ones owing beers."

The colonel brought the Cessna to stop where indicated by the ground flight controller. The Raptor had led the way in, along the runway, and once the pilot had observed the safe landing, he had communicated his congratulations, waggled his wings, and accelerated to return to his home base. But not before Sophie had obtained his contact details. If she had an opportunity, she'd promised him as much beer as he could drink.

Emergency vehicles accompanied the Cessna in the last section of its landing run, and MP vehicles were waiting at the Air National Guard Base.

"Congratulations, Colonel," Sophie said. "That was a smooth landing. I can breathe again. I think we'll be telling our story for a while." She indicated the waiting vehicles. "They'll be entertained, especially as it's MP to MP." She watched as the colonel went through the shutdown procedure. At some stage in her near future, she promised herself, she was going to add more hours, as many as she could afford.

Schmidt opened the cockpit door and said, "Well done, both of you. We're going to be here for a while. I've been in touch with the base's senior officer and he's promised to process us as quickly as possible. That means we need pilots—I don't suppose you know of any?"

"I think we should wait on the genuine ones, those who came with us," Colonel Hunter replied.

"They're in recovery mode. No long-term harm done, apparently. It will be another day before they're okay to fly, though. Depending how much paperwork we have to go through here, we might continue by car. It all depends."

"General, I'm sure we'll get to rescue Mark before too long."

Chapter 42

Mark waited for the psychologist to recover from her sobbing. He held no sympathy for her; there was no captive-bonding or Stockholm effect in their relationship. Whenever he thought of the torture he had endured, he had to force down the flood of anger to prevent himself from doing harm. To either or both—the psychologist or O'Hare. He had no interest in her full name or in her background. O'Hare was— Mark was confident—going to pay for the pain, drugs, and agony inflicted at his command. Somehow, somewhere, sometime. Mark had sworn that oath.

At last Emma raised herself from off the floor. Mark continued to wait. The hammering had ceased. He thought whoever was trying to gain admission had re-grouped, possibly to try other means of forcing an entry. Given the metal structure of the small building, he expected those outside would either use a cutting torch to get access or set a fire near or under the CHU. He hoped they tried the cutting torch first—it would mean they wanted himself and Emma alive—or at least, one of them. He lacked data.

At last Emma managed to regain control of her emotions. She washed and dried her face and returned to the narrow office. She had hiccups.

"I'm so sorry."

"You've already said that."

"I—I want to help."

"How? I've searched for a weapon. There's the other exit but it's likely to be guarded."

"They only have two guards."

"Can you guarantee they haven't arranged reinforcements? Are you sure they're O'Hare's people?"

"N—No. I never thought of that."

Mark shrugged. "They could have more people involved; they could be arranging for a cutting torch; they could start a fire and roast us. The possibilities aren't endless, I suppose, but they can do us harm."

The hiccups worsened. Mark walked the length of the CHU and back, lost in thought. He paced the circuit again.

An hour passed. Followed by another. The hammering resumed. It sounded as though they were using a heavier implement. Mark checked the steel door. There was no sign of damage. He sat for a while, lost in thought. He resumed his pacing along the forty feet length of the CHU and back. The hammering ceased.

It was another hour before the hammering began again. Mark wondered at the intention of whoever was outside: were they simply trying to disturb them or was it a serious intent to penetrate the container? He resumed pacing. He did not notice as Emma raised her hand as though to attract his attention. He repeated his circuit. This time she reached out and touched his arm. He turned.

"Yes."

She bit her lip. "I—I lied to you earlier."

"What? Which one?"

"I said I didn't have a weapon."

Mark was close to losing control of his anger.

"Well, it was true—I didn't have one here, in the CHU."

"And that's changed, how?"

"I brought my pistol with me when I came back. It's in my handbag."

"Now you tell me." He held his hand out.

Emma fumbled with her handbag and drew out the pistol. It was a Glock. He snapped out the magazine—six bullets, .38 caliber.

"Any more?" He indicated the magazine as he inserted it back into the Glock.

"Two." She felt around in her bag and found the two magazines and handed them over.

Mark checked. He had another twelve bullets. Not enough to start a war, but probably as many as he needed. He tucked the spare magazines into his pants pocket.

"I'll go out the other door—their attention is probably on this one. Come with me and lock the door behind me. I'll come back via the other door. Wait until I knock, understand. Two raps and a pause and then one."

"Don't—don't go." She tugged his arm. "I'll be alone."

Mark ignored her entreaty. He tucked the handgun into his belt and headed to the other door. With luck, the locking levers would open without a sound. Otherwise—he shrugged. He'd spent more than enough time in this metal prison.

He turned off all the lights as he walked along the length of the CHU. It would be dark outside, he assumed, and light suddenly shining through a doorway would attract attention—unwanted attention. When he reached the end of the narrow corridor, he turned the corner to reach the locked door. He grabbed hold of the lever and slowly applied force. The lever and its attached bars moved a fraction of an inch at a time. There was no noise. He maintained pressure and continued to ease the lever until it reached its unlocked position. He hoped the fit of the door did not add a noise risk when he attempted to push it open. He turned the lock and leaned against the weight of the metal structure, moving it in small increments. He sighed with relief when he had a gap wide enough to fit through; the door had performed flawlessly.

Mark waited minutes before moving the door any further.

He hoped he had controlled the opening process with enough caution that the movement had not attracted anyone's attention. He dropped to his knees, and with even more caution, moved his head and body until he could see outside. No one. He pushed the door out another six inches. Still no one. He moved the door and checked again.

There. A man was standing about twenty feet away, his back to the CHU. He was smoking a cigarette. He carried a weapon; it looked like a miniature machine gun. Mark couldn't identify it. The overhead lights did not provide much illumination. As far as he could determine he was in the middle of some kind of container farm; he did not know whether they were CHUs or proper freight containers. There were rows of them, stacked three and four high. He heard, in the distance, the roar of diesel motors followed by a long train whistle. This certainly was not Gitmo, he decided.

Mark pondered for a moment how to handle the watcher with his cigarette. If he tried to sneak up on the man, he was liable to be detected. If he fired at him from the CHU doorway, he might miss and the noise would alert other guards. He decided to sneak up on the man, at least until he moved. He stepped out onto the concrete, closed the door, and with utmost care, moved towards the guard. Mark held the Glock ready, aimed at the back of the man's head.

The guard inhaled smoke and dropped the cigarette on the ground. He twisted his boot on the ember, squashing the butt. He straightened up and shifted his weapon. Mark was only ten feet away. He continued to move, inch by inch, a leopard stalking its prey.

His target yawned and leaned against a steel support, a vertical beam of some kind. Mark stayed focused. He stopped when he was two feet away.

"Turn around, slowly. No, don't move your weapon."

"*Govno!*" The watcher jerked his weapon around.

Mark didn't debate whether the movement was an attack or an involuntary movement as a result of surprise. He fired the Glock. At a distance of two feet he was not likely to miss. The guard fell, his weapon clattering onto the concrete. Mark cursed under his breath—the noises were startling in the quiet of the night.

A shout from the other side of the CHU indicated someone was concerned. He wasn't sure what the language was and didn't know whether it was a question or command. No one replied. He headed to a shadowed area some yards away, where lights did not reach. He hoped the shadows would hide him from whoever came to investigate the shot and subsequent silence. He didn't have to wait for long.

A dark figure came from the far side of the CHU, displaying caution with each soft step. The man called out again. It was the same word, perhaps the name of the watcher Mark had shot. He didn't reply. He waited, certain he had blended into the shadows and was partially protected by another steel beam. Mark used his pistol to track the newcomer, ready to fire when he was certain of a successful shot.

The man stepped into a lighted area. Mark fired. The bullet hit the man's weapon and a bullet exploded. Cursing, the man fell backwards. Mark waited. The bullet's impact at least had discouraged the stranger even if it hadn't injured him. Patience, Mark cautioned himself. Time moved ever so slowly. Minutes passed. The mix of light and shadows created a hallucinogenic effect. Shadows moved. Some regressed, some came forward. The body of the second man was half in light and half in shadow. Mark looked again. The body now was all in shadow. Mark aimed and fired.

The man cursed and clutched at his leg. Mark fired again. The man called out, presumably to a companion. There was no reply. The injured man cursed again; his voice contained a sob. The gunshot wounds, Mark assumed, were painful.

A sound, a soft slide of a step across loose crumbled concrete, alerted Mark. He spun around and fired; his reaction was instinctive, the shot not consciously aimed. Twenty feet away a man dropped to the ground, his weapon clattering as he fell. That was three, Mark thought. How many more were there? He had fired five shots. There was one left in this magazine. He released the magazine and replaced it with one of the spares.

A shout from the other end of the CHU drew his attention. There was a scream and a sound of a scuffle. A voice called out. "Hey, we have the woman. Come here or we'll kill her."

Mark shrugged. He wondered how they had enticed Emma to exit her office. He decided he could take advantage of the situation and slowly moved back towards the container. He reached the corner and, cautiously, peered around. An overhead light illuminated the area around the entrance to the CHU. A man held Emma; his pistol was pressed against her temple. Mark wondered if he realized a shot from that position would probably backfire, wounding the shooter, too.

He stood and walked out into the light, his pistol down by his side. His movement alerted the gunman. Mark knew he was taking a risk; however, he thought the odds were with him, that this man was the sole survivor.

"You want me?" he asked as he kept walking towards the man who was trying to hold the struggling Emma.

"Yes." The stranger turned, using the psychologist as a protective barrier. Mark could not see her face because of the poor lighting but assumed she was frightened—unless he was being set up. He kept walking.

"Stop!" the man shouted, waving his pistol towards Mark. "That's close enough." Mark couldn't place the man's accent—foreign, he thought, not American.

Mark slowed his pace.

The man aimed his weapon at Mark. His left arm was around Emma's neck; her struggles were fruitless, causing only minor distractions.

"Drop your weapon."

Mark raised the small Glock and looked at it. "You mean this?"

"Of course I fuckin' mean your gun. Drop it."

Mark snapped his arm up and fired two shots. Two bodies fell to the black top. The gunman's legs twitched and stilled. Emma looked up at him with unseeing eyes. Mark ignored the accusatory expression now frozen on her face. He searched the man for a cell phone. He found two—one was a flip top, presumably a burner and disposable, while the second was a more typical flat cell phone.

He checked. The burner switched on without a pass code. The second phone required entry of a numeric code. He tried all zeroes. Nothing. He tried all nines. The code worked. He shook his head—the lack of security indicated the quality of the group trying to extract him from the CHU.

He checked the time—it was three in the morning. Either too late or early to call. He could wait, he thought. He looked around. The building was old, poorly lit, and as far as he could see, held nothing other than containers. It would be imprudent to wait here, with four dead bodies and an injured man near the office unit. Presumably his attackers had dealt with any watchman or security for the building. Possibly there would be a shift change later in the morning, probably at 6:00 a.m., when all hell would likely break loose.

Mark heard a scuffle and realized he had not checked on the man whom he had shot in the leg. He checked the area in front of the CHU and found no one. He moved, with extra caution, towards where the shadows had earlier hidden the wounded man. There, against the steel beam. Mark raised his pistol and fired. The man collapsed, soundlessly, and his legs jerked for a few seconds and then stilled.

He had no idea of where he was. Linda Schöner's people would track the location of cell phone, if he used it to call Maeve. He was prepared to wait—as long as it wasn't for too long.

###

Mark explained later to Maeve. Agent Gordon, the senior FBI agent in charge of his rescue team, had telephoned to report once they had extracted him from the warehouse. Gordon had handed her phone over to Mark after providing an update to Maeve. The FBI team had avoided the local police who seemed perplexed by the entire affair; at least, based on their radio traffic, which the FBI team had been following.

He said, "I walked to the other end of the warehouse building, where there was an old deserted office in a corner. The door was unlocked. As far as I could tell it seemed unoccupied and unused. I blocked the door with a broken chair and lay down on the floor. I couldn't help it—I fell asleep. I'm still weak, I suppose. Anyway, I woke to all kinds of noise and activity. I assumed the warehouse security people, after discovering the bodies, had called the police. That's when I called your office."

Maeve said, "Linda's team enjoyed the challenge of locating you. They tracked the cell phone you used to call me. They located the local cell tower without difficulty; however, there are ten or more warehouses and acres of stacked containers in that facility. That's when we decided to deploy FBI agents. We couldn't take a risk that the local police might treat you as armed and dangerous."

"Which I probably was."

"Undoubtedly. We've been monitoring their cell phone and radio traffic. Apparently the in-house security management are somewhat embarrassed at the discovery of the CHUs set up by O'Hare. He had bribed a number of their people to look the other way. He had four container units in place, so he was planning for more than your kidnap."

"Naming the unit Gitmo was a stroke of genius."

"I agree. We need to talk more, but not by cell phone. I'm in transit to Newark airport. You're not far away from there. Are you up to meeting with me for more discussions? We can talk on the way to Boston. I'm sure Anna wants to see you as soon as possible. I have a lot to cover."

Intrigued, Mark replied, "Of course. As long as we're heading to Boston. I'll call Anna and tell her to expect us. If you can follow-up and let her know our arrival time?"

"I will. Now hand me back to Agent Gordon; I'll give her a time and place to meet up. In the meantime, she can organize breakfast for you."

"Oh, I need more than that—a shower and clean clothes and possibly a shave. Do I have time for all that?"

"Yes, there should be time. Pass the phone over and I'll arrange it all."

Maeve, via Agent Gordon, funded his quick shopping expedition, after which he checked into a small hotel where he was able to shower and change. He also shaved. Refreshed, he ate two breakfasts while he and Agent Gordon waited for Maeve's arrival.

Chapter 43

It was a family gathering, thought Mark, as he sat down to dinner. It was a day after his escape from the container unit and he was feeling relaxed. Anna sat next to him, jumping up every so often to bring out more dishes for their meal. The three Welsh teenagers were on one side of the table and Gabrielle, Niland, and Alex sat opposite them, while Ladder was at the end. An interesting group and full of potential and challenge. He had shaved and showered three times through the day; his urge to be clean was compulsive. He knew he had not fully recovered physically. Mentally? He shrugged.

He'd spent some time with both Maeve and Linda describing his torture yesterday as they drove to Boston, which refreshed memories he did not enjoy. It was bad enough to experience the pain and degradation the first time, without having to re-live the details. They had also brought him up to date with their activities, including their explanation of why the psychologist was immune to his influence, an analysis he found alarming. Someone in Cerberus had stolen vaccine for O'Hare, who had used it to treat Emma. As a result, she was able to resist Mark's mental pressures. There were still issues to resolve, he realized.

He owed Ladder—no, he owed all of them. Somehow, they had each participated in or were involved in his rescue.

They now needed to return to some degree of normalcy; at least he did, and he suspected Anna did, too. He was unsure what could be defined as normal, given their different backgrounds.

Anna returned from the kitchen and seated herself beside him.

"You're looking serious?" she said.

Mark nodded.

"Thinking."

He looked at Lewis. "How did you get out of school? It's not vacation time? Will I get fined or something?"

The three Welsh teenagers looked at each other. Lewis nudged Owen and said, "You're the eldest, you tell him."

"By two minutes. Unfair."

Carys said, "You are the eldest. I'm the youngest, so you need to protect me. Besides, it was you—" She nodded her head instead of completing the sentence.

Owen said, "Ah—Mark, we promised a donation to the school." Cerberus UK had taken over the old building in London where the three siblings lived, and the organization provided housekeeping and security. Mark paid their school fees.

"Can we take it out of your allowance?" Mark asked.

Owen paled. "Um—no, I don't think so. It's too much for that."

Anna innocently said, "Why, how much is it?"

Owen tried to speak but couldn't find his voice. Lewis put his hand over his mouth. Carys looked at her two brothers and said, "You're both supposed to protect me."

Mark, hiding his amusement, said, "Come on, Owen. You're the oldest."

Lewis laughed. Carys looked at her older brother and patted his shoulder.

Owen swallowed and said, "Fif—fifty thousand pounds."

Everyone around the table stared in shock at the three siblings. Mark gasped and said, "That's sixty, seventy thousand dollars. For letting you take time out of school?"

Anna said, "Surely that can't be right?"

Lewis said, "Well, no, not only for time away."

"It's to repair the lab. One of their experiments blew it up. There." Carys looked at her two brothers in turn. "That's the way to do it."

"Totes emoshe," Mark said.

Half the group burst into laughter while Anna, Alex and Ladder looked bewildered. The three Welsh teenagers wore embarrassed expressions while trying to hold back their laughter.

Owen said, "I—I think you won that, Mark. But it really was an accident."

Lewis commented, "Yes, someone misread the formula. We were lucky—"

"To only lose our eyebrows," finished Owen.

Carys added, "I looked odd for a month, until mine grew back."

Mark shared a wry look with Anna. "What do you think? Do we cast them out into the cold?"

"I think not." She reached for Mark's hand. "They brought the British Army here to rescue you, so they can't be all bad." The three British officers had decided to go sightseeing and weren't expected back for another hour or so.

"There is that. All right. This once, I'll agree to donate to the school."

Lewis, Owen and Carys sat back in their chairs. They were holding hands. Carys said, "Mark, we thank you, all of us. If ever you need rescuing again, I'm sure Lewis and Owen will lead the way."

Mark realized Ladder was probably wondering what all the discussion was about. "Ladder, when we were in London, my sister introduced Anna and me to these three rebels. We offered to support them through school and university. It seems they have issues reading directions, thus the need to repay their school."

Ladder grinned. "Thank you. I thought I'd caught the wrong train somewhere. Are you planning to go to London?"

"Ah. An interesting question. Anna, my dear, what say you?"

Owen and Lewis said, "London." Carys nodded her head, watching Mark.

Gabrielle and Niland added, in unison, "You have responsibilities with Cerberus UK."

Anna waited for a moment and asked, "What do you all vote?"

Alex said, her voice tiny, "London, only if Ladder comes too."

Everyone looked at Alex.

She said, "He helped. He knocked out one of the terrorists. And he read your code, even if it was a red herring."

"Doesn't Ladder live in Redmont?" Mark asked.

"Yes, Mark, I do. But—" He looked around the table, at all the faces looking back at him. "I—I'd enjoy England, I think. I've heard their universities are good. I want to study a challenging course. I don't know how I'd pay my way, though."

"That's it. Ladder comes too." Alex decided.

Anna said, "What's the vote?"

She listened to the shouts and turned to Mark.

"We all say London. What do you want?"

"London, of course. Well, to be correct, Bankton House, in East Sussex. It's not that far from London."

"You'll sell the property at Redmont?" Anna asked.

"Damn, I haven't spoken to the architect. Yes, we'll sell the land. I'd like to keep this apartment, though."

Their conversation was interrupted by a knock on the door. Mark said, "That must be Schmidt. He said he might visit."

The visitors were Schmidt and Maeve. Linda had returned to Washington in the late afternoon. The general had received his medical clearance for his return to duty and had brought a bottle of champagne to celebrate. Maeve and Schmidt joined in the London conversation.

"You're taking Ladder?" Schmidt asked.

Alex was firm. "Yes, we are. I know, he's too old to be my boyfriend, so he's now my big brother. Mark said he's always wanted a family, and I think he has one now, even though we're a chaotic mix."

"Well, if you ever want to join us, Ladder, you're welcome," Maeve said. "We were all impressed—Linda's team and my people." She paused. "By the way, I never did find out why you're called Ladder?"

Alex burst into laughter, Ladder's face turned red, and there was a mix of laughs and questions.

Ladder said, "No, only Alex knows."

The lighthearted conversation was interrupted by the buzz of Mark's cell phone. The caller ID was for the ground floor security desk.

"This is Mark." He held his hand up to quieten the group.

"Four visitors? Captain Hudson and her two sergeants and a friend? Can you repeat that? It's noisy here. Yes, they can come up to my apartment."

He caught Schmidt's attention as he disconnected the call. "We have an issue. Three people went out, four are returning. Hudson should simply have returned to your apartment. Also, the ranks are incorrect."

Schmidt reacted. "Everybody except Mark." He pulled his apartment key from his pocket. "Head down the fire escape to my apartment. Stay there until we say it's okay to return. Quickly."

The apartment was cleared in seconds. Mark and Schmidt sat in the study, waiting. Both were armed. Mark did not comment when he realized Maeve had not joined the group heading to Schmidt's apartment. He didn't know where she was.

"We'll know in a minute or two," Mark said. "Any thoughts as to the extra person?"

"No, none at all. Someone looking for you? For me?" Schmidt shrugged. "Waiting is a curse."

The door buzzer interrupted their discussion. Mark released the lock and stood back, out of the way of the opening door. Schmidt remained in the study, handgun drawn. Colonel Hudson entered the apartment first; she was trying to signal, her expression full of alarm. She was followed by Thomas. Laura and the fourth person came in last; the newcomer was holding the lieutenant's arm. With a start, Mark recognized his kidnapper.

"O'Hare!" He spoke loudly, warning Schmidt. "We thought you'd been caught in the explosion that took out the Saudi spy—Dr. Chaborz."

"I'm not that easily defeated." O'Hare's face was partially bandaged. He pushed Laura away and she stumbled and nearly fell. Thomas steadied her.

Laura said, "He's badly burned and suffering pain. I—I can feel his agony."

O'Hare ignored the comment. He said, "Shut up. Move away from the door—all of you."

Evelyn said, "I'm sorry, Mark. He latched onto Laura and we couldn't risk her life."

"Stay where I can see you all or I will shoot someone. Where's a room we can use?"

"There's a study," suggested Mark. "It's quite large." He pointed. "It's through there."

"Hudson, you first. Then you, boy, whatever your name is. You—" He motioned at Mark using his handgun as a pointer. "Follow them. Laura, my dear girl—keep in front of me. Come on, walk."

There was a second door to the study and Mark wondered how Schmidt was going to handle the likely ambush. He hoped the general would come around behind O'Hare—that would give everyone an opportunity to escape O'Hare if he started shooting. He thought the man looked forbidding, angry. He wondered at his sanity.

"All right—sit down. We're going to get Schmidt here. I know he's somewhere in Boston. You, Midway."

"Yes?" Mark replied.

"You call him. Ask him to come here. Tell him it's urgent. Don't say why. Then I'll have both of you."

Schmidt's voice startled O'Hare. "Why call me? I'm right here."

O'Hare spun around, forgetting his need to keep Linda under threat. Two shots blasted simultaneously. O'Hare's body crumpled to the ground. Seconds later, Schmidt also collapsed, his unfired weapon sliding across the floor. Mark checked O'Hare. The shot had hit his left temple; his death probably immediate.

Maeve checked Schmidt. She shook her head.

She said, "Archimedes is dead. O'Hare's shot hit him in the chest—his heart."

Mark said, "I tried to shoot O'Hare before he could fire his weapon."

"Schmidt's hands were shaking earlier, I noticed. He was still suffering from the attack on his apartment." She touched Schmidt's cheek. "We'll miss him, all of us."

Mark looked at the pistol in his hand and back at Maeve. She nodded her assent to his unspoken question. He pushed Schmidt's handgun across the room towards Maeve. He said, "Pick that up, please. It should be disposed of as soon as possible."

"I agree," Maeve said as she dropped the weapon into her large handbag.

Mark said, "All of you—please move away."

He waited for the British soldiers to move. Maeve was already out of harm's way. He ignored their unspoken questions. He placed his pistol in Schmidt's dead hand and fired a shot at the wall behind where O'Hare had stood. He dropped Schmidt's hand; it still held his Glock.

Maeve came over to stand beside Mark. She looked at the visitors. "I support what Mark's doing. They shot each other. O'Hare was wanted for a number of crimes, including murder and for kidnapping Mark. We—speaking for Cerberus—

would prefer to minimize the newspaper headlines. We'll keep Mark out of the glare of public exposure—no one needs to know he shot O'Hare."

Mark said, "It's simpler this way."

Maeve added, "I think it's time to call 911." She dialed the number.

Colonel Hudson said to Mark, "We'll support you, of course. Do you think the authorities will accept the apparent shootout?"

"We'll all provide them with supporting eyewitness details. You'll need to give statements—tell the truth except for the fatal shots. Schmidt killed O'Hare."

"I think Cerberus UK is going to be an experience for all of us," the colonel said. Her two companions nodded. They were still in shock.

Maeve finished her call. "We'll have FBI agents here in a minute or two and there'll be police. All Cerberus, of course. The story is simple. They shot each other after O'Hare threatened you at gunpoint to force his way in. Agreed?"

Colonel Hudson looked at her two junior officers, who each nodded. She said to Maeve, "We're agreed."

I'm relieved that Anna and the children decided to move to London. I might be able to have a more peaceful life, there.

That was something he could enjoy.

oooOOOooo

Thank you for reading Mark Four. I hope you enjoyed the story—and if you did, please share your experience by adding a review to Amazon or to the reseller site where you purchased the book.

Keep up to date by subscribing to my newsletters: John Hindmarsh

Check my web site for details of all my books: http://johnhindmarsh.com/

More Details

Newsletter
Learn more about John Hindmarsh and his books—sign up for John's newsletter.

You'll receive: updates on John's writing schedule, the occasional freebie (e.g., books, short stories, excerpts from John's current work in progress), advance details of discounts, and be part of John's street team for new releases.

Subscribe here: John Hindmarsh

You can unsubscribe anytime - NO SPAM guaranteed. [John should be far too busy writing to send out spam].

Reviews
Thank you for purchasing and reading this book. Reviews, whether positive or negative, are indispensable to an author, so please add your review on Amazon, Kobo, Barnes and Noble, or other vendor site where you made your purchase. Or send John an email. Or indeed, do both!

John's email address is: John@JohnHindmarsh.com

About John Hindmarsh
John writes science fiction and thrillers, sometimes with crossover. Well, he claims you need a thrill in your science fiction and an occasional touch of science in your thrillers.

John originates from Australia, has lived in England (plus a number of other countries—it's a long list), and now lives in the High Sierra region of California where he is writing full time. He could be hiking, kayaking, or skiing, when he's not writing.

John's books generally are written with an American voice [well, he tries], although he prefers to write British English. So he gets mixed up.

Check his Author's page on Amazon - viewAuthor.at/JohnHindmarsh

Let him know about possible errors—send your email to John@JohnHindmarsh.com

Also by John Hindmarsh
Science Fiction
Glass Complex Trilogy
Book 1: Broken Glass
Book 2: Fracture Lines
Book 3: Diamond Cut [Check web site for release date]

Shen Ark: Departure

Contributor to Quantum Zoo (anthology); published by Orion's Comet

Thrillers
Mark One
Mark Two
Mark Three
Mark Four
Mark Five [check web site for release date in 2017]

Explore further details - Go here: http://johnhindmarsh.com/

64377827R00175

Made in the USA
Charleston, SC
25 November 2016